CONQUEST OF THE VEIL BOOK III

A WITCH'S BREW

MICHAEL SCOTT CLIFTON

BOOKS BY
MICHAEL SCOTT CLIFTON

Book Liftoff
1209 South Main Street
PMB 126
Lindale, Texas 75771

Interior's book design by Champagne Book Design
Cover design by Evelyne Paniez www.secretdartiste.be
www.secretdartiste.be / digital-art
RESOURCES:
Witch cottage: depositphotos 230579434
Table: www.cheshirestudios.uk
Flame effect: www.deviantart.com / tamilia
Cloak: depositphotos 451948008
Sword: shutterstock 224197540
Model: www.fantasybackgroundstore.com
Armor: shutterstock 621720590
Potion: www.kickassrenderstock.com
Kettle: depositphotos 73608805
Witch hands: depositphotos 334749208

Interior's illustrations by Nancy E Durham
www.facebook.com / artistnedurham

Library of Congress Control Number Data
Clifton, Michael Scott
A Witch's Brew / Michael Scott Clifton
Magical Realism / Fiction.
Dragons & Mythical Creatures / Fantasy / Fiction.
3. Paranormal / Fantasy / Fiction
BISAC: FIC061000 FICTION / Magical Realism
FIC009120 FICTION / Fantasy / Dragons & Mythical Creatures.
2021906206

ISBN: 978-1-947946-71-2 (Kindle Direct Publishing)
ISBN: 978-1-947946-73-6 (Ingram Spark)

www.michaelscottclifton.com
http://www.bookliftoff.com

Double, double toil and trouble;
Fire burn, and cauldron bubble.
Macbeth

Nancy E. Durham

CHAPTER I

A CLOAKED FIGURE FLITTED DOWN THE NIGHT-DARKENED ALLEY. Pausing, the shape flattened against a vine-covered wall. And waited.

No one followed, and no sounds of stealthy pursuit disturbed the nocturnal silence. Clutching the cloak tighter, the figure turned and scurried to a broad door at the back of an immense, multi-storied building. Two soft taps on the door produced the clank of a bolt being shot back.

The door swung open to reveal a diminutive gnome with large, violet eyes. He scratched his head, bald except for a few stubborn, straggly hairs.

"Come in."

Hurrying inside, the cloaked figure threw back his cowl.

The gnome shut the door. "Really, Pandathaway. Aren't you a little old for this nighttime skulking?"

"How are you, Bedrosian? And yes, I'd rather have this meeting under more normal circumstances, but my shop is being watched," Pandathaway replied.

Bedrosian stroked his pointed chin. "Watched? By whom?"

"My guess is Dorothea, the duchess."

Bedrosian frowned. "Dorothea? What possible interest could she have with a gnome like you?"

"She suspects I aided Lady Alexandria."

Bedrosian's eyes flew open wide. "You—you helped her escape Wheel?"

Pandathaway shrugged. "Dorothea suspects everyone. Anyone who had even casual contact with Alex over the past month is on her list, including me."

Bedrosian leaned closer, his eyes suspicious. "Alex is it? How curious you refer to the duke's daughter in such a familiar fashion."

Rather than answer, Pandathaway pulled an object from underneath his cloak. Four feet long, it represented an intricately carved cane. Lodestones were embedded up and down the length of wood. "Do you recognize this?"

"A Staff of the Test. I haven't seen one of those in—"

"Not here. You're the Chief Archivist for the Library of Wheel, aren't you? I'm sure you can find a better place we can talk."

"Great stars above! What have you gotten yourself into now, Pandathaway?"

At his fellow gnome's stern look, Bedrosian waved off his own comment. "Never mind. Follow me."

They made their way through a labyrinth of row after row of books, manuscripts, and scrolls, each neatly stacked in labeled cubbyholes. The summit of the bookcases rose to lofty heights to disappear in the upper reaches of the darkened library. Bedrosian led them unerringly through the maze of dozens of tables and hundreds of chairs. Surrounded on all sides by the floor-to-ceiling bookcases, the area reminded Pandathaway of a valley flanked by mountain peaks.

Picking a table, Bedrosian activated the light crystal fixed to the tabletop. He pointed at a chair, and both gnomes sat.

"Okay. What is so important you couldn't have paid me a daytime visit?"

Pandathaway placed the Staff of the Test on the wooden surface. "I want you to taste the magic of this Artifact. Although much of it has faded, enough residue remains you'll understand why I make such an unusual request."

"Here I was happily ensconced in *The Travels of Revel Riversmith*, a glass of my favorite wine in hand, and you interrupt me for this?"

Bedrosian grabbed the staff. "Let's get this fool's errand—"

The archivist's mouth clamped shut, a look of astonishment on his face. He grabbed the staff with his other hand as well. Eyes closed, his lips moved soundlessly.

His eyes snapped open.

"What—what magic is this?"

Pandathaway smiled at his friend's reaction. "Precisely. You've never felt a charm or enchantment like that have you?" He moved closer. "The staff lay dormant in my shop for years, its lodestones drained of magic. In Alexandria's hands, the staff lit up like a festival bonfire."

"There is such…such power," Bedrosian added in wonder. "Pure, like spring water."

"Now you understand why the duchess is so upset," Pandathaway said. "And it has nothing to do with step-motherly love. She wants Alexandria. Somehow, Dorothea knows of her latent power and wants to use it for her own purposes."

"Surely you jest," Bedrosian scoffed. "What purposes do you speak of?"

Pandathaway steeled himself. "I believe both she and Lord Regret are in league with the Veil Queen. Lady Alexandria must have a part to play in the Dark Queen's plans."

"You speak treason!" Bedrosian hissed. "I hope you haven't mentioned this to anyone else, or you'll find yourself in one of the duke's dungeons. What proof do you have of this conspiracy?"

Pandathaway shook his head. "None, except for what Alex told me and my own observations."

"Well, Lady Alexandria is no longer here to validate your claims, nor is anyone likely to believe you."

"I know. This all sounds implausible. So, I just have one question—do you trust me, old friend?" Pandathaway asked.

Bedrosian tapped the table. He ran a hand over his bare scalp. "You are not one to chase rumors, legends, and ghosts. You were the duke's weapons master, and one does not rise to that position without both trustworthiness and competence."

He sighed. "And, for as long as we have known each other, your honesty is unmatched. So, yes, I trust you. Which means I must also believe you."

Pandathaway rubbed his hands together. "Good! We need to find out why Alex's magic is so important to the duchess."

"How?"

Pandathaway grinned. "That's where your skills as chief archivist comes into play. There must be something in Lady Alexandria's lineage, something you can find. Magic such as hers doesn't occur randomly. There must be an ancestor she inherited her power from. If we find this ancestor, we'll know why Dorothea and Lord Regret want her so badly."

"You want me to research her genealogy? The Duvalier line is an ancient one. It will be like trying to find a single seashell on a shoreline full of them!"

"You can narrow it down a bit. Remember the unusual magic you felt in the Staff of the Test. Look for an ancestor who possessed similar magic."

Bedrosian snorted. "The Duvalier's have a long history of powerful nobles. The difference between one magic-wielder and another is likely to be scant indeed."

Pandathaway stood and placed his hand on Bedrosian's shoulder. "Nevertheless, I can think of no one more qualified for this task than you. Once we discover why Alexandria's magic is coveted by Dorothea, I can take this information to the Court Grand Master, Alabaster John. I know he is suspicious of the duchess as well."

Pandathaway tightened his grip. "But you must hurry. I fear events are already afoot, and we are playing catch-up…we may already be too late."

CHAPTER 2

MARKINGHAM LAY BEFORE THE IMPERIAL ARMY.
Almost three weeks of travel from the breach in the Veil, and they finally reached the city from which they planned to launch the empire's war against the Veil Queen.

Tal studied the walls. Some sections were formidable. Rising more than one hundred feet from ground level, their foundation was sturdy and solid. Other sections leaned precariously and looked like a solid blow would bring them tumbling down. Still other segments had succumbed to damage and neglect, and lay in crumbling piles of debris. Gaping holes existed in the perimeter an enemy could easily ride through.

"How has this city managed to stay free of the Dark Queen's clutches?" he asked Bozar.

"We don't know who controls Markingham," Tal's *Eldred* and First Advisor answered. Lips pursed, he continued, "We must make sure no one leaves or attempts to send a message."

He turned. "Lord Gravelback, signal Lord Tarlbolt. Have his men place the dampers around the city."

"Aye," Gravelback growled. The grizzled commander stood up in his stirrups and waved a blue flag. Moments later, one column after another of flying horses took to the air in orderly fashion. Soon the sky above them was dark with beating wings. Each cavalryman carried a long pole. One end was a pointed like a lance, while on the other end, a circle of metal turned in the wind like a weathervane.

As Tal watched, the spear-like shafts were released. Falling, the magical devices plunged into the ground. Spaced at regular intervals, the Artifacts jutted from the ground a hundred paces from the walls.

"We will encircle the entire city with the dampers," Bozar said. They would prevent any form of magical communication from being sent, and also detect the movements of anyone trying to sneak in or out of Markingham.

"I have patrols in place all around the city," Gravelback said. "We would catch anyone trying to slip by regardless of these precautions."

Bozar shook his head. "Until we know more about the situation within Markingham, we will proceed with utmost caution."

He speared Tal with a hard look. "It is unfortunate we have to take such extreme measures, but our 'spy' got diverted on his way to Markingham."

Heat rose in Tal's face. Of course, his *Eldred* was referring to his rescue of Alex, first from a flock of gargoyles, then from a band led by a dark lord. He recalled the first time he saw her smile, how it lit up her face with snow-melting warmth, and the irresistible attraction of her sky-colored eyes. Although guilt weighed heavily on him, he wouldn't change a thing.

He would do it all again.

Anxious to change the subject, Tal cleared his throat. "What do we do now?"

Bozar turned his horse. "The only thing we can do. We wait."

Tal jumped off his mount and tossed the reins to a groom.

Before him lay a sea of gray tents, the sprawling army encampment filling the area before the gates of Markingham like the flood plain of a mighty river. Knowing the path by heart, he hurried to a tent which rose above the others like a giant cedar. The pavilion—the size of a large house—had colorful pennants flapping from its apex.

Nodding at the sentries posted outside, he pushed the flap aside and entered.

"Tal!"

A warm, soft, and fragrant form hurtled into his arms. Alex's breathless face, inches from his own, beamed at him.

"I've missed you."

Tal laughed. "It's only been an hour."

"Which seems like days when I'm stuck inside."

He waved at the opulent interior. "I can think of worse places to be 'stuck' in."

"A prison is still a prison whether the bars are made of canvas or iron."

Tal led Alex to a nearby table. They sat down and he took her hand in his. "Look, we've talked about this. Until we know more about the situation inside Markingham, this is for your own safety. I've already rescued you once from a dark lord. I'm not anxious to repeat the experience. If, as you have told us, your stepmother and Lord Regret are in league with the Veil Queen, then they may have agents in the city. They could try again."

"I have you and an entire army to protect me," Alex pointed out. "I don't think I have anything to worry about."

"My *Eldred* has said many times that we must prepare for the worst even if it looks like we have the best at hand."

Alex stroked Tal's arm. "I suppose you're right. You need to listen to Bozar more closely. He loves you, you know. You're like a son to him."

She leaned forward and kissed Tal. "But I love you more," she murmured.

Alex stood and grabbed Tal's arm. She pulled him through the pavilion and to her bedroom. She pushed him onto the bed. "This is more comfortable than a chair."

Tal lay back, his arms behind his head. Eyes closed, he said, "Yes, it is. I could fall asleep right here."

Alex grabbed fistfuls of Tal's tunic and pulled him to her. "Sleep is not what I have in mind."

Laughing, Tal drew Alex to him, and they rolled together onto the bed.

A cough came from outside the curtain separating Alex's bedroom.

Tal sat up and smoothed his clothes. Alex bolted upright and pushed the hair away from her face.

"Yes?"

"May I approach the prince?" a familiar voice asked.

Tal stood and pulled the curtain aside to reveal a figure with snow-white hair and eyebrows.

Pulpit.

The monk, a powerful magic-wielder of the priestly Order of the White, wore an apologetic look. "Forgive me, Lady Alexandria, but the First Advisor has sent me to fetch Prince Tal."

Tal tilted his head. "Why?"

"Riders approach from Markingham."

CHAPTER 3

TAL COUNTED THE MEMBERS OF THE SMALL PARTY APPROACHING: FIVE men and one woman.

The six proceeded toward them carrying a parley flag. As they drew near, he shifted his attention to the woman and the two horsemen next to her. Dressed identically, each wore a black vest, pants, and cloak. Each was heavily armed with broadswords, cutlass, and daggers. Despite the mannish clothing, it did nothing to conceal the lush curves or full bosom of the woman. Thick, toast-colored hair cascaded down her back.

Tal turned to the other three men. One carried a staff with the white parley flag. Frayed and worn, the pennant also contained a blue and gold crest with twin gryphons sewn into the fabric. No doubt the leader of the group, the tall, spare rider carried himself in the saddle with a ramrod posture. Hair streaked with gray, he was much older than the woman and her companions.

The final two men in the company couldn't have been more different. One was obviously a soldier. The sword and dagger at his belt carried an oft-used, well-conditioned look. Shorter, the military man was thicker, heavier, and cast an aura Tal recognized immediately; One familiar with violence.

The last one in the group didn't look much older than the woman and her youthful companions. He exhibited none of their swagger. His eyes darted back and forth, tension evident in his features. Brown hair protruded in an untidy mess, his tunic wrinkled and ill-fitting.

"Hail!" their leader proclaimed. "To whom do I have the pleasure of addressing?"

Bozar urged his horse ahead and raised a hand to return the greeting. "Hail and good health to you, sir. I am Bozar, First Advisor to Talmund Edward Meredith, Prince and Heir to the throne of Meredith."

He motioned and Tal inclined his head to the leader. Then Bozar introduced each of the rest of their party: Lord Gravelback, Lord Tarlbolt, Artemis Thurgood, and Pulpit.

The parley leader's eyes widened at the sight of Pulpit. "A White Monk! My grandfather described the members of your order to me, but I've never seen one."

Abruptly, he caught himself. "Pardon me. I forget myself. I am Bartholomew York, the Earl of Markingham." He pointed at the soldier and rumpled young man. "These are my advisors, Garth Morehead, the Lord of the City Guard, and Practius Bolt, my court magister."

Bartholomew turned. "And this is my daughter, Lady Margaret York, and her companions, Terrell Simmons and Bradley Sikes."

The trio displayed none of the polite deference shown by the earl. Instead, they regarded Tal, Bozar, and the others with narrowed eyes.

Lady Margaret fixed Tal with a sharp stare. "If you're a prince, then I'm a faerie queen." Simmons and Sikes snickered.

"Margaret!" the earl thundered. "Hold your tongue!"

Margaret curled her lip. "Tell me, Father, how many people have come to Markingham claiming to be long lost royalty? I've lost count. This Talmund is just one more example of the pretenders we've had to endure. Send them on their way!"

Gravelback's eyes flashed. "And who will send us on our way, eh, girl? From the looks of your walls, you couldn't stop an incursion of goatherders."

"Are you prepared to try?" Morehead asked in a dangerous voice. His hand inched closer to the pommel of his sword.

"Hold!" Bozar cried. "We are here to parley, not start a battle." His eyes drilled into Gravelback. "The lord commander misspoke. Let us start again."

The earl bowed his head. "We are at your service." This produced a loud snort from Lady Margaret.

Heat crawled up Tal's neck. He'd heard enough. Dismounting, he approached Bozar. "May I provide a demonstration?"

Caught off guard, Bozar raised an eyebrow. "Demonstration?"

"Yes, to prove to our delightful faerie queen I am indeed who you say I am." Tal's anger continued to build and he didn't wait for Bozar's answer.

He reached inside himself to draw on his well of magic. A sharp intake of breath came from Artemis Thurgood, the grand master sensing the cresting power. Eyes glowing blue, Tal pointed at Margaret.

She flew off her horse and straight up into the air. Screaming, she tumbled over and over, and continued to rise until her form was only a dark speck.

Then she fell.

Like a brick, Margaret plummeted toward the ground, her screams rising in intensity. Before she landed with crushing impact, her momentum abruptly stopped.

And she glided into Tal's arms.

Her face white, Margaret clung to him as he carried her back to her horse. Her soft curves reminded Tal of Alex, but there was also an underlying hardness of sinew and muscle. *Lady* Margaret was no woman of tea and pastries.

He lifted her back into the saddle.

Hand on her leg, he asked, "Is that proof enough for you?"

Blue eyes blazing, she ripped his hand away. "It proves nothing except you're good at levitation!"

Tal smirked. While Margaret's stubbornness wouldn't allow her to admit any mistake, the looks on the faces of her father and the others told a different story.

They were convinced.

In fact, Earl York looked giddy. "I don't understand the circumstances that led you to Markingham, but we welcome you. You come at a most opportune time."

Tal hoped the earl's enthusiasm would temper the lecture sure to come from his First Advisor. Regardless, he got what he wanted.

I sped up the negotiations.

A pavilion was erected on the broad road leading into Markingham. Exactly halfway between the army encampment and city, chairs and tables were placed in a circle, the two groups facing each other. Once refreshments were served, Bozar opened the discussions.

"The empire's purpose is to destroy the Veil, then find and execute the Veil Queen and King. We will use Markingham as our initial base of operations. It will take time to build our forces until we are ready to face the Dark Queen. We will expect your cooperation."

Earl York rubbed his chin. "Ah, of course, but could you further define *cooperation* for me?"

"By decree, Queen Celestria Meredith, Ruler of the Empire, has restored all laws, rights, and privileges that existed before the creation of Veil. However," Bozar paused, "fealty to the Crown is expected, and until such time as we have secured victory, I am the queen's representative. My word is final and will be followed to the letter."

"Aha!" Lady Margaret spat. "There you have it! The velvet glove slipped over the iron fist."

Unperturbed, Bozar continued. "Our army will quarter inside the city. Utmost secrecy will be maintained at all times. The

Veil Queen must not know we are in her midst until we are ready to strike. Therefore, no one will be allowed outside the city walls without my permission."

"How will we eat?" Lady Margaret snapped. "We must gather food or our people will starve."

Bozar frowned. "Gather food? You speak as though you are hunters gleaning the countryside for game."

Earl York quickly jumped in. "Our situation is, ah, unique. It is much more dire than you think. Perhaps now is not the time to explore this."

"Enough nonsense! The question I want answered is how?" Lord Morehead demanded. "How is it you are even here? Does the Veil not still exist? An imperial soldier has not set foot on this soil in over a thousand years, yet you claim to field an imperial army."

Bozar smiled. "Ah, that is the most important question of all— and the glorious answer is a breach has been found through the accursed barrier."

Stunned silence followed his remark. Then everyone in the earl's group began to talk and shout at once.

Holding up his hand, Bozar waited for silence. "Do not ask for details. Again, I cannot stress strongly enough that the Veil Queen must remain ignorant of our presence."

"Well, I think you're full of shit. And I pledge no cooperation." Lady Margaret stood and stalked off.

CHAPTER 4

ALEX RODE THROUGH THE GATES OF MARKINGHAM WITH TAL BY HER side.

Trash lined the streets, some piled high enough the refuse obscured smaller alleys and byways. They passed abandoned structures to their left and right. The air was heavy with hopelessness, and thick was the unsavory mix of rot, decay, and above all, the pungent odor of human waste. Rats boldly scurried about in broad daylight, and the few residents they passed wore clothes little more than rags.

She glanced at Tal and by the hardness of his jaw, knew the sight upset him. She reached across the space between them and squeezed his hand.

"I did not expect this," he said.

Alex didn't know what to say. In her former alternate life as Mona Parker, the scenes were eerily reminiscent of the videos she'd seen featuring famine and poverty-stricken regions on earth. Those images were filled with hollow-eyed children, their stomachs as empty as their prospects for hope. Anger boiled within her.

The Veil Queen caused all of this.

This rage gave her insight into how Tal must feel…and he had seen worse—far worse. The empire's inability to protect its most vulnerable citizens was an ongoing nightmare that plagued him every day. *This* was the reason he took such risks, why he felt he must do something, anything. The alternative was to give in to helplessness, and the Tal she knew would never consider that an option.

The result was a festering, visceral hatred for the Dark Queen and all things associated with the Veil. It consumed him. Like a cancer, it ate at him and threatened to leave him void of everything but anger and bitterness. Her heart broke to see him in such a state.

She squeezed the reins until her knuckles turned white. *I'm not going to let his emotions destroy him.*

They crossed a moat, dry except for scattered puddles of scummy water. Hooves clopped across the wood and iron drawbridge leading to the earl's keep. Located atop a hillock, the sturdy keep overlooked Markingham and offered an excellent view of the entire city. Smoke from numerous cookfires rose like strands of yarn from parts of the city.

While other sections were dark and silent.

Unlike most of the buildings they'd seen, Earl York's keep was well-maintained. Shrubs and trees were clipped, the grass kept low, and the structure itself looked formidable. A high wall studded with sharp pikes surrounded the fortified manor, and twin barbicans flanked the portcullis allowing entry. Even the outbuildings, including the stables, looked to be in good repair.

Bozar, Tal, Artemis Thurgood, Pulpit—most of the original parley group including Alex—would be staying at the earl's stronghold as his guests. The exceptions were Lords Gravelback and Tarlbolt. As the expedition's military leaders, they planned to stay billeted with their men.

Grooms ran up to take the horses, and Earl York led them inside. Spacious, the interior reminded Alex of the duke's manor in Wheel. It would be easy to get lost in the large, multi-storied structure.

An opulent balustrade flanked a wide, winding staircase. Tapestry-covered walls depicted hunting and battle scenes of long ago. The earl led them up the staircase as liveried servants carried their few belongings.

"There are plenty of empty rooms for your party," the earl said to Bozar. "We welcome the company." Wistfully, he added. "It will be nice to have this place filled with life and conversation again."

On the second landing, lengthy corridors stretched to the left and right. A woman in a long, blue gown waited for them. Middle-aged, she was a younger version of the earl, her brown hair pinned into a bun.

"This is my sister, Patrice. She runs the household," the earl said. "Without her, I would be lost."

"Welcome lords, lady, and Prince Talmund," Patrice said with a curtsey. "We have looked forward to this moment. I will be happy to take care of any of your needs. You have but to ask."

She approached Alex and covered Alex's hand with her own. A smile crossed her face. "And you must be Lady Alexandria. You are far more beautiful than my brother described."

Alex felt her own smile tug at her lips. "You are too kind."

"Nonsense! I simply speak the truth." Her warmth was infectious, and Alex liked Patrice immediately.

"Come with me. Brother, show our lords to their rooms." With that, Patrice led Alex down the long hallway.

After going some distance, she stopped and opened a door. Inside was a large, canopied, four poster bed. Windows flanked the bed, allowing abundant light into the room. A pair of doors led to a small balcony overlooking the courtyard. Next, Patrice showed her the bathroom. The opulent fixtures were gilded in gold, the tub large enough for two people to comfortably bathe.

Alex followed Patrice back into the hallway. The earl's sister turned and said, "Dinner will be served this evening. I'll send a servant to fetch you. Is there anything else?"

The hallway, empty and silent, retained an air of vacancy so thick, Alex felt compelled to ask, "Are any of the other rooms occupied?"

A troubled look appeared on Patrice's face. "Only one. Lady Margaret, my niece, occasionally stays here."

Aware she had touched upon a sensitive topic, Alex quickly said, "Thank you for showing me to my room. I look forward to dinner this evening."

Patrice gave her hand a final pat, then turned and left. Alex returned to her room, unpacked her things, and then went in search of Tal. Crossing to the other corridor, she followed the sound of his voice to a large room similar to hers. She found him talking to Pulpit. They both looked up as she entered the room.

The monk smiled. "I shall see you both at dinner." He left, closing the door as he did so.

Tal still wore a haunted look.

"Come here," Alex said.

Tal moved closer, and she held his face with her hands. "Let it go."

"Did you see them? This city? It looks like a pestilence has struck—"

"Tal, let it go."

"But—"

She pulled him to her and hugged him with every ounce of her strength. A grunt spilled from Tal over the fierceness of her effort. Then his own arms encircled her.

When at last they parted, Alex said, "You can't change the past." Tal tried to speak, but she placed a finger against his lips.

"Listen to me. It's what happens from this point forward that's important, right?"

Tal nodded.

"Then we need to help these people."

Tal raised an eyebrow. "What do you have in mind?"

"How about food, clean water, shelter, and decent clothing? That would be a good start."

"Alex, we're in the midst of an invasion. Our resources need to be focused on winning, not baking bread."

"War always has unintended victims. If we can't provide for those in need now, then why are you here? Why go into battle?"

A look of frustration crossed Tal's face. "You have a way of putting things that I should know but somehow escape me. My priorities always seem askew, don't they?"

Alex caught Tal's arm, and they sat on his bed. "No. Don't talk about yourself like that. Despite all your bluster, you have a tender heart."

She took a deep breath, then stood and faced him. "I want to help. I want to be part of any meeting concerning Markingham and its people."

Tal snorted. "My *Eldred* would love that! Why not also ask for jewels to fall from the sky?"

"I'm serious. I want to actually *help*, which means getting out into the city and among the citizenry."

"No. Doing so places you in danger."

Alex rolled her eyes. "If it makes you feel any better, send a score of guards with me everywhere I go."

She ran her fingers through his hair. "I want to be useful, Tal, not some ornament to be displayed on rare occasions. I am the heir to the Duchy of Wheel, lest you forget. I need to start acting like it."

Alex moved closer, slipping between Tal's knees. She draped her arms around him, his head nestled between her breasts. "Must I charm you to get my way?"

Tal's response was to move his lips across her sensitive flesh. The room suddenly became hot and close.

All other thoughts fled from her mind.

CHAPTER 5

WHETHER HER "CHARMS" OR SENSIBLE ARGUMENTS WON THE DAY, the next morning, Alex rode out of the keep and into the city. With her was Tal, Pulpit, a dozen mounted soldiers, and a wagon laden with food, blankets, and barrels of water, all requisitioned from the army.

At first, the few residents they encountered watched them from the shadows. Fear and suspicion filled their faces, and none would willingly come forth to meet and talk with them.

They came across a small boy, thumb firmly planted in his mouth, standing next to a backstreet littered with rubbish. Alex dismounted and knelt beside him. Face smudged with dirt, and his clothing ripped and torn, the little boy glanced left and right, ready to bolt.

"What is your name?" she asked. The boy's mother appeared silently and stood behind him. Hands on his shoulders, she prepared to pick him up and flee.

Emboldened, the boy said, "Brighton."

"What a beautiful name for such a beautiful little boy," Alex remarked with smile. She licked her thumb and rubbed it across his dirt-streaked face. Taking a kerchief from her pocket, she wiped away most of the grime. "There. That's better." Brighton grasped one of her fingers with his hand.

And grinned.

Like sunlight breaking through a grey, cloudy sky, the jittery atmosphere dissolved. "We named him Brighton because he was born on a bright, sunny day," his mother said.

"We have something to give you," Alex told her. Immediately, the mother's face radiated suspicion.

Alex signaled and Pulpit approached carrying a cloth sack. The monk held the bundle out. "This is for you."

Brighton's mother eyed the bulging sack with narrowed eyes. "What's in it?"

Pulpit opened the sack and showed her the contents. "A loaf of bread, a wedge of cheese, and salt pork. We also have fresh water. We can wait while you retrieve a bucket."

The woman stared at the food, her look first of disbelief, then of stunned delight. "Wh—what do I have to do for this?"

Alex stood. "This is freely given. The food and water are for you and your family. You have but to take it."

The mother grasped Alex's arm. "Thank you." She took the sack from Pulpit and whirled to leave. Stopping she looked back. "I know other families. Can they have some bread too?"

"Of course," Alex said warmly. "Go get them as well."

Brighton's mother picked him up and ran.

A short time later, the wagon was surrounded by dozens of men, women, and children. The wagon's supplies were quickly depleted. Those who came late wore disappointed faces.

Tal, seeing that a multitude would leave empty-handed, ordered the teamster to turn the wagon around and requisition more. "If the supply master gives you any trouble, tell them the order comes directly from me."

Alex searched Tal's face. At first, she was hesitant to have him accompany her as she went into the city. She feared he would react as he had when he first saw the rundown city and its ragged population. Instead of anxiety and anger, however, his eyes sparkled, joy evident in the wide smile he wore.

Pulpit moved to stand beside Alex. "Well done, Lady Alexandria."

Alex lifted an eyebrow at the monk. "For what?"

"For showing the young prince another way."

Alex jumped as Lord Gravelback, face red, pounded the table.

"This city is a deathtrap! We have been deceived. Markingham is ready to be picked like a ripe fruit. It should have fallen to the Veil Queen's forces long ago."

He pointed a shaking finger at the earl. "They must be in league with the Dark Queen! How else to explain why they still enjoy independence?"

Lord Morehead shot to his feet. "You dare to make such an accusation? We owe no allegiance to that foul bitch!"

"Liar! I—"

"Lord Gravelback!" Bozar's voice thundered across the table. "We have spent a week evaluating the city and its resources. Your task was to assess the military readiness of Markingham and its suitability as a base of operations. *Not* to question the loyalty of others!"

Gravelback glowered at Lord Morehead. Grimacing, he growled, "My apologies."

"Good!" Bozar snapped. "Are you ready to give the rest of your report *absent* other commentary?"

Gravelback swallowed. "Yes."

"Then proceed."

Alex sat on one end of a long conference table next to Tal. At Tal's insistence, Bozar had reluctantly included her in the meeting. The initial negotiators, minus Lady Margaret, made up the rest of the individuals.

Before Gravelback could continue, the door banged open

and Lady Margaret entered. She surveyed the group and her eyes settled on Tal. She swaggered to an empty chair, dragged it across the room and pushed it next to him, then sat down.

She scooted nearer to Tal until her knees brushed his. "I'm not going to float away am I, *Prince*?"

Margaret placed a hand on his arm. "Do I need to hang on to something?"

Alex's heart raced. *She's flirting with him!*

Suffocating jealousy rose in her, and she found it hard to breathe.

Tal's lips formed a thin line. "Lady Margaret. What a pleasant surprise. I thought you had decided to be uncooperative."

Margaret leaned closer. "Oh, there are some things I can be very cooperative about...and as you have no doubt surmised, I am no lady." She snorted. "Call me Maggie. No one calls me Margaret except Father."

"Margaret, now is not the time for this," the earl warned.

Ignoring him, Maggie caught Alex's eyes with her own. Stroking Tal's arm, she said, "Perhaps I can repay your demonstration with one of my own."

Alex's fingers curled like the talons of a raptor. If Tal weren't between them, she didn't know if she could stop herself from scratching Maggie's eyes out.

"Oh dear. I think I have offended your...mistress? Concubine? What would you call her, Prince Tal?"

"Alexandria!" Alex spat. "My name is Alexandria, the daughter of the Duke of Wheel."

Maggie clapped. "A prince and now a princess. We are showered with royalty."

"Enough!" Bozar's voice cut through the animosity like a sharp blade. "Lady Margaret, you are welcome to participate, but I must insist you maintain the decorum of this war council."

"I told you the name is *Maggie*." Her chair screeched as it was pushed back. "Sooner or later, you'll come asking for my help. My advice? Don't waste your time."

She stalked to the door, then paused and turned around. She pointed at Tal. "But I will talk to him. Who knows? I might change my mind."

Maggie swept out onto the main floor of the keep.

Although it was enjoyable watching the reaction of Alexandria to her flirtation with Tal, a deeper feeling ran through her, one she had tried and failed to ignore.

When the prince's magic had launched her into the air, terror filled her—multiplied tenfold as she plunged back to the ground.

Then he caught her.

He carried her as though she were a feather. Through the fog of her shock, she could feel the ripple and play of his muscles. Lifting her onto her horse with the ease she would pick up a twig, he had placed his hand on her leg. A quiver ran through her whose journey ended at her groin. Never had she felt such an instant and intense attraction. Even now, if she closed her eyes she could still smell Tal. The memory of his musky scent sending butterflies into flight through her stomach.

Her reverie was broken by a voice. "Well?"

Bradley waited for her at the door. She brushed by him and he followed her outside.

Maggie scowled. "Message delivered."

She swung into her saddle. "Now we'll see if they reply."

They cantered off.

Momentary silence took hold as the door slammed behind Maggie.

Tal watched the earl's face turn by degrees from pink to red at his daughter's display. Then, below the table, a hand clenched his leg above the knee, fingers digging painfully into his flesh. He turned to find Alex glaring at him.

Bozar saved him from further discomfort. Clearing his throat, his *Eldred* said, "Lord Gravelback, please continue."

The lord commander stood. "The fortifications protecting Markingham are in complete disrepair. Whole sections of the wall need shoring up, or worse, need to be replaced. The majority of ballista, scorpions, and other weapons mounted on the battlements are damaged, many beyond repair. I found only seven working blacksmiths in the entire city, and their smithies are barely adequate to straighten a bent horseshoe. To use them to repair or replace weapons such as those needed on the fortifications would be next to impossible."

"What of billeting our army in the city barracks?" Bozar asked. "The longer they are camped in plain sight in front of Markingham, the greater the risk of our discovery."

Gravelback shook his head. "Although there is more than enough room to quarter our soldiers within the city, the barracks are falling apart. There's not a roof that doesn't leak, and the latrines will need to be completely dug out and replaced. The stables are in such bad shape, our horses are better off pastured outside the city. If we attempt to use these facilities in their present state, we'll be battling disease long before we engage the enemy."

Gravelback leaned forward, palms placed flat on the table. "With an army twice the size we have now, I could not defend this city."

Bozar took the news with stoic silence. Hands steepled together, he said, "I see. Can we supplement our forces with those of the earl's?"

Heads turned. Instead of the previous shade of red, Earl

York's face was now pale. "Ah, you see, it's a little complicated," he stammered.

Bozar pursed his lips. "Come, come. Surely you know how large your city guard is?"

The earl looked at Lord Morehead. "Might as well get this over with," the guard commander growled. He pushed away from the table and stiffly took to his feet.

"We have maybe two hundred in the city watch. On a good day, we might get an additional twenty-five to show up."

Tal's jaw dropped.

Gravelback's loud cursing echoed off the walls. "Two hundred! You'd be hard-pressed to protect even the keep with such small numbers!"

Tal couldn't believe his ears. Between the crumbling battlements and the scant number of guards in the city watch, Markingham was essentially defenseless.

To his credit, Bozar remained calm. "We still have more reports. Please be seated, Lord Gravelback." The grizzled commander bit back another curse and collapsed into his chair.

"Artemis. What of the magical defenses?"

The grand master rose, his face grim. "I'm afraid my assessment is worse. Much worse."

He paused at the raised brows questioning what could be worse than a city without crumbling defenses.

"Markingham is essentially a city devoid of magic."

CHAPTER 6

THE CREAK OF CHAIRS AND RUSTLE OF CLOTHING GREETED THE GRAND master's pronouncement.

Tal finally found his tongue. "What do you mean? Magic is everywhere. How can none exist here?"

A sad smile creased Thurgood's face. "I didn't say magic didn't exist, I said *Markingham* is bereft of magic. Let me explain."

With a sigh, the grand master continued. "We all know the most common conveyance of magic is through the use of Artifacts. These objects, in order to function, need lodestones. They must be recharged periodically as the magic within them is exhausted.

"I have found not a single Artifact that works. Why? Because there's no magic left in their lodestones. That's why the city walls are in such disrepair. The lodestones embedded in them are depleted of magic."

"Why haven't they been recharged?" Bozar asked.

Thurgood spread his hands. "I don't believe there is anyone left in Markingham who knows how to wield magic. There's no one here to renew the magic of the lodestones."

In the stunned silence that followed, Tal had a hard time believing his ears. "Impossible. There must be at least one."

The grand master sighed. "I wish I was mistaken, lad."

Bozar pointed at Practius Bolt. The court magister shrank into his chair. "What of him? Isn't he your magical advisor, Bartholomew?"

Rubbing his face, Earl York released a sigh. "Yes, but you see, he has had no special training. Practius is," the earl swallowed, "the closest thing we have to a magister."

Artemis Thurgood speared the young man with a hard look. "Is this true, lad? You've had no training?"

Practius sank lower. "Yes," he squeaked.

"Then what qualifies you as a magister?"

The young magister looked like he might faint from the attention focused on him.

"I-I can move objects," he stammered. "Sometimes I can spontaneously light a candle. I can also sense magical beings like faeries and trolls."

Earl York's shoulders drooped. "There has been no one in Markingham to instruct others in magic since my grandfather's time. Practius has the talent, but not the schooling."

The grand master took a step back. "And yet you have allowed him use this talent?"

Thurgood slapped the table. "Listen to me! The boy must not attempt to use magic in any way. Without the discipline gained from formal training, he's as much a danger to others as himself. Down through the ages, countless numbers have been killed by uncontrolled, wild magic, precisely *why* its practice is forbidden."

The grand master nudged his chin at Bolt. "How many accidental fires have you started trying to bring the flame on a candle to life?"

Bolt licked his lips. "Uh, does this include my own clothes, or just the other objects in the room?"

"Blood of My Ancestors!" Gravelback roared. "Does this nightmare have no end?"

The normally unflappable First Advisor seemed at a loss for words. He cleared his throat. "This news is unexpected. I think we need time to absorb what we've heard. We will adjourn and—"

"You haven't heard my report."

Bozar's eyes widened at the sight of Alex standing. "My pardon, Lady Alexandria, but I don't recall assigning you an investigation."

"I decided to take the initiative, First Advisor. I hope you don't mind."

Bozar coughed. "Under the circumstances, I think we have far graver matters to consider."

Tal rose to stand beside Alex. Pulpit did the same. "I think we need to hear what Lady Alexandria has to say." He glanced at the monk. "Particularly since we helped Alex."

Pulpit nodded. "I concur with Prince Tal."

Bozar looked from Tal to Pulpit. The corners of his mouth tugged into the hint of a smile. "Very well." He folded his hands. "My lady, the floor is yours."

Alex took a deep breath. "I will try to be brief. Each day, we ventured into the city, and each day, we met the citizens of Markingham. We brought with us a wagon full of food, water, and warm blankets. Within an hour, no matter where we went, our supplies were rapidly exhausted."

She continued. "These people are on the verge of starvation. What's more, many have no source of clean water, and they live in areas where raw sewage runs out onto the streets. If something isn't done soon, many will die."

Gravelback, his eyes narrowed with suspicion, asked, "And where did you get these 'supplies,' Lady Alexandria?"

Alex paused, aware of the intense scrutiny now focused on her. Before she could answer Tal spoke up.

"We requisitioned them from the army's provisions. By my order."

"What!" Gravelback's cry crashed off the walls. His face rapidly transitioned from red to purple. "You take the bread out of the mouths of our own soldiers? This vixen has caused you to take leave of your senses!"

Tal's nostrils flared. Before he could blurt a retort, Alex placed a hand on his arm. "Perhaps you should explain why," she said.

Jaw clenched, Tal nodded. He surveyed those around the table.

"Everyone knows of my hatred for the Veil Queen and King and the magical abomination that has separated our people over the long ages. I would gladly carve Marlinda's black heart from her chest and serve it to her while still beating."

He looked at Alex. "But it was pointed out to me that the citizens of Markingham are our responsibility—just like our people on the *other* side of the Veil. If we turn our backs on them, if we let them starve or die from neglect, then we are not here to save them. We are hypocrites motivated only by vengeance and no better than Marlinda."

"If we lose this war, what then, Prince Tal?" Gravelback spat. "How does that work into your equation? Then we're right back to murder, slavery, and endless raids. *Everybody* suffers!"

Pulpit spread his hands. "We have been given a glorious opportunity to stop a long reign of pain and misery. Shouldn't we also have the faith to know helping others is part of this plan?"

"Spare us your pious platitudes, monk!" Gravelback barked. "It doesn't wield a sword or send an arrow into flight."

"There might be another way. One which helps the people and still prepares for war." Eyes riveted on Alex. Her knees quaked from the sharp attention.

Tal leaned closer and whispered in her ear, "You're doing fine."

Alex swallowed, the tension a taunt cord within her. "Why not rebuild the city, fix the sewers, repair the aquifers, and restore the population to full health?" she continued. "Then you have a ready-made pool of citizens prepared to join the fight. How long would it take to equal their number, to replicate the potential resources of this city—especially if forced to transport everything through the Veil and the long distance it would take to get here?"

"Sheep! Cowards! The populace runs at the sight of an unfamiliar shadow," Gravelback shouted. "We can expect no help from them."

"Yes. I imagine when one lives on the edge of starvation, when hope has been absent for generations, it is easy for fear to take root." Pulpit's calm gaze met the lord commander's flashing eyes. "One might even say folk with less mettle would have succumbed long ago. Yet, here the city still stands, its inhabitants' survivors in the vicious and black world created by Marlinda. I'd say that must have taken an inordinate amount of courage, a feat unmatched in the long annals of our history."

Bozar tapped his lips. "Intriguing. Your saying by rebuilding Markingham we would be helping ourselves?"

Gravelback's eyes bulged. "Surely you're not entertaining this fantasy? You'd have us delay the growth of our army, spend precious resources on chattel, all the while praying the Dark Queen remains unaware of our presence?"

Earl York pounded the table with a closed fist. "Lord Commander, my people are not chattel!"

Face red, his breath coming in shaky gasps, the earl gestured at Bozar and Gravelback. "I admit we deceived you and offered far more than we could ever deliver. Even the food and accommodations of my keep were hastily cobbled together, an illusion meant to keep you from realizing just how desperate our situation is. But what would you have done in my place? I was afraid once you knew how broken Markingham was, you would leave and never return."

He rubbed a weary hand across his face. "You have to understand. We've been isolated for so long, fought so many desperate battles, given everything we have, and with no hope the bitter struggle will ever end. What else did we have to look forward to other than our inevitable doom?"

Tears appeared in his eyes. "Then one day, an army camps outside our gates, one not of the Dark Queen, but made up of our long-lost brothers. It was the most magnificent sight my old eyes have ever seen." He turned to Bozar. "I beg of you, please help us. In return, I swear I will do all in my power to direct the resources of Markingham to aid in the war against the Veil Queen."

A heavy silence fell across the room. The scrape of a chair being pushed back echoed like a thunderclap as Bozar stood.

"I will communicate to Queen Celestria and her advisors that we need to alter our original plan. I will propose we continue build up our army, but dedicate a portion of our efforts to helping the civilian population and to rebuild Markingham. If the Queen agrees, then we will adjust the flow of personnel and supplies now coming through the Veil."

Earl York gripped the edge of the table with palpable relief. "Thank you, First Advisor."

Bozar held up his hand at the cry of protest from Gravelback. "My proposal continues to increase the number of our legions and prepare for war—although admittedly at a slower pace."

He looked at Alex then Tal, studying them both. "My thanks to Lady Alexandria for showing us what we should have seen all along." He turned to Earl York. "Every life is precious…including those here."

Lord Morehead cleared his throat. "May I approach the lord commander?"

Still fuming, Gravelback barked. "Say what's on your mind."

The lord of the city guard walked around the table to stand beside him. The veteran campaigners sized each other up as if warriors seeking a chink in an opponent's armor. Then Morehead extended his hand. "I'd be honored to serve in any way I can. I'll dig privies if that's what's needed."

Gravelback's hesitation was brief before slowly grasping Lord Morehead's hand. A tight smile appeared. "I think we can come up with a better use of your skills."

A wolfish grin appeared on Lord Morehead's face. "Will it involve killing Veil filth?"

Gravelback's savage smile matched Morehead's. "Oh, most assuredly."

"Then count me in."

CHAPTER 7

"**H**AVE YOU FOUND SOMETHING?"

Even as he asked, Pandathaway bounced on his toes in keen anticipation.

Bedrosian sighed. "Will you please sit? If I must endure these nocturnal liaisons, the least you can do is allow me the courtesy of normal conversation."

Harrumphing, Pandathaway took a seat. Once again, they occupied one of the tables in the middle of the cavernous reading and research area within the Library of Wheel. Bedrosian flicked his wrist, and a book appeared out of the dim recesses of the library. Wheeling in midair like a bird in flight, the tome glided to the table and settled in front of the gnome.

"I did as you asked and limited my research to anyone in the ducal line of Duvalier who exhibited or practiced an unusual form of magic. Sad to say, my efforts came up fruitless."

The archivist leaned forward, eyes sparkling. "Then I decided to look into the marriages of the Duvaliers—in other words, to those who became part of the ducal genealogy through matrimony, not directly by blood."

Bedrosian lifted the book before him. "This is the chronicle of Philbus Court, a minor historian known for his accounts of life in small villages and towns. He lived a hundred years before the creation of the Veil."

The gnome snapped his fingers and the pages flapped by in a blur. They stopped at an entry beneath which the picture of a woman had been sketched. Statuesque, the woman had long hair the color of gold. Azure eyes peered above gentle cheeks and a strong chin.

Pandathaway pursed his lips. "An excellent illustration."

Bedrosian nodded. "Court was an accomplished artist, noted as much for his illustrations as for his historical accounts. Whether he actually saw this woman or drew her from descriptions is an open question. However, that's not what's important. *This is.*" He pointed at a passage and began to read.

"Traveling through the township of Haversham, I was regaled at the local tavern by the tale of a noblewoman possessed of unusual healing powers. Rather than powders, potions, or other philters, the noblewoman—a Lady Diana—restored health by touch alone. Determined to see if this was fact or simply another fanciful local fable, I managed to locate two individuals who claimed to have been 'healed' by Lady Diana. One, an elderly woman afflicted with bloody bowels, claimed the noblewoman placed the flat of her palm on her stomach, and moments later, her ailment disappeared. The second, a wheelwright, had his hand crushed when the wagon he was repairing slipped and fell from its cradle. Lady Diana touched his hand and his shattered bones instantly knit. The wheelwright showed me his hand, and I could see no evidence of a previous injury. Both likened the curative magic as akin to 'pure, clean water.' Despite vigorous efforts to learn more, my inquiry into Lady Diana revealed nothing additionally of note save this.

All the villagers commonly referred to her as a 'Healer'."

Bedrosian closed the book with a *thump*. His eyes glowed. "I found her, Pandathaway! I referred back to the Duvalier genealogy, and a Diana Dane married Corbin Duvalier, the Twenty-Fifth Duke of Wheel, during this same time period."

Pandathaway felt his own excitement mounting. "And you believe her to be the same Diana referred to in this account?"

"She must be!" Bedrosian waved his hand, and the book rose

and flew off to disappear in the dark, upper reaches of the library. "Court's referral of the villagers to Lady Diana as a 'Healer' struck me as a title, not a description. So I did more research. It turns out a Healer is an ancient term whose origins can be dated back to the founding of the empire. It refers to individuals whose magic is virtuous and restorative."

The two gnomes looked at one another. "Just like the magic we felt in the Staff of the Test!" Pandathaway blurted.

"Precisely. But throughout the entire history of Meredith, there have been only a few accounts of the actual existence of Healers. They are so rare, in fact, Diana may have been the last one."

The Archivist leaned closer. "Although this revelation is stunning, it gets better."

Bedrosian snapped his fingers and another book winged its way to their table. Pages fluttered and came to a stop, the name, *Corbin Duvalier,* at the top of the section. Beneath the name, the duke's wife, Diana, was listed, and that of their children.

Bedrosian pointed at the list. "You can see Duke Corbin and Duchess Diana had four children, two sons and two daughters. Their youngest child, Elisa, married a minor noble with holdings in southwest Dalfur." The gnome flicked his hand and the pages in the volume turned to another section.

He moved his finger down the page and came to a stop beside another genealogical entry. "Do you recognize this name?"

Pandathaway's lips moved as he read to himself. His eyes grew wider. "Impossible. That can't be."

"It's true, my friend. I found the seashell you had me search for. *Here* is the connection and why the Dark Queen seeks Lady Alexandria. Diana Duvalier is the great grandmother of Sonja Salterhorn.

"The creator of the orb."

Silence fell and stretched into long moments between the two gnomes. Finally, Pandathaway shook his head. "No. Marlinda killed

Sonja and her husband when she took the orb. They had no children. Therefore, no direct connection to Alex exists. She couldn't have inherited any of Diana's magic and would be useless to the Veil Queen."

"It would seem so," Bedrosian agreed. "But what if Sonja had a secret, one she wanted no one to know about?"

Pandathaway cocked an eye at his friend. "What are you saying?"

"Sonja Salterhorn is one of the most researched individuals in the history of Dalfur. For years, the dukes and grand masters of Wheel have scrutinized every detail of her life in a vain effort to find a way to destroy the Veil."

"And?"

"And we know she suddenly left the Academy of Magic at Locus midway through her second year. Then she reappeared a year later and re-enrolled. We have meticulous accounts of every year of her enrollment at the academy except for the twelve months she was absent. Although the subject of much fruitless speculation, these twelve months remain a blank page."

He turned to his fellow gnome. "I think something happened. Something so profound, she had to keep it a secret."

Pandathaway sat back. His stunned mind tried to grasp the enormity of what he just heard. His mouth went dry and he had to swallow several times to remove the lump in his throat.

"Let's say everything you've said is true. What secret could be so important she had to disappear for a year?"

An exasperated chuckle left Bedrosian's lips.

"Indeed. Now we must find another seashell—on an even larger shore."

CHAPTER 8

"IF YOU GO TO SEE THAT, THAT *WOMAN*, I WILL NEVER SPEAK TO YOU again!"

Alex and Tal were alone in the courtyard of the earl's keep. Fuming, Alex crossed her arms and turned her back on Tal.

Tal threw his hands up. "You're not listening. Lord Morehead told my *Eldred* that Lady Margaret leads a group called 'Maggie's Marauders'. They number well over a thousand. He said although they're not a regular militia, they are the closest thing to a military force in Markingham. They know the countryside, where to hunt, where wild cattle graze, and have been supplying food to the city. We need their help."

Stomping her foot on the worn cobblestones, Alex whirled on Tal.

"Then somebody else can meet with her. Why does it have to be you?"

Tal shook his head. "You heard her. She said I was the only one she would talk to."

Alex stabbed a finger onto Tal's chest. "Oh, yes, I heard every word. I also saw Margaret throw herself at you—right there in front of everyone including me! *Send someone else.*"

Tal's jaw clenched. "*You* were the one who convinced me we needed to help the citizens of Markingham. That's all I'm trying to do."

"Throwing my own words back at me isn't helping you," Alex shot back.

"You're being impossible!" Tal snapped.

Alex barked a laugh. "I'm being impossible? What have you said to reassure me? How do I know the moment that Margaret's alone with you, she won't throw herself at you again?"

Exasperated, Tal ran a hand through his hair. "I already told you Pulpit is going with me. Surely the presence of a white monk will be proof of my continued virtue."

He draped his arms over Alex's shoulders. "You know how I feel about you. Why are you making this so hard?"

Alex felt her cheeks burn. *I'm acting like a fool.* With a sigh, she gripped Tal's waist and lay her head on his tunic. "I hate it. But, I suppose you must do your duty."

Abruptly, she pushed him away, and again, planted a slender finger on his chest.

"But make sure duty is *all* that you do."

Tal and Pulpit made their way through winding streets, the clip-clop of hooves echoing off empty storefronts and houses.

Their destination, a tavern in the eastern part of the city, was in a part of Markingham controlled by Maggie's militia. Although Lord Gravelback had conducted a cursory inspection as part of his original report, neither Tal or Pulpit were familiar with this part of the city. Despite the gathering gloom, it was clear to see the nearer they drew, the cleaner the streets and surroundings became. Even abandoned structures looked in better condition than those in the more populated part of the city.

They stopped, and Tal squinted at the scrawled directions on the paper in his hand. "We're almost there." With a flick of the reins, they continued.

Turning a corner, they came across a boulevard ablaze in light. Dozens of men and women, many around Tal's age, spilled outside a tavern and onto the street. Numerous torches were fixed to posts along the avenue. The flickering flames revealed stares of surprise, curiosity, and in some cases, open hostility.

A freshly painted sign hung above the pub. There were no words, just the depiction of a hand grasping a bloody sword.

Tal cast a wry glance at Pulpit. "Looks like we're at the right place." He snorted. "And look. We have a welcoming committee." They dismounted and tied their horses to a railing in front of the alehouse.

A large, swinging door allowed entry into the tavern. When Tal tried to enter, a familiar figure blocked his way. "Only Marauders allowed in."

Tal flashed a tight smile at Bradley Sikes. "We have come at the invitation of Lady Margaret."

A number of young men and women gathered around Tal and Pulpit. Sikes nodded at them and smirked at Tal. "Pity she's not here—and I don't know anything about an invitation. Now, turn around and go back." Snickers broke out around them.

The smile disappeared from Tal's face. "I'm afraid I must insist. I need to talk to Lady Margaret."

Sikes took a step forward and thrust his face toward Tal. "Maggie don't want nothing to do with you." He looked Tal up and down. "Empire royalty my ass. You and your snowflake get the hell out of here while you can still walk!"

Seated near the door, Maggie heard voices.

Her heart beat faster at the prospect of seeing the prince once again. This time, however, it would be on her terms, not his. She would listen to whatever proposal he presented, but she had her own demands. Chief among them was that her Marauders must be allowed to come and go as they pleased. They had not been allowed outside the city since the imperial army appeared, and the grumbling among her followers became louder each day. If she didn't get some sort concession from the prince, sooner or later a hot-headed Marauder would attack an imperial soldier.

A disaster she must avoid at all costs.

The problem was, every time she was around Prince Talmund, he stirred a passion inside her, a veritable tempest tossing her steely determination to the winds.

Sikes' angry voice interrupted her meanderings. *What is he doing?*

"Bradley! Shut up and let them in!"

Wet, choking noises were the only response she received. A moment later the prince entered, her lieutenant held aloft like a banner in the wind. Sikes feet kicked at empty air, Tal's hand around his throat shaking him like a terrier would a rat.

Maggie shot to her feet, the chair toppling over. "Release him, Prince Talmund."

"I'd get a better guard dog. This one only knows how to bark." With a final shake, the prince dropped Sikes. Prone on the floor, the Marauder massaged his bruised throat, gasping like a fish out of water.

Prince Talmund turned to Maggie. "Call me Tal. No need for honorifics here."

Sikes staggered to his feet, a dagger in his hand. Pulpit cried a warning and pulled a baton from his belt. Instantly, the baton grew to the length of a staff and he swung, striking Sikes' wrist. The Marauder yelped and dropped the knife.

Molten anger rose in Maggie, and she grabbed Sikes by his tunic. "You fool! You don't do anything unless I tell you to!"

Sikes rubbed his sore wrist. "But I thought—"

"Who told you to think? Now, get out!" She shoved him and he stumbled away.

Maggie turned to the prince. "I'm sorry...Tal."

His sea-green eyes probed hers. She stared, aware the throb within her had started anew. She wrenched her attention away and pointed at the table. "Please be seated."

She waved, and a burly Marauder brought three tankards and placed them on the table. Maggie thrust her chin at the foaming liquid. "Best ale to be had in all Markingham...not that anyone in this shithole city knows good beer from muddy water."

Tal remained silent, and she could feel his eyes on her again. To fortify her nerves, Maggie picked up her mug and took a long swallow. Wiping her mouth with her sleeve, she pointed at Pulpit.

"I know nothing about your order, monk. Do your vows prevent you from imbibing?"

Pulpit picked up the tankard and drank half the stein. He belched and smacked his lips. "No."

Maggie snickered. "A monk that drinks and a prince that immediately picks a fight with one of my best men. What a way to begin a discussion." She placed her hand on Tal's arm. "You are here to negotiate, aren't you?"

Tal smirked. "To be fair, Sikes initiated the confrontation. I just decided to end it as judiciously as possible. And yes, Lady Margaret—"

"Maggie."

"—Maggie, we are here to negotiate."

Maggie ran her fingers up Tal's arm. "Everything has a price, Tal. It will cost you something to begin our talks."

Tal squinted at her. "What?"

Maggie stood. "Push your chair back," she ordered. Puzzled, Tal did as she asked. She dropped into his lap, arms around his shoulders.

"My price is a kiss," Maggie whispered in his ear.

Leaning forward, she covered Tal's mouth with hers.

CHAPTER 9

AUGHT BY SURPRISE, TAL TRIED TO PULL BACK.

Maggie's unexpected strength forced her lips to his until she broke away. Her kiss carried the tart taste of ale.

She placed her hand on Tal's chest. "*Hmm.* We should do that more often."

Quickly Maggie shifted and moved her legs to straddle him. "Shall we open the negotiations?"

Maggie's warm weight settled uncomfortably on his crotch. Tal clutched her waist and pushed her back, only to discover the maneuver positioned her breasts just below his chin. Dressed in Marauder black, she wore only a thin tunic unbuttoned to display firm cleavage, her nipples jutting through the lightweight material like spear points.

Thoughts of Alex's warning, *do only your duty*, galvanized Tal into action. He picked up Maggie and placed her back in her seat. Spinning, he bent to Pulpit's ear. "Not a word of this to anyone," he hissed.

The monk wore an amused expression. "Certainly, my prince." He pointed. "But what might they say?" Tal looked over his shoulder and stifled a curse.

A hundred or more Marauders filled the alehouse, all of them following Maggie's overt display with keen interest. He swallowed and fell back into his chair.

Maggie chuckled and patted his arm. "Don't worry, Tal. I can *probably* make sure none of this reaches the ears of your sweet, precious, Lady Alexandria."

Blood pounded in his ears. "You did that on purpose. You knew exactly what you were doing." His anger grew. "And what would the price be to make sure you can 'probably' keep your little spectacle from Alex?"

Maggie traced her finger alongside the curve of his jaw. "I'll take it into consideration and let you know."

Tal caught her hand. "Enough games. Are we here to talk or not?"

He took a heavy purse from his belt and dropped it on the table. It landed with a metallic thud. "A hundred gold crowns? A thousand? What's it going to cost?"

Maggie wrestled her hand away. She opened the purse and took out a gold coin. Turning it over and over, her shoulders shook with laughter. "You must be joking. Money? Coin hasn't been used in payment for anything since before my great-great-grandfather's time."

Chuckling, she hurled the gold crown away. With a *ping*, it landed on the floor and rolled to the crowded bar. "Barter is the coinage of choice here. You give me something, I give you something back."

Maggie boldly held Tal's gaze with her own. "For example, if I wanted something of a more physical nature, would you be able to furnish that?"

Temper smoldering, and his patience wore parchment-thin, Tal lost any semblance of diplomacy with Maggie. Pulpit must have sensed the same thing because he placed a warning hand on Tal's arm.

Tal forced himself to pick up his tankard and take a long drink. Putting the ale down, he wiped his mouth with the back of his hand and looked past Maggie to the pub's ballroom-sized interior.

An arched ceiling, stained black from years of cook fires and torches, stretched high above their heads. Stout wooden beams traversed the width of the ceiling. Old wagon-wheels formed candelabra, and hung from the beams. The wheels, layered with the tallow of countless tapers, were tied to thick ropes so the candelabra could be raised or lowered for lighting and replacement.

A rough-plank bar ran the length of one side of the tavern. Three leather-aproned Marauders filled tankards from a row of casks stacked on a thick wooden counter. The common room ran deep into the bowels of the pub. Scores of mismatched tables and chairs were scattered throughout, most occupied by the black-clad Marauders.

A large fieldstone fireplace occupied one wall. A deer carcass turned slowly on a spit, grease dripping into the flames with a hiss. The aroma of roasting venison wafted past Tal's nose. On the far wall, a group of Maggie's followers were engaged in a contest. Groans and cheers followed one another in rapid succession.

Impatient, Maggie took the dagger from her belt and flipped it expertly into the air. It fell back to the table and quivered, the sharp tip buried in the wood.

"I want my Marauders to regain the privilege of traveling to and from Markingham as we please," she said.

Tal returned his attention to Maggie. "And I want your followers to help rebuild this city. We need your knowledge of the land, sources of food and water, and strategic landmarks of military value."

"Then it seems we both want something," Maggie purred. "Tell your soldiers at the gate to let us pass freely."

Tal cast a steely glance at Maggie. "You know we can't allow that. The Dark Queen must not discover we have found a way through the Veil."

Maggie snatched the dagger. Eyes flashing, she stabbed the blade into the wood. "You think we are traitors? That we would tell the black-hearted bitch? My followers hate her as much as I do!"

Tal leaned forward, nostrils flaring. "What I *think* is irrelevant here. The fact remains Marlinda must remain ignorant of our presence. We can take no chance that might alert her."

Maggie shoved the bag of gold back at Tal. "Then take your worthless money, empty promises, and leave!"

Pulpit spoke up. "Perhaps a compromise is in order?"

Tal and Maggie glared at each other. Tal's sharp hearing detected the *thunk* of metal on wood. Distracted, he looked past Maggie at the gaming group he spied earlier.

Maggie turned and followed Tal's eyes to the Marauders at the back of the common room. A cunning smile formed.

"I think your proposal has merit, monk. A compromise that satisfies both of us."

She turned to Tal. "I offer this: let us come and go from the city unhindered, and in return, my Marauders will cooperate."

Tal's fist struck the table. "I've already told you—"

"Accompanied, of course, by soldiers of the empire," Maggie added.

Tal reined in his temper and considered her proposal. "You mean wherever your followers went, they would be escorted by imperiallegionnaires?"

"Yes."

"And they wouldn't try to lose their escort?"

"You have my word."

He could find no holes in it. "Agreed...as long as you honor the agreement. If even one Marauder tries to slip away unnoticed, none will be allowed beyond the walls until the war against the Veil Queen is concluded."

"Of course. But there is one condition."

Lips pressed flat, Tal tilted his head and studied Maggie. "And what would that be?"

"Play a game of daggers with me. Win or lose, our agreement remains. However, if I win, I get something else I want."

Leaning back, Tal crossed his arms. "What is it you want?"

"A night alone with you."

A long moment of silence followed. Finally, Pulpit spoke. "Lady Margaret, this is most inappropriate—"

"I told you the name is Maggie, and this is between me and the prince, monk. Stay out of it!" She turned to Tal. "What say you? Shall we play?"

Tal snorted. "Why should I? I've got what I came for. We have an agreement, and I have no more need of your games."

Maggie leaned closer. "The Blood Prince, the anointed heir is afraid to compete against a woman? I had no idea your pride is so easily bruised." She flicked her hand. "Go then."

Although he knew she was provoking him, red anger filled Tal. "Tell me the rules of this game," he spat.

"Follow me." Maggie pushed away from the table, and sauntered to the back of the common room. Tal and Pulpit followed. The Marauders parted to reveal two thick corkboards. A life-size representation of a man was outlined on each corkboard. Targets of different colored paint circled each vital area of the figures—the eyes, throat, heart, groin, and a painted spot on the thigh that Tal assumed was an artery. The cork was scored around each of these painted areas, evidence of the Marauders' accuracy.

Each board, suspended from a metal peg hammered into the wall, was attached to a thin rope. When pulled, the rope caused the wooden figure to swing from side-to-side.

"You are given five daggers. The object of the game is to place the knives in the painted areas on each figure. Hitting any one of these places on a real man would, of course, immediately kill or disable him. You get three points for a dagger strike on any part of the man, eight points for placement inside a circle, and ten points for a perfectly centered throw. You take the target on the left, I'll take the one on the right. Stand here." Maggie indicated a white line on the floor.

She added, "Oh, one more rule especially for you, Prince Tal. No magic. You hit or miss the targets solely on skill."

Tal walked to one of the targets and wrenched a dagger free. He flipped the knife in his hand to test the weight. Perfectly balanced. He pointed the sharp tip at Maggie.

"Let's play."

CHAPTER 10

A CROWD GATHERED, ALL JOSTLING FOR THE BEST VIEW OF THE contest.

Tal stepped up to the white chalk line. He estimated the distance to be at least twenty-five paces to each corkboard figure. Not difficult to hit with a dagger, but placing the knives inside each painted circle would take considerable skill.

Before he could take his first throw, Pulpit spoke up. "Who judges accuracy?"

"Are you questioning my honesty, monk?" Maggie snapped.

"Oh, not at all. But it seems there could be some, *ahem*, disagreement over which dagger is closer to the center. I offer my services as an impartial arbitrator, if that meets with your approval."

"As will I."

Terrell Simmons pushed his way through the crowd of Marauders. Her other lieutenant, a taller, thinner version of Sikes, stood beside Maggie, arms crossed. "My judgement is as good as the monk's."

With a smug look, Maggie turned to Tal. "Two judges then to determine each throw's accuracy?"

Tal shrugged. "How you lose—with adjudicators or not—doesn't matter to me." He stepped back from the line. With an exaggerated bow he swept his hand forward and said, "Would my *lady* like to go first?"

As he expected, dark anger colored her face. She brushed by

him. "I'll be glad to show you how to throw a blade," Maggie snarled. Tal chuckled at Maggie's reaction.

Toe on the line, Maggie took a deep breath, her brow furrowed in concentration. Snatching a dagger from her belt, she snapped her wrist forward.

Thunk. In rapid succession she hurled the other four daggers.

A blade pierced the middle of each colored circle, the last still quivering from the impact. The crowd cheered. Pulpit and Simmons inspected each target. Maggie's lieutenant glanced back at Tal. "Direct strike, each one," Simmons stated with smug assurance. Pulpit nodded in agreement.

Pivoting, Maggie sauntered up to Tal. Her hand trailed across his chest. "Your turn," she purred.

Tal strolled to the white stripe. He frowned. "Too easy." He moved back five paces, then shook his head. Ten paces produced another negative shake, and Tal backed up an additional ten steps. He nodded. "This will do."

He thrust his chin at Pulpit. "Would you take the rope and move my board?"

Pulpit smiled. "Of course, my prince."

Maggie stared at Tal. "You're going to try to hit the targets at double the distance—with them moving?"

Tal cocked an eye at her. "Yes. Does that break any rules?"

The Marauders howled with laughter. Maggie tossed her head, a victorious smirk on her face. "No, but save up your strength, Prince Tal. You are going to need it for the night I have planned." The tavern shook as her followers brayed their appreciation at the bold comment.

Tal ignored the remark and tumultuous response. He nodded at Pulpit. The monk pulled the rope and the corkboard figure began to rock side-to-side.

Tal studied the movement of the wooden figure and timed each pendulum-like swing. His hand whipped the first dagger from his belt, followed in a blur of motion by the other four.

Thunk, thunk, thunk, thunk, thunk.

All five blades protruded from the target circles.

Each perfectly centered.

The jeering ended suddenly, the Marauders gaping in disbelief. Simmons, gawking along with his companions, approached the corkboard and studied the targets. He turned to Maggie, incredulous. "Each dagger is dead-center."

Pulpit stepped forward. "A draw. No one wins."

"No!" Face scarlet, Maggie jabbed her finger at Tal. "You cheated! You used magic! No one could have made those throws otherwise."

"I can and I did." The temptation to goad the earl's daughter proved too much to resist. He added, "I don't need magic for such an easy contest. Next time, pick a more difficult game."

The look of fury on Maggie's face warmed his step as he and Pulpit turned and left.

Once outside, they mounted their horses and rode back to the keep.

Imperial sentries stood outside the broad doors of the earl's manor. They snapped to attention and Tal nodded as he and Pulpit entered.

"Lady Margaret is not someone to prod," Pulpit said in continuation of a discussion they'd carried on for most of their trip back. "You may have caused her to be more difficult in the future."

The monk had already made this point repeatedly. Tal scowled, "You sound more and more like Bozar. Are you sure the two of you don't have a common ancestor?"

Pulpit chuckled. "Just pointing out that stirring the hornet's nest is not always the wisest course of action, especially since we received the agreement you sought."

Exasperated, Tal stopped, "You heard Maggie and what she really wants. If I need to bed her for the good of the empire, I'll gladly oblige—"

Tal's jaws clamped shut. At the foot of the stairs, Alex stood, arms crossed. His heart raced.

Did she overhear what I said?

His answer came when she spun and stormed up the staircase.

"Alex!" he shouted. After a moment's hesitation, Tal swarmed up the steps after her. He caught up to her just as she reached her room.

"Alex, I—"

"Don't!" She whirled on Tal, angry tears streaming down her face. "You would sleep with a woman you barely know when you haven't even, even..." her voice trailed away.

"You don't understand. I just said that so Pulpit would stop lecturing me! I didn't mean it."

"Leave, Tal. I don't want to see you." Alex entered her room and tried to slam the door.

Tal grabbed the door and blocked it. "I'm not leaving until you listen to me. *I meant none of it!*"

Alex stalked to her bed and sat, arms held tightly against her chest.

Tal followed and sat beside her. "Why don't you believe me?" he pleaded. Alex refused to answer, and they sat in silence.

Alex finally stirred. "Have you ever loved someone before, Tal?"

The question took him by surprise. "Other than family and friends, no," he managed to answer. "Not until I met you."

She nodded. "Close the door."

Confused, Tal got up and did as she asked. When he turned around, his breath caught in his throat.

Alex was stepping out of her gown.

With a whisper of fabric, it slipped to the floor. She turned. "Unlace my bodice."

Mouth dry, Tal stumbled to her. His nimble fingers, suddenly clumsy, struggled with her stays. Midway through the task, he found his tongue.

"Why are you doing this?"

Impatient, Alex yanked the bodice off. Her breasts sprang free, covered only by a thin undergown. The diaphanous material did little to conceal her body.

"I've never loved another either. But even before I saw you for the first time, I knew you were the one. You haunted my dreams. I can no more help loving you than a river can stop returning to the ocean."

Fierce desire gripped Tal at the sight of Alex's partially exposed body. Before all rational thought fled, he managed to ask, "Is this because of Maggie?"

Alex tugged Tal's tunic up and over his head. She tossed it aside, then unbuckled his pants. The material pooled at his ankles, caught by his boots. Alex pushed him onto the bed and pulled one boot off, then the other. His pants flew through the air as she ripped them off.

She stepped back and shed her undergown.

Tal, propped on his elbows, drank in the sight of Alex. She climbed on top of him and pushed him back down. Straddling him, she kissed him, her long hair falling on either side of his face like a warm curtain.

She whispered, "I've discovered love to be a breathless wonder, indescribable in the breadth and depth you make me feel. But I've also learned how much it can hurt, how it scalds when I think of you with someone else. So, I want you to know this isn't because of Maggie. It's about me and what I want. And right now, I want you."

Heat raced through Tal's veins like wildfire. He crushed Alex to him, her moans stoking his ardor. Rolling over on top of her, he felt her hips positioning beneath him.

Then, a knock came from the door.

CHAPTER II

T HEY PAUSED, THEN RESUMED THEIR PASSIONATE GRAPPLING. ALEX'S moans grew louder.

Another knock.

Tal glanced toward the door, his breath coming in deep, husky gusts. Impatient, Alex yanked his head back to her breasts. They immediately forgot the irritating distraction.

A stronger rap rattled the doorframe.

"Lady Alexandria? I'm looking for Prince Tal."

Tal groaned at the sound of the familiar voice. "Bozar."

Alex placed a finger on his lips. "Shh!"

"Ignore him," Tal whispered. "He'll go away."

"Is that you, Tal?"

A louder groan escaped Tal. "I forgot he has the ears of a cave bat."

"I need to know the results of your meeting with Lady Margaret."

"We have to get dressed!" Alex hissed. She pushed Tal off and scrambled for her clothes.

With a heavy sigh, he rolled off the bed. "Give us—ah, I mean me—a moment."

"Of course. Take all the time you need."

A flush warmed Alex's face. She was certain she heard amusement in Bozar's voice. She slipped on her undergown as fast as possible, then struggled with her bodice.

With a growl, she ripped it off and shook the stiff fabric in Tal's face. "Whoever designed these, hates women!" She hurled the bodice under the bed. She wriggled into her dress while Tal—fumbling into his pants and tunic—thrust his feet into his boots.

Tal walked to the door, stopped, and looked back. Arms crossed over her chest, Alex nodded.

He threw open the door.

Bozar's neutral expression didn't quite mask the sparkle in his eyes.

"Yes, my *Eldred*?"

"I hoped we could talk about your meeting with Maggie." He paused, "But perhaps another time would be better."

Alex stepped forward. "No need, First Advisor. Tal will join you shortly."

"Very good." Bozar inclined his head, then turned away. The click of his bootheels faded down the hallway.

Tal leaned against the door. "I'll be back as soon as I can."

Alex waited on her small balcony. The night air cooled her passion and with it, clearer thinking returned.

She reached a difficult decision—the hardest she'd ever had to make.

A tap came at her door. "Enter," she called.

Tal rushed in, and eagerly grabbed her hand. "C'mon."

Alex pulled back. "No."

He blinked. "Why not?"

Alex took a deep breath, and tried to organize the jumble of thoughts plaguing her since Tal left for his meeting with Bozar. *Please help him to understand what I'm about to do.*

"Do you realize that since I recovered from the scorpion dog's sting and first saw you, we have never been apart? From being chased across the wilderness by a dark lord, to traveling to Markingham, we've been inseparable."

"So?"

Alex swallowed. "We need some time apart."

"What?" He stared. "Why would you want that?"

A vise gripped her heart at the confusion in Tal's eyes. "I just think it's for the best. At least for now."

Tal didn't move as if shocked into paralysis. He cleared his throat. "I don't understand. We were just together."

He retreated a step. "If you don't want to see me, that must mean—"

He paused, his words laced with pain. "Have your feelings for me changed?"

While they were hunted by Stefan, Alex had witnessed repeated acts of Tal's fearless bravery—from slipping into the dark lord's camp and killing a dozen of his band, to battling the vampiric Night Walkers. Few men could match his courage. Yet now, dejected, he looked intensely vulnerable and every bit as young as his twenty years. It broke her heart.

Alex struggled to keep her feelings at bay, to stand her ground. "Oh, Tal, I love you so much at times it's almost more than I can stand."

She put her hand on his arm. "I want you, Tal. In every way a woman can want a man, that's what I feel every day for you. But I have a dream, one I won't retreat from, that when we finally make love it will occupy a place in our hearts forever, something so special we'll never forget. And yet tonight, I came close to throwing my dream away. After you made your comment about Maggie, I was hurt, angry—and determined *no one* would have you before me. Instead of the love and intimacy I so desperately wanted to share with you, it became instead a cheap race, a contest."

Tal stalked back into Alex's room. Jaw clenched, he turned.

"How many times must I say I didn't mean what I said about Maggie? I love *you*, no one else!"

Alex followed Tal and stopped beside him. "I know."

Tal threw his hands up. "Then what else do you want? I'm sorry I made such a stupid remark."

Alex caressed his cheek. "I want my dream. But the only way it means anything is if I know you share it with me."

A sigh of resignation escaped Tal. He caught her hand and kissed her fingers. "I hurt you and I'm a fool. If this separation will make things right between us, then even though I'll be miserable every day, I'll go along."

A sad smile came to his face. "I'd ask how long our self-imposed isolation is to last, but I'm afraid of what your answer would be."

He paused at her door and looked back. "I already feel like I'm leaving part of myself here."

The door shut behind him.

His comment burned. It blazed through her like liquid fire.

Alex already regretted her decision to temporarily stop seeing Tal, but knew she made the right choice. She would not be taken for granted. Not now. Not ever. And the best way to achieve that was to force Tal to step back and fully appreciate their relationship. Knowing she was right didn't fill the hollow emptiness within her though.

How long could she bear to stay away from him? A day? A week? It didn't matter.

It would still feel like years.

CHAPTER 12

"A ND YOU'RE JUST NOW TELLING ME THIS?"

Maggie slammed her fist on the table. Her tankard jumped, ale spilling down the side. Mid-morning, the few Marauders in the tavern eating breakfast looked up at the commotion. Her eyes speared Bradley Sikes. "How long?"

Sikes gulped. "A week…maybe longer."

Maggie jumped up and grabbed Sikes' tunic. "The Prince and his whore have a falling out and I'm the last to know? What the hell is wrong with you?"

He squirmed in her grasp. "I didn't think you would care."

"Listen, you worm. I've told you that *I* do the thinking." Abruptly, she released her lieutenant and dropped into her seat. She snatched up the tankard, drained it, then wiped her mouth with the back of her hand.

"Are the imperial soldiers letting us pass through the gates?"

Sikes wore a look of palpable relief at the change of subject. He nodded. "Yes, but no one leaves without an escort. We were warned not to get separated."

Maggie snorted. "Yes. It wouldn't do if a Marauder went off on his own. They trust us no more than we do them."

She twirled the mug in her hands. With a *thump* she ground the base of it onto the tabletop. Her lips stretched into a smile.

"What?" Sikes asked.

"I think I've been far too remiss in my duties as a daughter. I need to visit my dear father at his keep.

"And this time, I plan on staying awhile."

Tal followed the progress of a crew of men struggling to replace a huge block of stone back into Markingham's perimeter wall.

An iron and timber gantry swung the slab of masonry into position. Cradled aloft in a thick leather sling, it inched closer to the gap in the wall. Overseeing the restoration was Anders Bower, a construction engineer, and part of the nonmilitary support personnel. Stocky and possessed of a full head of wiry-gray hair, he directed a mix of imperial soldiers drafted for the task, and city residents who worked for food, fresh water, and other necessities.

"Put your backs into it, lads," Bower called to the sweating, swearing work crew. "Now, slowly lower. Yes, that's it."

The huge square of masonry—nestled between two similar-sized blocks of stone—now filled what had been a gaping hole. Bower moved closer and ran a critical eye over the placement.

He nodded in satisfaction. "Grand master?"

Artemis Thurgood, along with his new apprentice, Practius Bolt, sat astride horses beside Tal. The garrulous grand master, red hair and beard appearing like embers in the bright morning light, dismounted and smoothed his ale-stained robe. He approached a nearby cart holding crates of lodestones, and selected one half the size of a man's head. With a grunt, he lifted the gem, carried it to the wall, and with a word of power, fused the lodestone to the new-laid block. Next, he placed both hands on the gem, arcs of lightning sparking from his palms. Within seconds, the crystal glowed a bright blue. The seams disappeared to become a solid wall.

"And *that*," Thurgood said with a wink at Bolt, "is how you charge a lodestone." He dusted off his hands. "Now, apprentice, please explain to Prince Tal what you have learned about why magic is only part of the construction."

Bolt, gangly with thin arms and legs, scratched the back of his neck. "Certainly, Grand Master." His spiky hair still poked at odd angles, but his robes were clean and for the most part, unwrinkled. Forehead furrowed, he quoted, "Magic works best and endures longer when paired with physics."

Thurgood waved a hand. "Elaborate."

Bolt's larynx bobbed as if he'd swallowed an entire hard-boiled egg. "Uh, yes. That means any physical object shaped, made, moved, or positioned by natural means, when infused with magic, retains its properties longer. The enchantment is stronger and more durable."

Thurgood lifted himself back in the saddle. Eyes twinkling, he said to Tal, "I'll make an adept out of the lad yet."

Tal chuckled. "I have no doubt." He called out to Bower who was still inspecting the repaired section of wall, "Good work. Anything else you need?"

The engineer cast a wry glance at the numerous sections of crumbling, weakened fortifications. "Other than a hundred more work crews, more engineers, and at least a year's time to complete restoration of the city's walls, nothing, Sire."

Tal's chuckle turned to laughter. "Bozar assures me more help is on the way from the empire. But it takes time to get through the breach in the Veil and to Markingham. Until then, I'm afraid you'll need to make do." He directed his horse beside the engineer, his expression turning serious. "As long as these walls remain porous, we cannot defend the city."

"Aye," Bower growled. "We'll do our best, Sire. I'll start with the most serious breaches, then work back to the less compromised sections."

He squinted at Tal. "More workers will help, but what we really need is time. You can't cut corners, and forcing the pace is liable to get someone killed. Those unstable portions of wall can fall and squash a man flat in the span of time it takes to release a breath."

Tal shook his head. "I'm afraid time is a commodity we have

the least of." The sound of drumming hooves caught his attention. Curious, he turned his mount and spied a cavalryman approached at a gallop.

The rider pulled up and saluted, palm from head to heart. "Sire, the First Advisor requests your presence at the earl's keep. A soldier was attacked and suffered a broken arm and several broken ribs."

"A soldier attacked? By who?"

"Not who but what, Sire. A troll. There's a troll in the sewers."

❖

Alex rode beside Pulpit as the monk skillfully directed the team of horses pulling their wagon back to the earl's keep.

They were returning from an abandoned shop in the old central market they had converted into a food and aid station. In addition to the food and other necessities, they now carried antiseptics, clean bandages, and needles and thread to stitch up cuts and abrasions. As usual, they ran out of supplies by mid-morning.

Alex found she had a knack with minor injuries. She especially enjoyed soothing the children with whispers and hugs while wiping away tears and dressing their hurts. Her gentle words seemed to have an immediate calming effect. Despite the fact that Alex had no medical training and could offer little more than comforting words, her rudimentary first aid skills were soon in great demand. Parents lined up with sick children.

The wagon rolled into the keep's expansive courtyard, and Pulpit helped Alex down. Their escort of soldiers saluted and trotted away.

The day, warm and growing warmer, presaged spring giving way to early summer. Alex was eager to wash up using her enchanted water basin and pitcher. Embedded with tiny lodestones, she could control the temperature of the water issuing from the pitcher, while the basin kept the selected temperature constant.

As she entered the fortified manor, Alex was surprised by the sight of Bozar, Earl York, and lords Gravelback and Morehead in the great hall. They were huddled together over a diagram spread out on a table. They were so engrossed in a heated discussion, they didn't register her presence.

"It's a maze. There must be leagues of aqueducts and sewer channels. That damn troll could be anywhere," Gravelback grumbled.

"Do you have a more recent chart of Markingham's sewers," Bozar asked Earl York.

The earl spread his hands. "I'm sorry, Bozar. You must understand, Markingham's water and sewer system were laid out before the creation of the accursed Veil. I was lucky to find even these old plans."

Alex stood frozen in place, not wishing to distract them. Bozar finally looked up, his eyes widening. "Lady Alexandria." The others joined the First Advisor in greeting her.

"Don't let me disturb you," Alex said. "I'm just going to my room to freshen up."

"Now, m'lady?" Earl York cast his eyes upstairs. "Wouldn't you like some refreshments first? I can have a servant bring them to you immediately."

Bozar nodded eagerly.

Why are they acting so odd?

"No, but thank you for your kind offer. Perhaps later."

Alex felt their eyes follow her as she mounted the stairs. She reached the second floor landing, stopped and looked down. The men below quickly averted their gazes back to the sewer chart.

Shaking her head at their peculiar behavior, Alex continued to her room. Just as she reached the threshold, a door opened down the corridor and a woman stepped out. Alex's breath caught in her throat as the woman turned and flashed a cold smile.

"Greetings, dear Alexandria," Maggie purred. "Where's the prince?"

CHAPTER 13

A LEX'S EYES NARROWED. "I'M NOT IN CHARGE OF TAL'S COMINGS and goings. I don't keep up with where he is."

Maggie approached wearing a gown rather than Marauder black pants and tunic. The bodice was low-cut to display a daring amount of firm cleavage, the gown's tight fabric hugging her small waist and trim hips.

She sauntered up to Alex. "Oh, that's right. You two are no longer together." She shook her head. "I'm *so* sorry." Her insincerity dripped from her like syrup.

She moved closer. "How do you do it?"

"What do you mean?"

"How do you resist him? Eyes the green of spring grass, and a body tall and hard as a sentinel pine. One can only imagine what the prince looks like beneath his clothes." Maggie fanned herself. "Well, I blush to even think about it."

Alex fought the urge to slap the earl's daughter. "Somehow, I doubt you've ever blushed about anything."

Maggie laughed. "Oh, you have no idea." She tapped her lips. "I think I'll find out."

Alex couldn't help herself. "Find out what?" she snapped.

"What it's like to fish in the waters you abandoned."

She spun and with hips swaying, made her way down the staircase.

Alex growled, and took a step after Maggie's retreating back. A river of jealousy frothed and boiled within her. Her breath came in explosive gasps, spots appeared in her vision, and she started to hyperventilate.

Stop it, stop it, stop it, she screamed in silent frustration.

She managed to rein in her emotions—only to come to the sudden realization that by spurning Tal, she had opened the door for Maggie. "What have I done?" she whispered.

Sick to her stomach, she rushed to the privy and emptied her breakfast into the chamber pot. Staggering to her charmed pitcher, she poured water and splashed the cool liquid on her face. The cold water allowed her to regain a measure of calm, and she sat on the corner of her bed.

Tal loves me. I know he loves me.

"And if he loves me, I've got nothing to worry about," she told herself. Like a mantra, she mouthed it over and over.

Then why did you refuse him?

The errant thought rebuffed every attempt to dismiss it, burrowing into her conscience and taking root.

"I wanted him to feel the same pain I felt," she breathed. "To teach him a lesson. But I'm the one who's hurting." Alex buried her face in her hands. "I'm such a fool."

In her haste to reach the privy, she had left her door wide open. Voices drifted up from the floor below. She sat up at the sound of a voice she knew well.

Tal!

Alex rushed from the room.

"Where did the attack occur?" Tal asked.

Bozar tapped a section on a chart of Markingham's sewer system. "Right here. A squad of soldiers was escorting a magister restoring spent lodestones, when a troll appeared out of nowhere and clubbed the nearest soldier. The other soldiers rushed to the fallen man's side to render aid, but the creature disappeared into the darkness before they could capture it. Needless to say, our efforts to repair the city's water and sewer system have come to a halt."

"You could hide an army down there," Gravelback groused. "Finding this creature will be nigh impossible."

Bozar pursed his lips. "If we don't restore the water and sewer systems, we won't need to worry about the Dark Queen. Disease will take us first. The troll threatens all of us."

The First Advisor turned to Tal. "Because trolls are faerie creatures, they're resistant to all but the most powerful magic. Besides Artemis, I have no one but you who can find and kill it. The grand master needs to continue recharging the thousands of spent lodestones in the city."

The First Advisor cocked an eyebrow at Tal. "Unless you want to take over Artemis's task to let him hunt the troll?"

"No!" Tal blurted. "I'll lead the search."

Bozar chuckled. "I thought so."

"I'll go with the prince."

Maggie strolled boldly into the gathering. She eyed the small lodestone marking the section of the chart indicated earlier by Bozar. "Yep. I've been there before."

Earl York looked askance at his daughter. "You've been down there?"

"Marauders move above and below ground, Father. Yet one more thing you didn't know about me."

She moved next to Tal and brushed her hip against his. "Few know the underground ways of the city better than I do."

"I'm going too!"

Breathless, Alex skidded to a stop several paces away.

Tal stared at her. "Uh, you want to join the search? For a troll?"

Alex swallowed. "Yes."

"Pardon me, Lady Alexandria," Bozar interjected, "but have you ever seen a troll?"

"No," Alex said with a tight smile, "but there's always a first time."

Tal shook his head. "Absolutely not. They're big, and they're dangerous. I don't want you anywhere near this creature."

Maggie moved closer to Tal. "Besides, its damp and dark. And the smell...much too much for the delicate senses of a sophisticated lady."

Alex's eyes flashed. "I'm going!" She jabbed a finger at Tal. "And don't you try to stop me, *Prince* Tal!" With that, she spun on her heel and stamped up the stairs.

Uncertain as to what just happened, Tal stared until Alex disappeared out of sight.

Maggie clapped. "I can't wait." She looped her arm through Tal's.

"This is going to be fun."

Alex waited with Pulpit beside a squad of helmeted soldiers armed with shields, swords, and crossbows. A thick iron grate had been removed from the bed of a cobblestone road not far from the keep. A rusty, filth-encrusted ladder reached down into the gloom below.

Although she tried to prepare herself, the reek arising from the opening was so putrid, Alex gagged and turned away.

"What's the matter? Never smelled shit before?" Maggie quipped. Dressed again in the Marauder black pants and tunic, she clearly enjoyed Alex's discomfort.

Eyes watering from the nauseous stench, Alex snapped, "No, I suppose I don't have your tolerance. But then, I don't frequent the low places where you spend so much of your time."

Tal overheard the exchange and cast a furious glance at Maggie. He walked over to Alex. "Here," he handed her a pair of thick leather gloves. "You'll need to wear these. They'll protect your hands from nicks and cuts."

Tal pulled a white kerchief from his pocket. He puffed on the fabric, and it briefly glowed blue. He handed it to Alex.

She took the cloth and sniffed. "It smells like wildflowers."

Tal smiled. "Tie it over your nose and mouth, and it will block the worst of the odor. The enchantment is temporary but should last long enough for us to finish this foul business."

He signaled the officer leading the squad, and the soldiers began to scramble down the ladder.

Tal turned back to Alex and grasped her shoulders. "Stay near me! If we find the troll, you will go to the rear and nowhere near the creature."

Maggie smirked. "Wouldn't want you to get scratched." She fingered her sword handle. "Or get in the way of us who can actually kill the troll."

"Maggie! That's enough," Tal snapped.

The Marauder leader raised her hands, chuckled, and backed away.

Tal's eyes met Alex's. "You don't need to do this."

Alex glared at Maggie's retreating form, then back at Tal. "Yes, I do. But don't worry. I won't get in the way."

They stood in silence for a few moments longer. Then Tal leaned in and whispered in her ear, "I miss you." He pivoted and followed the soldiers down the ladder.

Numb, Alex gathered her tattered emotions and waited her turn. The entire surreal situation—her feelings for Tal, her anger at Maggie's attempts to seduce him, and now, pursuing an underground troll—rattled her. It reminded her of a book she once read as a child back on earth, *Alice in Wonderland*. Now she, just like Alice, was going down the rabbit hole.

CHAPTER 14

ALEX DIDN'T BELIEVE IT POSSIBLE, BUT THE SMELL GREW WORSE.
When she reached the bottom and dropped onto the
brick-lined surface, she hastily tied Tal's kerchief across her
face. The scent of daffodils, lavender, and wild rose replaced the
rotten-egg stench. After a moment, her eyes adjusted to the dim
illumination produced by the newly activated lodestones. Spaced
at intervals, the magical gems revealed the circular contours of
the sewer system. The roof of the culvert rose more than ten feet
above their heads, and double that in width. A sluggish stream of
muddy, brown sludge oozed through the center leaving plenty of
room on each side to walk.

Once the entire party was gathered, Tal led them forward,
Maggie and Pulpit close by his side. Alex hurried to join them.

"It will be easy to locate where the attack occurred," Tal said.
"All we need to do is follow the active lodestones. Where they go
dark, the real search will begin."

Alex watched her step, careful to walk along the side of the
culvert so she didn't slip into slimy, slow-moving muck. "Why are
the lodestones so important to the sewage system?" she asked.

"Lodestones are attuned to absorb specific kinds of magic. In
this case, their magic is designed to purify the wastewater carried
by the sewers. But it takes the entire system to function properly.
We need all the magical gems working to purify the water. Until
we kill the troll, we can't restore them."

There was little conversation after that. The clink of weapons, creak of leather, and the scrape of booted feet were the only sounds.

Following twists and turns, the armed group went on for quite some time. Alex lost all sense of direction, and focused on keeping up and well away from the rancid stream. They rounded a curve and the light from the activated lodestones came to an end. Tal stopped and cursed.

Three culverts branched in three different directions.

"The troll could have taken any one of them, and we would be none the wiser," he hissed through his teeth at Pulpit.

"Perhaps the faerie creature left traces of which path it took," the monk suggested. "A cursory search might reveal this."

Tal nodded. He approached the nearest channel entrance and twirled his finger. A blue luminescence issued from the digit and hung in the air like smoke. It reminded Alex of neon lights back on earth.

With a snap of his wrist, Tal propelled the glowing fog into the duct. Twisting like a corkscrew, the azure luminescence deposited a thin layer of radiance across every surface. Quickly, the tunnel lit up in a soft glow. He repeated the process for the remaining channels.

Tal turned to the soldiers. "We'll go a short distance into each channel. Search for any clues of the creature's passage." He picked five of the legionnaires. "You will stay with Lady Alexandria. Do not allow her to wander off."

"Tal, I'm not a child!" Alex protested. "I can take care of myself."

Maggie stepped beside Tal and smirked at Alex. "And how would you do that? You have no weapon, and even if you did, you wouldn't know how to use it."

"I wasn't talking to you!"

Tal approached Alex. "She's right. We don't know how the troll will react when we find it. I want you safe and well out of harm's way."

Alex stabbed a finger at Maggie. "She goes, but I don't?"

Tal groaned. "Of course she does. Maggie is familiar with these sewers and she's a better fighter than most legionnaires."

The triumphant look on Maggie's face was so infuriating, Alex spun and turned her back on Tal. She waved her hand. "Go on then. I'll wait here.

"As ordered."

Seething with fury, the second Tal disappeared with Maggie, Pulpit, and the rest of the soldiers down the sewer channel, Alex decided to inspect the center culvert. A corporal, the leader of her guards, blocked her way.

"I'm sorry, Lady Alexandria, but the prince was quite clear. You are not to enter. In fact, you aren't to move from this place." Though his slender build hardly made for an imposing figure, he wore a determined look.

Alex let out a frustrated sigh. "I just want to look at the tunnels, not go into them. What harm can come from that?"

The young corporal, brow furrowed, considered her request. At last, he nodded. "Very well, but we will be with you every step of the way." He motioned, and the soldiers formed a semi-circle around her.

Alex rolled her eyes and headed for the center culvert. "Follow me."

The group shuffled toward the mouth of the channel. Matching her every step, Alex stifled a laugh at the ridiculous image they presented. Stopping just outside the entrance, she studied Tal's magically produced light. The eerie luminescence left no shadow, and the smooth sewer walls provided no cover where a troll could hide.

Satisfied, she led her little band to the last opening on the left.

Identical to the other two and lit up in the neon-like light, she spied no evidence a troll had used the passageway.

Alex sighed and was about to turn away, when a burning sensation creased her left hand. She yelped and rubbed her palm but the pain refused to go away.

"What's wrong my lady?" the young squad leader asked.

Alex shook her head. "Nothing. Just a strange pain in my hand." As they moved away, the discomfort disappeared. She smiled at the corporal. "There. It's gone now."

Puzzled, she stopped and looked back. *The burning itch started near the tunnel, but vanished when I moved away.*

With an abrupt pivot, she reversed course almost colliding with the soldiers. She ignored the corporal's cries and ran to the channel entrance.

The pain returned.

She moved a step closer. Her hand throbbed.

Another step.

The stinging pain increased.

A hand grabbed her arm and pulled her back. Red-faced, the squad leader shouted a warning at her. Alex, mind churning, ignored him.

She gripped the corporal by his collar. "Go find Prince Tal… now!"

"What? Why?" he stuttered.

"Tell him I know where the troll is."

The squad leader's mouth worked, but no sound came out.

"And tell him I can lead him straight to the creature."

CHAPTER 15

A LEX WAITED IMPATIENTLY.

Hemmed in by soldiers, she wasn't allowed to move. The sound of boots echoed from the tunnel that Tal had disappeared into. Moments later, he burst from the entrance at a dead run, Pulpit, Maggie, and the rest of the soldiers struggling to keep up. He spotted Alex and veered toward her.

He slid to a stop. "Where?" he demanded. "Where's the troll?"

Before she could open her mouth, he turned angry green eyes on her. "And I told you not to venture anywhere near these sewer channels." The corporal shrank from the heated look Tal drilled into him.

Alex took Tal's arm. "They followed your orders. Every step I took, I was encircled by soldiers. All we did was look into each culvert."

Tal blinked. "Then how do you know where the troll is?"

Alex held up her hand. "I feel his pain." She turned and pointed. "And the troll is wherever that passage leads."

"What?" Maggie, breathing heavily, stared at Alex. "You claim to somehow sense this creature? The sewer gas has addled your mind!"

She rounded on Tal. "We ran all the way for this? Send this delicate flower back before she loses more of her petals. I—"

"Shut up, Maggie!" Alex snapped. "I felt the creature. I *still* feel him."

Maggie, fists clenched, stepped toward Alex but was blocked by Tal's arm. "Don't!" he barked.

"You mean you believe her?"

Tal's eyes narrowed. "Of course I do."

Maggie pushed Tal's arm away. "Then you're as big a fool as she is."

A laugh bubbled from Tal. "I *am* a fool." He glanced at Alex and their eyes locked. "But not for any reason you would understand."

His look galvanized Alex, and she shoved her way through the soldiers to stand beside him. "The troll's down that sewer pipeline, Tal. I don't know how or why, but I sense he's injured."

Pulpit joined them. "May I examine your hand?" Alex nodded, and the monk probed her palm with his fingers. "Hmm."

Tal tilted his head. "What?"

Pulpit pursed his lips. "Members of my order have a sensitivity for magical creatures. There's something here."

"You're aware of the troll too?" Tal blurted.

The monk shook his head. "No." He looked at Alex in wonder. "I sense pain…but it's being channeled through her."

The scrutiny of the entire company was suddenly on Alex. She jerked her hand back.

"I'm not sure what you mean, Pulpit, but I know one thing."

Pulpit inclined his head. "Yes, Lady Alexandria?"

Alex whirled and pointed at Maggie.

"When we find the troll, *she* is going to eat her words!"

A groan escaped from Alex. The vicious ache in her hand grew worse the further they moved down the brick-lined culvert.

Tal's eyebrows drew together. "Is the pain increasing?"

Alex nodded.

"We must be getting close. There's no reason for you to

continue and your pain to worsen. We know the direction now so you can stay—"

"No!"

Tal spread his hands. "Alex, be reasonable. Trolls can be dangerous creatures, especially when they're trapped and injured."

"You'll just get in the way. Unless of course, you've led us on this merry chase for nothing," Maggie snorted.

This time Tal had to restrain Alex. He wrapped an arm around her waist and held her as she moved to confront the Marauder leader.

It was the first time Alex had been this close to Tal since she put their relationship on hold. With his strong arm around her, for a brief moment, all was well and life was as it should be. The feel of his closeness, the warmth of his body, even his familiar muskiness, all came rushing back.

Distracted by the familiar intimacy, the anger she felt toward Maggie melted away

She turned and placed her hands on his chest. He didn't release his hold and she didn't to push away.

"Tal, let me finish this with you…please."

He puffed out his cheeks. Finally, he nodded, "Very well. But once we find the troll, you *will* move a safe distance away."

Alex nodded. Reluctantly, Tal released her.

They continued the hunt.

The huge contours of the sewer channel—big enough to drive three wagons abreast through—curved and meandered. They rounded a bend, and a roar greeted them. It reverberated off the circular walls, gathering momentum to wash over them with ear-spitting intensity.

The culvert ended at another junction of sewer lines. A large, cavern-like opening formed at this intersection.

And right in the middle stood the troll.

At nine feet tall, the troll had a thick body the color of amber.

Its large, hairless head rested on massive, muscular shoulders. Fierce lavender eyes peered at them above a blunt nose and a wide mouth with thick lips. Naked except for a loincloth of fur, the creature brandished a truncheon the size of a small tree.

The troll bellowed another ear-shattering roar.

I hurt.

The words rang in Alex's mind.

Tal shouted orders, and the soldiers spread out. Cautiously, they streamed out of the tunnel and moved a safe distance away to flank the faerie creature.

Boorba hurt.

Again, the words echoed in Alex's head.

"Stay here!" Tal ordered her.

Brandishing his sword, Tal approached the troll. Pulpit flanked one side, Maggie on the other. Tal's eyes burned blue, specks of magic appearing like azure fireflies in the air around him.

Alex's teeth clenched, the pain in her hand a red-hot ember. She managed to put the agony aside, and studied the troll. She noticed one anvil-sized hand cradled close to its body. Although everything about the creature was huge, the appendage appeared swollen and distended.

"Tal, don't!" she cried.

Alex ran toward Tal, and he looked back, eyes growing wide in alarm.

"Stop! Go back!" he shouted.

She ignored him and continued until she was between Tal and the troll. She waved her hands. "Don't kill him," she pleaded. "He's just hurt, that's all."

Tal froze. "Don't make any sudden moves. Slowly, very slowly, walk back to me."

Alex shook her head. "Not until you listen to me. He's in such pain he can't think straight. Look at his hand! It's swollen to almost twice its normal size. That's why he attacked the soldier."

Tal hissed, "Alex, move away. Now!"

Pulpit cleared his throat. "It does appear the creature is injured. Perhaps we should listen to Lady Alexandria."

Angry, Tal spun to face Pulpit. "That's your best advice?"

"And how does this change the situation, monk?" Maggie snapped. "The troll is still a threat."

"Tal, please. Let me try to help Boorba," Alex begged.

Maggie pointed at Tal. "I told you she's not in her right mind. Who the hell is Boorba? A pet's name she has given the troll?"

Pulpit stepped forward. "I'll go with Lady Alexandria and assist her."

Incredulous, Tal shook his head. "And get you both killed? No!"

The monk took a deep breath. "Think of the chain of events that has taken us to where we are now. Do you think they are accidents of fate, mere random acts with no logical pattern? Or rather, a design we're meant to be part of? Faith is what's needed now."

Maggie snorted and waved her sword. "This is what I have faith in. And whatever drivel you spout, monk, a dead troll is still that. *Dead*."

Tal glanced back and forth between Alex, Pulpit, and the troll. "You are asking a lot, Pulpit."

Alex knew Tal would never agree to risking her life, much less Pulpit's. She spared him the decision and walked to the troll. A growl issued from the troll's lips. Ignoring Tal's cry, she moved to within an arm's length of the creature.

She held out her hand.

The growling increased.

Then without warning, the troll extended its hand. "Boorba hurt." The voice, a deep bass, sounded like gravel pouring from a bucket.

Alex took the spade-sized hand and examined it. A deep gash ran down the palm, pus-filled and stinking. The wound needed to be lanced and drained before the infection spread further.

"The source of your pain," a voice said by her ear. She looked up and Pulpit stood beside her. Before she could answer, Boorba growled, jerked his hand back, and raised the club.

She turned and a nimbus of cobalt magic surrounded Tal.

"Stop!" Pulpit cried. "You're endangering our lives."

The halo of enchantment faded.

Alex smiled at Boorba.

"Let's get your hurt fixed."

CHAPTER 16

"**T**AL, DO YOU HAVE ONE OF THOSE MAGICAL BAGS?" ALEX ASKED.

"Bags?" he asked, puzzled.

"You know, when we—"

She clamped her mouth shut and motioned him over. Tal moved to her side, one eye on the hulking troll. Alex leaned closer and whispered, "The bag you had so much stuff in when you saved me from the dark lord."

Comprehension dawned in Tal's eyes. "Oh. You mean a Deep Pocket."

"Yes. That's it."

A chuckle spilled from his lips. "I also remember when you asked me to share your bed at that abandoned farmhouse."

Heat crept into Alex's cheeks. "Do you have one or not?"

Still laughing, Tal gestured to one of the soldiers. The legionnaire removed a satchel tied to his belt and tossed it to the prince.

Tal caught the bag. "What do you need?"

"A sharp knife, alcohol, bandages, and a needle and thread."

Tal nodded, handed her his dagger, then pulled out the other items. Alex kept the dagger and handed the rest to Pulpit. She motioned for Tal to move away.

"No. I'm staying right here. I don't trust the troll."

"Tal, please. I can do this, but not with you beside me. Your likely to mistake the wrong way anything Boorba does and attack him."

Tal stayed rooted by her side. At last he pulled her close and spoke into her ear. "I will move a small distance away. But understand this; I will not let you be harmed. If the troll makes any move I consider threatening, I will kill him where he stands."

A shiver crawled up Alex's spine. Tal's words carried no malice, but rather, a cold and lethal intent. She rarely saw this side of him, the part honed by the cruel realities of the struggle against the Dark Queen. It was a stark reminder of how dangerous Tal could be.

He took three steps back.

"I don't believe this!" Hands on hips, Maggie fumed. "We came all this way through muck, slime, and shit, and now you're going to let the delicate flower play healer to the very monster we came to get rid of?"

Boorba growled.

"Stop it, Maggie. You're upsetting him," Alex snapped.

Maggie ripped her sword from its sheath. "I'll do more than that. If no one else has the balls to kill the troll, I'll do it myself. Get out of the way!"

The growl turned into a roar. "Boorba no like female." He hefted the club with his good hand.

Alex whirled toward the troll. "Boorba, no! She's not going to do anything."

"The hell I'm not!"

"Maggie!" Tal's voice boomed like thunder. "Sheath your sword." When Maggie made no move to comply, his lips formed a thin line. "Don't force me to disarm you."

Muttering, the Marauder leader slammed the sword back into her scabbard. "Don't blame me when the brute pounds the delicate flower into paste."

Alex ignored the remark, and doused Tal's knife with some of the alcohol. She craned her neck to speak to the towering troll. "Boorba, do you trust me?"

The troll scratched his head. "Fix hand?"

"Yes…but it's going to hurt."

Boorba nodded. He pointed at the gash, "Boorba know. Fix."

Alex took a firm grip of his injured hand. With a deep breath she slashed with the knife. Pus spurted from the infected wound in a greenish-yellow geyser, the smell like rotten fish. Boorba raised his head and howled, a cry so loud it hurt Alex's ears.

Tal started toward them, his sword partially unsheathed.

"No!" Alex motioned him back. "We're in no danger."

With obvious reluctance, Tal backed away.

Alex poured more alcohol onto the wound, eliciting another ear-splitting yowl. She soaked one of the cloth bandages and thoroughly cleaned the laceration. Boorba gnashed his teeth as she stitched the gash with thread, then wrapped clean bandages around the wound. She stepped back to inspect her work and nodded.

"Boorba, you'll have to keep the dressings clean. I'll come back in a couple of days and change them."

The troll dropped his club and patted Alex's head. "Give you something."

Before she could respond, the troll turned and trotted deeper into the dark hollow. When Alex hesitated, he waved. "Come."

She moved to follow when Tal snagged her arm in an iron grip. "We'll go together or not at all," he told her firmly.

The entire group shadowed the troll until he came to a stop at a corner of the wide intersection of pipes. Tucked up against the side was an odd collection of bright, shiny, and in most cases, broken, objects. A shattered mirror, cracked iron tankard, and the snapped blade of an old sword were among the things Alex recognized. It reminded her of a packrat's collection.

Among the baubles was a giant bird's nest. Constructed of twigs and branches, leaves, rags, and dry grass, Alex realized this was Boorba's den, the bed he slept in.

One item in the troll's hoard that didn't sparkle was a rolled tapestry that lay close to his crude bed. The troll picked up the tapestry with reverence and dangled it in front of him. About the width of a shield and embroidered with silk thread, the rich brocade fell past his waist

Boorba pointed at a woven image on the tapestry then at Alex. "You."

Alex gasped. The bottom half had been ripped off, but the remaining top half displayed an image. It pictured a woman in a green gown, golden hair, and long legs seated in an ornate chair. A woman Alex had seen before.

The Afterimage, Diana.

"She—she looks just like you," Tal exclaimed.

"Yours," Boorba said handing the tapestry to Alex.

Speechless, she took the drapery from the troll.

"We…" Boorba's massive forehead furrowed in effort, "friend," he managed to say at last.

Tears stung Alex's eyes. She motioned to the huge troll and he leaned down. She handed Tal the drapery, then took the faerie creature's face in her hands. "Friends. Always friends, Boorba."

An hour later, they straggled back to the earl's keep.

Alex was bone-tired and desperately wanted a hot bath to wash off the sewer's stench that clung to her like a second skin. Tal accompanied her up the stairs and they lingered at the landing.

Tal broke the awkward pause. "You continue to amaze me."

Alex flashed a weary smile. "I don't know if you mean that in a good way or not."

He shook his head. "I would have killed the troll. But instead, you tended to his injury and befriended him."

He moved closer. "Magic has been a part of me since the day of my birth. I've never known a moment of life without it, and there are few charms, enchantments, or magical Artifacts unfamiliar to me. Then I met you and learned of a new magic, one far more powerful than any I have ever experienced."

Tal placed his hands on her waist and pulled her close. Alex felt her resistance crumble. "What magic is that?" she murmured.

"It goes by many names. Compassion, empathy, mercy, kindness, and," he nuzzled her cheek, his warm breath caressing her ear, "love."

Tal's lips moved lower and he kissed her. "Against such formidable magic, there is no defense."

He pulled the rolled tapestry from the Deep Pocket tied at his belt and handed it to her.

Without another word, he turned and walked away.

CHAPTER 17

TAL DISAPPEARED FROM SIGHT.

Alex turned and entered her room. With a heavy sigh, she shut the door, leaned against it, and closed her eyes. Over and over she replayed the feel of Tal's firm grip on her waist, the warmth of his breath against her cheek, the taste of his lips on hers.

I'm such an idiot.

A knock startled her. Hoping it was Tal, she turned and yanked the door open.

"Tal, I—"

Her face fell. Pulpit stood on the threshold.

"Were you expecting someone else?" he asked with the hint of a smile.

Flustered, Alex flailed for an answer. Finally, she moved aside. "Come in."

The monk stepped in. "I'd like to talk to you about Boorba."

Alex almost told him no. She wanted to shed her foul clothes, soak in water so hot she could barely stand it, and most of all, think about Tal.

Instead, she pointed to a pair of chairs. "Of course."

When they were seated, Pulpit asked, "Do you know much about trolls?"

Alex shrugged. "No. I didn't know they existed until I heard about the soldier being attacked."

"I see. Part of my monk's training is a thorough introduction to magical creatures, especially those of the faerie kind. For example,

I learned trolls are notorious for their solitary habits with little tolerance even for the company of their own kind."

He leaned closer. "Yet, Boorba not only accepted you, he bore the painful dressing of his wound, *and* gave you a gift. Not the normal behavior of a troll, and in my experience, unheard of. How do you explain that?"

Alex fumbled for an answer. "I—I don't know."

"There is power in you, Lady Alexandria. I know this with absolute certainty. What I can't understand is why you hide it. Why you deny its existence."

Alex's mind raced. What was she supposed to say?

Okay, Pulpit, you got me. Here it is. See, my guardian angel, a snippy and rude man, offered me a chance to swap my old, miserable life on earth for that of rich and beautiful Alexandria here on Meredith. So I made the switch, and wow, what a ride. I've almost been killed twice, been chased across the wilderness by a dark lord, seen things I can scarcely imagine, and, oh, fallen in love with Tal, the heir to the Empire of Meredith. And now you want a detailed description of this magic or power within me? A power I don't understand or control? Sure, why not.

It was too much.

Alex buried her face in her hands and wept. She felt a gentle touch on her shoulder. "I'm sorry, Alexandria," Pulpit said, "I didn't mean to upset you."

Alex sat up and wiped her eyes. "It's not your fault. All of this—this *shit* has been building for a long time."

She fought back a second wave of tears.

"I'm tired of fear and not knowing what's next. I'm especially tired of this 'power' you, Tal, and others see, but I can't!"

"Perhaps it would help if you had someone to talk to?" Pulpit suggested.

With a sigh, Alex leaned back in the chair. "Yes. That would be nice. I mean I talk to Tal, but now…" she left the sentence unfinished.

Pulpit patted her hand. "The vows of the White Order require my celibacy, but that doesn't mean I can't recognize a young man and young woman in love."

He stood and made his way to the door. "I can tell you're tired. We'll talk again soon."

He reached for the handle and paused. "Might I add one more thing before I go?"

Alex nodded.

"Whatever chasm has opened between you and the prince, remember this: no matter how wide the divide, no gulf exists that can't be bridged by love."

He tapped the side of his head.

"And even a celibate monk knows that."

A week later, Maggie rode to the top of the knoll and surveyed the area.

Below, farmland spread into the distance. Trees, mostly second-growth forest, bordered the rich cropland. Faint outlines of crop rows stretched away from a farmhouse, barn, and equipment shed. A score of men were hard at work repairing the barn, irrigation well, and farm equipment. Even from a distance, the glint of lodestones mounted in the farm implements was clear to see.

Maggie had no interest in the beehive of activity. Rather, her presence was for one reason only. She pulled a spyglass from her saddle pack—a useful tool she managed to wrangle from the Imperial Army. Tiny lodestones encircled the tubular Artifact giving it a powerful magnification.

She put the spyglass to her eye and searched through the group of men. She stopped when she came to a muscular, bare-chested young man. Her breath caught in her throat.

Tal.

A short distance away, Bradley Sikes and Terrell Simmons lounged in their saddles. Sikes leaned forward. "Why are we here?"

"I don't recall asking you to come," Maggie retorted.

"You ride out like you have this great purpose in mind, and you expect us to stay behind?"

Maggie turned a baleful eye on her lieutenant. "I repeat, I didn't ask you to come. I gave you both imperial passes so you could go about Marauder business without need of an escort. *Not* to follow me."

Sikes pointed at the basket tied to the back of her saddle. "What's in the hamper?"

Maggie's temper boiled over. Her hand went to the dagger at her belt. "Would you like to open it and see?"

Sikes gulped. "Uh, no."

"Good. You can both leave now."

Simmons saluted Maggie. "Let's go." He grabbed Sikes' reins and led his horse away. They disappeared into the trees.

Maggie waited until she was sure they were far away. Then with a flick of the reins, she directed her horse toward the farmhouse below.

Toward Tal.

The wagon rumbled along the dirt road producing a trail of dust in its wake.

Alex sat beside Pulpit as the monk skillfully directed their team of horses through the worst of the ruts. The back of the wagon was filled with food for the farmhands, bread, salted meat, cheese, and fresh water.

"I bet they'll be glad to see us," she told Pulpit.

"Bozar told me they've been working nonstop on this farmstead for weeks," he replied. "The lodestones on the well and pump, like all the others, were drained of magic long ago. The mechanism is seized with rust and won't work even with freshly-charged lodestones."

He pointed at a canvas-covered bulge in the back of the wagon. "That's the new pump."

The monk eyed Alex, a smile playing across his face. "You seem excited about what is a rather mundane delivery. Could it have anything to do with the prince helping out also?"

Alex folded her hands. "Is it that obvious?"

Pulpit chuckled. "I'm afraid so."

"I can't help it. I miss him every day."

Pulpit tugged on the reins and brought the wagon to a stop. He tied them to the wheel brake and turned to Alex. "Then why carry on with this separation? You have made both yourself and the prince miserable."

Alex raised a defiant chin to the monk. "He said something that hurt me, something he didn't know I could hear. Tal needs to learn I'm not some breathless girl who follows his every whim."

Pulpit scratched his chin. "Forgive me, Alexandria, but from my perspective, Tal's not the one being taught a lesson.

"It's you."

He untied the reins, but Alex grabbed them. "Stop! What do you mean?"

Pulpit sighed and looked up at the sky. "If my fellow monks could see me now, I would be de-frocked and removed from the order."

"Enough!" Alex shook the reins in his face. "Tell me what you mean."

Pulpit pushed her hand away. "I mean only the Creator knows perfect love. We all make mistakes because we are imperfect creatures…and if you don't know by now that Tal is hopelessly in love with you, then you are as blind as a cave bat!"

Pulpit's hand flew to his mouth. "Oh, me. Did I say that? Please forgive me, Lady Alexandria."

But you're right, Pulpit. I've let my petty jealousy and stubbornness come between myself and Tal. But not anymore.

Alex threw her arms around him and planted a kiss on his cheek. She handed him the reins. "Go!"

"What?"

"Get me to Tal!"

<hr>

Maggie approached the band of workers and searched for Tal. She spied him in the distance beside a well. A wooden beam stretched across the top of the well with a rope tied to it and attached to a bucket. Thick vegetation had grown up near the well, and Maggie decided to surprise him.

She melted into the brush unnoticed by the busy workers. Reaching a spot parallel to Tal's position, she pushed aside the leaves and smiled. There he stood, bare-chested, muscles rippling and damp with sweat. His long hair was pulled back giving a clear view of his intense green eyes and handsome face. A burning ache spread from her groin.

She lifted the lid on the basket and checked the ale and food she had packed. *Perfect.* Before she could close the lid, the creak of wagon wheels rolling to a stop drew her attention. She parted the branches again.

And spied someone running toward Tal.

<hr>

Alex sprinted as fast as she could.

Ahead, Tal raised a bucket of water over his head and poured it out. Shaking his head, droplets sprayed in all directions.

Not slowing down, Alex barely gave Tal time to drop the bucket before she hurtled into his arms. Her momentum drove them both to the lip of the well and almost over the edge.

Alex covered his face with feverish kisses. Mixed with Tal's salty perspiration and water, she was soon soaked.

She paused only long enough to say, "I don't want us to be apart ever again."

Maggie's stunned mind absorbed the entire scene. A choked sob rose deep within her. "No," she moaned.

She dropped the basket and it overturned, spilling the contents onto the ground.

Eyes brimming with tears, she stumbled away.

CHAPTER 18

"LET'S STOP HERE." TAL VAULTED OFF HIS HORSE AND HURRIED TOWARD a large pavilion nestled between precise rows of smaller tents. Bozar watched Alexandria emerge from the pavilion. She wiped her hands on her apron, and broke into a run when she spotted Tal. He caught her and swung her up into his arms.

"The lad is quite taken with Lady Alexandria, eh?" Artemis Thurgood remarked.

"Why else do you think he insisted we take this route on our inspection tour," Bozar answered wryly.

"The hospital represents progress. Markingham hasn't had surgeons or proper medical care for generations," Pulpit observed. "When Lady Alexandria learned help was needed, she volunteered."

"I wish the same could be said about the city's defenses," Gravelback growled. "This diversion of resources has cost us dearly. Only a third of the city walls have been repaired, and despite blacksmiths working day and night, most of the defensive apparatuses still haven't been replaced. Markingham remains ripe for the plucking."

"Come, come, Lord Commander," Bozar admonished. "Even you have remarked on how the citizenry has responded to our efforts. We have no lack of those willing to work for food and other daily necessities. The army barracks and stables are near complete restoration, crops have been planted, and with a functioning sewer and water system, widespread disease is no longer a concern."

Gravelback's response was interrupted by Tal's approach. He leaped into the saddle, a broad smile on his face.

Bozar shook his head, and the group continued their tour.

The walls of Markingham slowly receded as Alex, Tal, and Pulpit rode north away from the city.

"I never thought I'd say this after we were chased all across the wilds by the dark lord, but I'm glad to get out of the city," Alex sighed. "And after a week at the hospital, I'm ready for some fresh air."

"You've been working too hard. I barely see you," Tal groused.

"There's a lot of need, Tal. I'm glad I can do something to help."

"You have provided comfort for many families, Lady Alexandria," Pulpit added.

"Thanks, but no one has worked harder than you, Pulpit," Alex said. "You don't ever seem to get tired."

Alex handed Tal a crude map with directions scrawled on it. "I was told blue moss grows near this old farm north of here."

Tal took the map and studied it. "Tell me again why we are looking for this moss."

"It has the medicinal qualities of reducing pain and fever," Pulpit answered.

Tal cast a wry glance at Pulpit. "More of your monk's training?"

"It does include a thorough instruction in the beneficial aspects of natural herbs and plants," he admitted.

They rode on for another hour with frequent stops while Tal consulted the map. The area around them, once cultivated, had reverted to tall grass, brambles, and young trees.

They came to a farmhouse with weathered gray siding. A section of its porch lay canted as if ready to collapse. The trio dismounted and gingerly walked across the rickety wooden porch, each step accompanied by creaks and groans.

Tal had to push hard on the warped front door to get it open enough for them to slip into the house. The interior was surprisingly intact. A single table, bench, and a few chairs, occupied the main room. A cursory search revealed several bedrooms, all empty except one containing a dusty bed and nightstand.

They found nothing of interest and walked out. The wind had picked up, and the sun disappeared behind a bank of clouds.

Alex stopped and pointed at a large building in the distance. "Is that an old barn? Maybe the moss grows over there."

"I'll stay here with the horses if you want to search the area," Pulpit offered.

Alex nodded, grabbed Tal's hand, and they walked through the knee-high grass. The barn, a two-story structure, was located beside a meadow filled with a riot of yellow wildflowers. An ancient oak grew from the middle of the meadow. It loomed over the field like a giant sentinel.

A rumble rolled across the sky. Alex looked up. Angry clouds frothed and billowed.

"A storm is brewing," Tal observed. As if in confirmation, lightning flashed followed by another boom of thunder.

They ran for the barn. Tal stopped abruptly. He reached down and plucked something from the sea of wildflowers. He held it up.

Alex's breath left her in a rush.

It was a lavender flower—just like the one in the future thread shown to her by Diana.

Tal tucked it behind her ear. "C'mon."

He pulled her along, and they continued their race for the barn. They burst through the doors just as a downpour started. Breathless and laughing, they listened to the pounding rain on the roof.

Alex walked to a ladder which led to the second-story hayloft.

She crooked her finger. "Follow me." She grabbed the rungs and began to climb, Tal right behind her.

They reached the loft. Old piles of hay lay in heaps, and dry straw covered every surface.

Except for one area.

A section had been swept clean and a thick blanket spread out. A magical light crystal and flagon of ale were perched by the blanket.

Tal blinked. "Somebody's been here—"

He stopped and folded his arms. "You did this. There's no such thing as blue moss is there?"

Alex reached for Tal and pulled him down onto the bedspread. "Of course there is."

"Is Pulpit in on this?"

"Who do you think told me about blue moss?" A smile tugged at Alex's lips as she recalled the white monk's words. *Even a celibate monk can recognize a young man and young woman in love.*

She unlaced her shirt and pulled it over her head. Then she pulled off her boots and wriggled out of her pants.

She wore nothing underneath.

Tal's eyes grew to the size of plates. He pulled at his own buttons, and in his haste, fumbled so much Alex had to help him get his tunic off. Arms wrapped around each other, they fell back onto the soft blanket.

"Not that I'm complaining, but why?" Tal asked.

Alex stroked his face. "I could tell you I've been stupid and jealous and wanted to make it up to you, but the real reason is I don't want to wait any longer. I love you and nothing's going to change that."

Tal ran his hands up and down her bare flesh. His mouth soon followed his hands. Alex shivered, her growing desire making further conversation impossible.

They grappled with each other in an explosion of passion. Tal's lips found Alex's breasts, his tongue teasing her nipples. Moaning, her fingers threaded through his thick mane of hair. Every place found by his lips and tongue scorched her flesh. Her hips bucked with each exquisite sensation.

At last, she could take no more.

She pushed Tal off and began to unbuckle his pants.

Whump!

The barn doors below flew open. Damp air filled the interior along with another scent.

A beast's wet fur.

In an instant, Tal clamped a hand over Alex's mouth. He put his lips next to her ear. "Don't make a sound," he warned.

He inched to the edge of the loft and looked down. Alex saw him stiffen. When he turned back, her heart filled with dread. His eyes were hard. She'd seen that look before.

Something dangerous lurked below.

Something he was going to kill.

CHAPTER 19

TAL PUT A FINGER TO HIS LIPS AND MOTIONED TO ALEX. SHE CRAWLED to him, and they both peeked over the edge of the loft.

A trio of beasts stood dripping inside the barn.

Their leader, at seven feet, stood a head taller than the others. He flicked pointed ears to shed them of rain. Covered in black, bristly fur, the beast growled to reveal razor-sharp canines that glistened in the dim, storm-tossed light. Red-rimmed eyes surveyed the barn's interior. Rainwater dribbled off his fur and the three-inch claws protruding from each hand. The two smaller beasts were identical to the pack leader, except for fur color. Both had brown pelts.

Tal motioned again, and they eased back out of sight. The wind and drumbeat of rain against the barn were accompanied by frequent lightning and thunder. "I don't think they can hear us over the storm," he said.

"What are they?" Alex whispered.

"Werewolves, shapeshifters who can transform from man to beast."

"They look vicious."

Tal didn't answer. He returned to the loft's edge and studied the scene below. A heavy chain with a hook swung like a pendulum in the stiff breeze swirling through the open doors. Intended to lift hay bales, the chain was looped through a pulley and secured to a crossbeam. Several feet away lay a hay fork partially covered in straw.

Tal saw no other implements he could use as weapons and scooted back to Alex.

He pulled her close and plucked the dagger from his belt. In a low voice, he murmured, "This is all I have. I could make short work of them with my sword, but I left it strapped to my saddle."

"Tal, you can't fight those things with just a knife!" Alex whispered. "Use your magic to deal with them."

Tal shook his head. "I can't. They've been warded. I sensed it the moment they entered the barn."

"What does that mean?"

"It means they have a layer of magic cast over them for protection. I can break it, but it would take too much time. The second I try to dismantle the ward, they'll know it and attack us."

"Then use your magic to—I don't know—pick them up and throw them far away."

Frustrated, Tal grit his teeth. "Maybe with one or even two of the lycanthropes I could manage that. But there are *three* warded werewolves. The blast of magic needed would demolish everything in the vicinity, including the barn."

Tal cupped Alex's face. "I'm not going risk your life."

"Then we can just wait here and not make a sound. Eventually, they'll go away, and you won't need to fight them."

"You don't understand. We're on borrowed time. The shape-shifters are going to smell us, and we need to surprise them before they do. It's our only chance."

"No, Tal, no."

Tal swallowed and did his best to ignore Alex's tears spilling onto his hands. He lifted her chin to force her gaze to meet his. "Alex, I need you to listen to me. Can you do that?"

She sniffled and nodded.

"Good. The only way to kill a werewolf is with silver or to behead the creature. I can transmute my dagger's iron into silver for a short time, but it's only temporary. The change should last long enough for me to do what's needed."

Tal pulled Alex's tear-streaked face closer. "Here's the most important part. If *anything* goes wrong, I'll keep the lycanthropes distracted long enough for you to escape. Run as fast as you can back to Pulpit. He'll know what to do."

"No. I'm not leaving you."

"Yes, you will!" Tal hissed. He pointed at the loft window. "Climb out and lower yourself. It's a long drop to the ground, so try to hang on and extend your arms to shorten the distance a bit. The rain has softened the ground, so bend your knees and roll when you land. Then run. Run faster than you ever have in your life."

Tal put his arms around Alex and crushed her to his chest. "I love you, and if you love me, you'll do exactly what I say." He paused. "Wish me luck."

He crawled to the loft edge and studied the lycanthropes' spacing and distance. He gathered his legs beneath him. There would never be a better time.

He dropped silently to the ground below.

Alex scrambled to the edge just in time to see Tal land nimbly among the werewolves. They reacted instantly.

But Tal moved even faster.

He stomped his booted foot on the tines causing the hay fork to flip up. Tal caught the handle in midair and launched the hay fork at the nearest werewolf. The fork caught the leaping shapeshifter in the chest impaling the beast and hurling it backward. Such was the force of Tal's throw, that the tines pierced the thick wooden support beam and protruded onto the other side. Pinned, the werewolf howled in agony unable to extricate itself.

In the next breath, Tal grabbed the dangling chain, swung it over his head like a sling, and released it at the next charging werewolf. Like the coils of a snake, the chain wrapped itself round and round the shapeshifter. The end with the hook rebounded to be caught by Tal. With the heel of his hand, he drove the sharp tip up into the ribs of the werewolf. Then he jerked the chain down, the pulley squealing, and the struggling werewolf shot into the air to hang suspended. He looped the chain over a cleat, yanked the dagger from his belt, and whirled to face the pack leader.

Alex, heart in her throat, watched in disbelief. The entire sequence of events took less than ten seconds. She had never seen anyone move so fast. At times, Tal's quickness made his image blur.

Now, however, Tal and the giant pack leader slowly circled each other like gladiators.

The werewolf darted in and swung a huge paw in an attempt to disembowel Tal. He dodged away and instead, the claws cleaved empty space. A howl of agony split the air as Tal quickly lunged in and slashed a bloody streak down the lycanthrope's ribs.

The open wound dripped blood.

Tal wore a savage smile. "Not healing is it?"

With a snarl, the werewolf struck again, missed, and Tal scored another bloody laceration across the beast's chest.

A squeal of metal jerked Alex's attention from the bloody contest. The impaled werewolf had drawn its legs up to push against the beam. By arching its back, the beast was slowly pulling the metal tines inch-by-inch out of the wood.

That thing is going to free itself, and Tal will have to face two werewolves at once.

The awful realization galvanized Alex into action. Still naked, she hurried down the ladder and desperately cast about for anything she could use to bend the tines. She caught the glint of metal in a corner. She rushed to the spot, and kicked away the hay to reveal a manure shovel, the handle broken midway down the shaft.

Alex picked up the shovel and dashed to the impaled werewolf. The shapeshifter clawed savagely at her, but she dodged past and darted behind the beast. She lifted the shovel and hammered at the protruding tines. Each blow bent the prongs a bit, and Alex sobbed with relief. She redoubled her efforts and swung again and again, her wild blows causing her long hair to fly in all directions.

So intent on her task, she didn't see the skewered werewolf reach blindly backward with sweeping paws where its claws caught in her hair. It jerked savagely, ripping strands from her scalp. She screamed in pain.

"Alex!" Tal shouted.

She pulled herself free, minus some hair, just in time to see the mammoth werewolf use Tal's distraction to strike. Bloody furrows plowed across his chest, the sharp claws digging deep. Tal cried out in pain.

"No!" Alex screamed.

The pack leader snarled with bloodlust and moved in for the kill. Lips stretched to reveal sharp fangs, the werewolf lunged to rip Tal's throat out. Instead, the slavering jaws snapped at empty air as Tal nimbly sidestepped. Before the beast could react, Tal's charmed knife struck a sweeping blow at the exposed head and neck. A red line formed below one pointed ear to the next. Throat cut, blood gushed from the werewolf's severed jugular. Tal stood ready to strike again, his gore-drenched dagger in one hand, his ripped side held with the other.

The werewolf swayed like a tree in the wind. The primal light in its eyes faded, and the shapeshifter toppled to the floor. It lay unmoving.

Then Tal collapsed.

CHAPTER 20

A LEX RUSHED TO TAL AND SLID TO A STOP BESIDE HIM.
She knelt and grunted with effort as she lifted his head into her lap. His blood streaked her breasts and dripped down her stomach.

"You're a sight," Tal mumbled.

Alex ignored him and examined his wounds. Parallel lacerations raked across his chest. There was so much blood, she couldn't tell how deep they were.

"I'm sorry, Tal. I should have run like you told me to," she sobbed, her tears mixing with his blood.

Tal reached up and touched her face. "You did what you had to do. If the beast had pulled itself free, we would both be dead by now."

He dropped his hand. "Help me up."

With Tal's arm draped over her shoulder, Alex struggled to raise him to a standing position. The two remaining werewolves thrashed about, and Tal grasped the enchanted dagger to end their lives. It slipped from his grip. He slumped more heavily, and Alex could barely hold him upright. She half-walked, half-dragged him to one of the broad support beams. He slid down, his back against the joist.

He waved weakly at the lycanthropes. "You have to get the monk. He needs to finish off those monstrosities."

Alex didn't want to leave Tal, not even for a second. But she needed Pulpit. They had to get Tal back to Markingham as soon as possible.

She dashed out into the rain.

The deluge had subsided to a drizzle. She screamed Pulpit's name over and over again until her throat was raw. *Please hear me, Pulpit, please.*

Not willing to wait any longer, she ran back inside.

The rain had washed most of Tal's blood from her skin, and he cast her a lopsided grin. "I repeat, you are a fair sight, dripping wet and bare-arsed. If I weren't so indisposed, I'd carry you back up to the loft so we could finish what we started."

"Oh, Tal, how can think of such a thing right now?"

He nudged his chin toward the barn doors. His grin grew wider. "It's easy, but I wonder what Pulpit will think when he sees you." The grin disappeared, and he groaned as a spasm of pain gripped him.

With a start, Alex realized Tal was right. She scrambled up the ladder and hastily pulled on her clothes and boots, then hurried back down.

She had just knelt beside him when she heard hooves splashing on the ground outside. Moments later, Pulpit rushed in, his *haloub* fully extended. He swung the weapon around and his eyes fell on Alex and Tal.

His mouth dropped.

"What happened?" he demanded.

Tal pointed. "They did."

The monk whirled and almost dropped his staff. One enormous werewolf lay nearby in a pool of blood, another squirmed in mid-air held tight by loops of chain, while yet another was skewered to a thick beam and struggling to free itself.

Alex put her arm around Tal and cradled his head to her chest. Between sobs, she managed to tell Pulpit the gist of Tal's battle with the werewolves.

"We need to get him to Markingham. We need to go now!"

Tal stirred. "No. Kill them first, Pulpit. They can't be allowed to get free and ravage the countryside." He gestured feebly at his dagger on the ground. "I think the transmutation still holds. You can use the blade to end the beasts' lives."

Pulpit answered with a grim nod. He held the *haloub* before him and a silvery cord erupted from the tip. It snaked along the ground and wrapped around the dagger's handle. The monk approached the suspended werewolf and snapped the staff. The cord whipped the dagger forward with such force, the sharp blade cleaved completely through the shapeshifter's neck. Before the severed head had even toppled to the ground, he repeated the process with the remaining werewolf. For good measure, he separated the dead pack leader's head as well.

All three bodies transformed into men, sightless eyes staring from their severed heads.

The monk deactivated the *haloub* and it shrank back to a baton. He shoved it in his belt, picked up Tal's dagger, and hurried toward his horse. He returned with a Deep Pocket.

Pulpit removed soft gauze from the magical bag. Gently, he wiped away the blood from Tal's wounds so he could examine the injury. The flow had slowed, revealing cuts so deep the white bone from Tal's ribs showed. Pulpit and Tal shared a grim look.

"We need to get him to the farmhouse," he told Alex. "It will be easier to bind his wounds in a bed than here on the dirt and straw. The prince can't afford to lose any more blood."

"When can we take him back to Markingham and to the hospital?" Alex asked.

Pulpit sighed. "I'm sorry, Alexandria. Tal is in no condition to travel. Any attempt to move him now would hasten—I mean endanger—his life."

With a grunt, the monk picked Tal up and carried him to the

horse. He lifted him into the saddle and then swung up behind him. Pulpit handed Alex the reins.

"You need to lead the horse while I hold onto the prince."

Alex ran through the wet grass leading the horse. When they reached the old farmhouse, she steadied Tal while Pulpit dismounted. The monk slid him from the saddle and carried him inside. Alex rushed to the room with the bed, and ripped off the old dusty spread. Pulpit gently laid Tal down and Alex propped a pillow under his head. He activated the *haloub*, planted the staff by the bedside and waved a hand over the knobbed end. A warm light filled the darkened room.

Pulpit placed the Deep Pocket beside him, reached inside, and pulled out bandages and alcohol. Alex stood beside him and they both worked to staunch the bleeding and clean Tal's wounds.

When they finished, bandages were triple-wrapped around his chest and pulled so tight that Tal feebly complained. Pulpit carried chairs into the room and they sat by the bed. Outside, the rain continued to fall, accompanied by an occasional roll of thunder.

Alex held Tal's hand shocked at how pale he appeared. His eyes were closed and his breathing was labored at times. Pulpit leaned forward and pulled an eyelid up. He shook his head. "The prince has slipped into unconsciousness."

"Is he going to be alright?" Fear for Tal filled her so completely Alex could barely get the words out.

Pulpit didn't answer.

Alex grabbed his arm. "Answer me!"

"The blood loss would have already killed a normal man. Tal is a Royal, moreover, a Blood Prince. Such men are not easily killed. If he survives the next few hours..." Pulpit didn't finish.

"You mean he might die?" The prospect left Alex so distraught that she became lightheaded. She swayed, and spots appeared in her vision.

"Alexandria!" Concerned, Pulpit took her arm. "Do you need

some water?" Alex nodded and Pulpit hurried from the room to return with a leather bladder.

Alex took a drink and handed the water container back. "It's all my fault. I planned this, planned to lure Tal to this place, planned to surprise him, planned everything."

Alex buried her face in her hands. "My fault, my fault, my fault," she cried.

"Alexandria, you can't blame yourself—"

He was interrupted by a loud sigh from Tal. They both looked up. His chest had stopped moving.

Tal wasn't breathing.

CHAPTER 21

Pulpit rushed to Tal and placed his face near the prince's mouth. No breath emerged.

He took Tal's wrist but could detect no pulse.

Alex shot up and pushed him aside. She put her ear to Tal's chest. "His heart's not beating. And he's not breathing!

"NOOOOOOOOOOO!" she screamed.

The volume increased. Pulpit clapped his hands to his ears, the decibel level threatening to deafen him.

The room—indeed, the entire house—began to shake. When he turned back to Alex, her mouth was slack, her eyes rolled back. The whites of her eyes glowed with an incandescent brightness. Pulpit staggered away from the apparition.

The vibrations increased, dust cascaded from the ceiling, and the entire house shifted up and down, backward and forward. Pulpit found it hard to keep his footing. Magic flooded all around the monk, a torrent more potent than anything he had ever experienced, more than anything he could have imagined. The room couldn't contain it, nor could the house. It was going to explode with everything and everybody in it.

Then, before his disbelieving eyes, all the magical energy rushed backwards into Alex's mouth. Silence, so abrupt it shocked his overwhelmed senses, fell over the room. Alex continued to shake like a mannequin whose strings were being plucked one after another.

Then the magic rushed from her again.

Pulpit flew backward and hit the wall with crushing impact.

The breath knocked from him, stars burst in his head. He bounced to the floor and lay sprawled, fighting to breathe. He swam in and out of consciousness and lay still for long moments, his entire body bruised.

At last, he rolled over and sat up. His vision swam, and he was forced to rest his head between his knees. When the vertigo passed, the monk stumbled to his feet. The first thing he noticed was Alex lying prone across Tal.

Pulpit blinked, then blinked again. A ghostly vapor emerged from one of her fingers. Then another and another. Soon tendrils grew from all her digits. They undulated and crawled across Tal's body. The mist emitted a soft glow, bathing Tal in an ethereal light.

As one, the vaporous wisps plunged into Tal's flesh.

"The Creator have mercy!" Pulpit cried. He staggered closer.

Tal's pallor was pink, not the deathly pale it had been before. He rubbed his eyes and looked again. The healthy glow had darkened to an even rosier hue!

A loud hiccup issued from Tal, and his chest expanded—then began a regular rise and fall. He was breathing!

"What?" the monk whispered.

Pulpit approached Alex. She lay with eyes closed, unconscious. He gently lifted her and carried her to the other side of the bed. He placed her beside Tal.

Pulpit returned his attention to the prince. He tried to persuade himself that Tal had been alive all along, not dead.

Except that Lady Alexandria believed him dead also.

Then he noticed the bandages.

Before, the fresh bandages were spattered with red. But now, they looked clean and spotless as if never touched by blood. Pulpit tugged the dressing loose and looked at the wounds. His knees wobbled at the sight.

Where ripped flesh should have been, now only healthy skin appeared. No sign of the horrible wounds existed.

He raised a shaky hand to his head. "I must be feverish." Pulpit pinched his cheek…hard. Then he pulled back the bandages again.

Smooth, unblemished skin.

Alex groaned. She sat up and looked around bleary-eyed. Pulpit rushed to her side. "How do you feel?"

"Like an entire army is marching through my skull," she moaned.

She went rigid. "Tal!"

"Right beside you, Lady Alexandria."

Alex rolled over and onto her knees. She ran her hands over his bandages, then put her ear to his chest. "His heart's beating! Tal's alive!"

"He is. In addition, there's this." Pulpit used Tal's dagger to carefully cut away the dressing and removed the bandages. No sign of his terrible wounds existed.

Alex threw her arms around Tal and held him in a desperate embrace. She rocked back and forth, cuddling him. "He's come back to me, Pulpit. My love has come back to me."

The scene touched Pulpit, and he decided to give Alex some time alone with the still unconscious prince. Curious, he left in search of the chairs mysteriously missing from the room. He found them at the table he had originally taken them from. It was as if they had never moved.

Then he noticed the door. Before it stood warped and ajar. Now it was closed. Curious, he turned the knob and it swung open easily. He stepped outside and blinked. He rubbed his eyes and looked again.

The porch, once leaning and in danger of collapse, was sturdy and straight as a plumb line.

The rain had stopped with rays of sunlight peeking through thinning clouds, so Pulpit stepped off the porch and faced the farmstead.

"By the Creator's love!"

Gone was the weathered and gray exterior. Now the house wore a coat of bright white paint, every board and nail appearing as if just recently installed by a carpenter.

The entire farmstead was brand new.

Eyes closed, Alex clung to Tal.

The brush of his warm breath on her skin was a constant reassurance. She moved her hand down to his bare chest and reveled at the strong beat of his heart.

"I thought I lost you," she whispered.

Pulpit entered the room carrying the two missing chairs. He placed them beside the bed. "Can we talk?"

Alex shook her head. She couldn't bring herself to let go of Tal.

"I can assure you the prince is well on his way to recovery. In fact, I believe you'll find that when he wakes, he'll feel wonderful. Perhaps better than at any time in his life."

With great reluctance, Alex released Tal and laid his head gently back on the pillow. She kissed him and scooted off the bed and into the chair next to the monk.

"What do you remember?" he asked her.

Alex twisted her hands in her lap. "Tal had stopped breathing. After that," she shook her head, "it's all a blank."

She clutched Pulpit. "I thought Tal had died. What happened?"

The monk patted her hand. "*You* happened."

Alex rubbed her temple, the pounding threatening to return. "I don't understand."

"I'm not sure I do either. But I do know one thing."

"What?"

"Tal was dead and you revived him. You saved his life."

CHAPTER 22

ALEX LISTENED IN STUNNED SILENCE AS PULPIT RECOUNTED THE sequence of events.

"And you remember none of it?" he asked.

She shook her head.

"Has anything like this ever happened before?"

"No, I mean maybe, I mean yes." She threw her hands up. "I don't know how to answer you."

Pulpit placed a hand on her arm. "Try. I'm a patient listener."

Hesitant at first, once Alex started, the words gushed from her. She told him how Rodric commandeered her handmaiden's body, how he attacked her and when she was near death, magic erupted from her to hurl him away and save her life. She described being stung by the scorpion dog, and Tal's description of how she leveled a wide area of forest.

"Then when the dark lord was chasing us, Tal crept into his camp and killed a number of his men and gargoyles. He was wounded, grazed by a javelin. I cleaned and bandaged it, but by the next day, the wound had disappeared—like the injury never happened. We were running for our lives, and I really never gave it much thought...until now.

She turned to the monk. "What do you think it means?"

Pulpit sat for long moments, hands steepled before him. At last he spoke. "You have power within you the likes of which I have never witnessed. At first, I thought it a new magic, but now—now I think it something else."

He leaned closer. "Not new but an ancient and rare magic."

"Is this magic Artifact, Elemental, or Locomotive?" she asked.

Pulpit shook his head. "None of these. In truth, I don't know how to classify your power."

Alex sighed and rubbed the back of her neck. "Then nothing has changed. I still don't know anything about this force inside me."

Pulpit wagged a finger. "Not so. Think of the circumstances by which your magic erupted—assaulted by Rodric and in fear of your life, then later, stung by the scorpion-dog and in incredible pain. That takes us to the present where you feared for Tal's life and indeed, thought he had died. But with the prince, we can add one more factor."

"What?"

"You love him."

Alex glanced at Tal lying on the bed. She reached out and stroked his face. "Yes, very much, but then you already knew that. What do my feelings for Tal have to do with my power?"

"Everything."

Alex grimaced. "I'm sorry, Pulpit, but you didn't answer the question."

The monk chuckled. "Oh, but I did. I believe in each case, strong emotions trigger the release of your magic."

Alex turned the monk's words over in her mind. "But what about Tal's spear wound? I was irritated with him for taking stupid risks, but it was a minor injury. I didn't display strong sentiment one way or another, yet the wound still disappeared."

Pulpit scratched his cheek. "What was going through your mind when you saw the prince's injury? When you cleaned and dressed the laceration?"

Alex sat back and sighed. She closed her eyes.

Tal had blood on his shirt when he returned from the dark lord's camp. I helped him take off his tunic and saw the wound. His skin was warm, and the light from the campfire displayed his muscles like a sculptor had chiseled them. He'd run most of the way back and he was damp with sweat.

Heat rose in Alex's cheeks. She glanced at the monk, uncomfortable. "Um, Tal took his shirt off, and I, um, looked at the graze on his side."

Pulpit nodded. "Right. We can add desire to the list."

The blaze in her face advanced to a wildfire.

He ignored her obvious discomfort. "Let me show you something."

The monk led her outside. Alex gaped at the bright paint and brand new exterior of the house. "I did this?"

Pulpit nodded. "The entire farmhouse has been restored inside and out—just like me. Your magic blasted me against the wall. Battered and barely conscious, by rights I should be lying in a bed like the prince. Yet here I stand, not a mark on me and more vigorous than I have ever felt in my life. Such is the power and reach of your magic."

Numb, Alex followed the monk back into the bedroom. She checked on Tal and brushed a stray lock of hair out of his face. Then she joined Pulpit, and they both sat beside the unconscious prince.

The monk studied her so intensely, she felt like a bug being examined under a glass jar. "What?" she blurted.

"There is more to you than simple acts of magical power. You have compassion for the less fortunate. Hunger, pain, and suffering in others move you. I have watched you interact with the population of Markingham, and you display unfailing kindness."

Uncomfortable, Alex waved the comment away. "Lots of people are like that."

The monk shook his head sadly. "You would be surprised how many people are not *like that*. There would be no need for my order otherwise."

A loud groan interrupted them.

Tal sat up.

"Alex, let me breathe!"

Tal firmly pushed her away and tried once more to put on his tunic. She hovered beside him as if he might collapse at any moment. "I'm fine, I tell you."

He stood and managed to pull on his shirt, but not before he examined his side one more time. No sign existed where the werewolf's claws had scored a jagged path across his chest.

Out of patience, he picked up Alex and sat her in the chair beside the bed. He motioned for Pulpit to join her. When both were seated, he said, "Now tell me what happened."

Alex and Pulpit, by turns, related the sequence of events after Tal had passed out. When they finished, he shook his head. "I remember the pain—then nothing, until I woke."

He gestured at Alex. "And you kept telling me you have no power."

Alex hung her head. "I'm sorry, Tal. I didn't know."

Tal mentally kicked himself for being so short with her. He drew her next to him. His arm around her waist, they sat together on the bed. "I'm the one who should be sorry. You saved my life, and here I am quibbling about things that don't matter."

"Her magic is unusual, Prince Tal," Pulpit interjected. "Unlike the magic flowing through you, Alexandria's is directly tied to her state of mind and feelings. That makes her control unpredictable, unstable. She cannot draw upon her power at will as all magic-wielders are trained to do."

Pulpit cleared his throat. "There is one more thing to consider, my prince."

Tal frowned. "I'm having a hard enough time absorbing everything that's happened so far. What else could there be?"

"Based on what Lady Alexandria has told us about the situation in Wheel, and why the dark lord tried so hard to capture her, we must assume she is crucial to the Veil Queen's plans. Now we know why. The Dark Queen desires her power, and wants to manipulate it for her own ends. But if, as I believe, this magic is tied to Alexandria's emotions, then it would be uncontrollable and useless to her. She must know this if she understands the nature of Lady Alexandria's magic. Why go to all this trouble for no gain?"

Tal leaned forward, intrigued. "What's your point?"

"The Dark Queen knows something we don't. Something that makes her believe she *can* channel Alexandria's power."

Alex shuddered, and Tal held her tighter.

"Marlinda will never get the chance!" he spat. "Her black heart and her head will decorate a pike so all will see her reign of bloody terror has ended."

Tal took several deep breaths to dampen his anger. "It will be dark soon. We need to get back to Markingham before Bozar sends out search parties."

"May I bury the poor souls in the barn first?" Pulpit asked.

Tal nodded. "I'll help you."

An hour later, the sun low in the sky, they finished burying the former shapeshifters.

Tal dropped his shovel, then stood with Alex as the monk prayed over the dead men. They mounted their horses but went only a short distance before Tal stopped. He turned back and studied the graves.

"What is it?" Alex asked.

"Something's been bothering me since we discovered the werewolves." Tal gestured at the fresh mounds of dirt. "The lycanthropes were warded."

"So?"

"Only a trained magic-wielder could ward them. They couldn't do that by themselves. So, who cast the magic?" He studied their surroundings. "More importantly, where are they now?"

They took off at a gallop back to the city.

CHAPTER 23

THE PACE TO REBUILD MARKINGHAM'S WALLS ACCELERATED AT TAL'S news of the warded shapeshifters.

Bozar ordered round-the-clock shifts, and the work never paused. Whole sections of the wall—formerly honeycombed with weakened foundations and crumbling gaps—now presented a formidable barrier against any attackers. In addition, new scorpions, ballista, and arrow slits sprouted from the battlements.

Tal walked with Bozar along the ramparts inspecting the progress. He nodded with approval. "Much has been done."

"Agreed," his First Advisor said. "Unfortunately, a considerable amount of work still lies ahead. Even toiling day and night, it will take months to complete repairs to the walls and defensive emplacements."

Tal gazed across the plain from their perch high on the wall. All the trees and brush had been cleared for half a league around Markingham's perimeter. No enemy could sneak into the city, and any armed force would be seen long before they launched an attack. This also created a clear line of sight for defenders to shoot arrows, hurl javelins, and other missiles at the attackers. Any assault would cost the enemy dearly.

Legionnaires drilled in the open plain, the bark of sergeants drifting to where he and Bozar stood. The soldiers responded with crisp precision. With such highly trained legions, Markingham would be unassailable.

If we can fully restore the walls and battlements.

Tal's nights had been restive since his encounter with the were-wolves. *Someone* had cast a spell of protection over them. A sense of foreboding pricked the back of his neck.

He glanced skyward. "The Dark Lord chasing Alex had squarks. The giant birds could make us vulnerable to an attack from the air. What is the strength of our flying cavalry?"

Bozar pursed his lips. "Not as many as I would like. Lord Tarlbolt has a garrison-strength complement of three hundred flying horse soldiers under his command. More trickle in from the Veil's breach, but as you know, flying horses are much harder to come by than ground-based mounts. Our invasion plans call for a minimum of a thousand airborne steeds. I won't feel comfortable until we reach that number."

Tal shook his head. The invasion force continued to grow at a snail's pace. The numbers coming through the Veil were reduced as civilians and supplies to rebuild Markingham took the place of soldiers.

Tal's troubled look caused Bozar to squeeze his shoulder. "It was the right decision. These are our people, and they are in need. Even Gravelback agrees that we benefit from the populace's support."

Tal kicked at a stone parapet. "Yet, it took Alex pointing this out for me to see. I was ready to let them starve in the rush to see Marlinda dead."

He glanced at Bozar. "Not much of a prince am I?"

"All of us were prepared to do the same thing," the First Advisor reminded Tal, "and you will be a fair and just ruler."

A harsh laugh erupted from Tal. "How can you say that after all the mistakes I've made?"

"Rare is the man or woman not guilty of errors in judgment. A good monarch admits to this and moves to correct them. From such comes wisdom. For example, you disobeyed me and saved the life of Lady Alexandria. I was wrong. *You* were right."

At the mention of her name, Tal's thoughts flashed back to Alex's smile at breakfast that morning, and how it made the day seem brighter. His lips stretched at the memory.

"You love her." Bozar's words were not a question but a statement.

Tal nodded.

"You realize the complications that come with this, don't you?"

Tal frowned. "What do you mean?"

"Lady Alexandria is the daughter of the Duke of Wheel. She has told us the duke arranged her marriage to another. He will not be happy she disobeyed him, fled Wheel, and now is with you."

Tal's frown deepened. "I am the prince and heir to the throne. That alone should please the duke."

"You forget the empire has been separated from Dalfur and the Duchy of Wheel for centuries," Bozar told Tal. "The old royal order means nothing now. You could be a peasant for all the duke cares."

"But we come to destroy the Veil, kill the Veil Queen and King, and reestablish the empire's rule," Tal spluttered.

"Have we accomplished that yet?"

"No, but we will."

"If you were the duke, having survived generations of war against the Dark Queen and her vile minions, would you accept that promise?"

Tal opened his mouth, then stopped. "No, I don't suppose I would," he admitted.

"Then there is your mother. You can do nothing without the queen's approval. Of course, she knows of Lady Alexandria, but not the depth of your, *ahem*, relationship. For good reason, my regular reports do not include your romantic entanglements. She thinks the only reason we have not returned Alexandria to Wheel is because our position here is not yet secure."

Tal held his arms stiffly against his sides. "I don't know where you are going with this, my *Eldred*, but I love her. I will not allow her to be sent back to Wheel, much less to wed a man she fears and loathes!"

"Love isn't enough, Tal. You aren't even into your majority. Both you and Alexandria have yet to see your twenty-first summer. Your youth blinds you to how the world works."

"I've killed enough men and monsters to be considered a man. I'm not some lovesick green lad!" Tal shouted.

"Then what is your plan?"

The question threw Tal off stride. "Wh—what do you mean?"

"What do you hope to do with Lady Alexandria? What's your plan? What if, the Creator forbid, you get her pregnant and produce a bastard child?"

Tal paused, his mind on their passionate couplings, near misses only because of fate's intervention. "I—I suppose we would wed," he stammered.

"You suppose?" Bozar asked incredulous.

"You know what I mean," Tal retorted.

"No, I don't, 'know what you mean'."

Tal turned his back on Bozar, anger coursing through him. For long moments, he stood and fought to rein in his temper. *What am I going to do?* He knew he loved her, and she loved him. Until now, that had been all they needed. But as Bozar had pointed out, it wasn't enough.

Not anymore.

He whirled to face the First Advisor. "I love her, my *Eldred*. Not with the infatuation of youth but as a man. She fills my mind and heart, my very flesh and bones. It grows stronger every day. I realize I'm young, but doesn't that describe love?"

Bozar sighed. "It does indeed."

"Then what am I to do? You are my advisor. Advise me!"

Bozar put his arm around Tal's shoulders and they continued their trek along the battlements. "There is only one answer I can give you."

Tal stopped. "What?" he asked eagerly.

"We must arrange your marriage to Lady Alexandria."

Astonished, Tal stared. At last he asked, "Are you serious?"

"When we win this war, your marriage to Alexandria would seal an alliance between the empire and the duchy of Wheel. Even the duke should see the advantage of having his daughter wed a prince and heir to the Crown. The queen will be anxious to end the long separation, and bring Dalfur back into the empire. I'm sure I could convince Celestria your marriage to Alexandria would speed this along."

Tal blinked. "You old goat. You've already given much thought to this. You provoked me on purpose!"

Bozar chuckled. "I admit to nothing other than deciding to face the inevitable."

The First Advisor's next comment quickly tempered Tal's growing excitement.

"First, we must secure Markingham, the most important step in our invasion plan. Then we'll discuss this farther. Agreed?"

Tal gave a reluctant nod.

Before they could resume their inspection, Tal heard a shout behind them. Practius Bolt, Artemis Thurgood's apprentice, ran up to them. Bent over, he tried to catch his breath.

"The grand master sent me," he puffed.

"For what purpose?" Bozar asked.

"The troll brought a dead body to the earl's keep. He refused to give it to anyone but Lady Alexandria."

Tal's foreboding flared, the sense of unease spreading to his entire spine. "Describe the body!" he demanded.

"It's a meld, sire. One of Marlinda's creatures."

CHAPTER 24

TAL AND BOZAR THUNDERED INTO THE KEEP'S EXPANSIVE COURTYARD. A circle of soldiers with Alex, the earl, and Artemis Thurgood in the middle surrounded a prone body on the cobblestones. Above them all towered Boorba. The club held by the troll was ominously smeared with blood.

Tal leaped from the saddle and rushed to join Alex.

She clutched his arm. "It's horrible, Tal. What is that thing?"

The troll nudged the figure with a toe. "Try to sneak by Boorba. I bring bad monster to healer."

Tal knelt and examined the battered body. The troll's truncheon had crushed the creature's head. Reddish-gray brain matter leaked from the splintered skull, but enough semblance remained he could tell the head to be that of a raptor. Black and white feathers covered the head and neck, a hooked, flesh-tearing beak where the mouth should have been. One "arm" was a wing sheathed with the same black and white feathers, the other a normal appendage of skin and flesh. A human torso was attached to legs ending in scaled talons.

Tal stood and spat on the body. "One of Marlinda's melds. But I've never seen one like this." Bozar joined him and examined the body.

"What do you think, my *Eldred*?" Tal asked. "The creature looks—"

"Incomplete," the First Advisor finished for him.

"May I?" Earl York asked.

Tal nodded, and the earl knelt beside the meld. He lifted the human arm and examined it. His face went pale and a gasp escaped his lips. He dropped the limb as if it had scorched his hand.

Alarmed, Tal asked, "What is it?"

The earl pointed a shaking finger at the arm. Quickly, Tal grabbed the limb and examined it. A tattoo was inked on the bicep.

One of a single, milk-white eye.

Varg ripped a chunk of meat from the steaming joint. Hot grease ran down his chin and he absently wiped it with the back of his hand.

The centaur was much larger than most of his melded kind. His equine withers stood at six feet, and when added to his brawny torso, his height reached nine feet. Varg's broad shoulders supported long, heavily muscled arms. He wore no tunic, the bare skin of his trunk marked by tattoos and scars acquired in battle against enemies and challengers to his leadership. These opponents always shared the same fate.

Death.

Varg tore off another piece of meat. Filed to sharp points, his teeth presented a frightening sight. On the rare occasions Varg smiled, an array of sharp, carnivorous teeth appeared like that found in some fearsome predator of the deep.

Varg's head was completely shaven except for a topknot of braided, inky-black hair that draped to his waist. Only when one looked at Varg's face was an imperfection found on the centaur. His right eye was perfectly normal.

His left eye was completely white and blind.

Because of that single flaw, he had been forced to join the Baleful. All who rode with the host had similar imperfections. A mere foal at the time, Varg and others had been driven out of Marlinda's caverns and to the waiting horde. In exchange for useful information and captives, the Baleful received all of Marlinda's rejected creations.

The Baleful then left on their nomadic trek across Dalfur. The newly joined were expected to keep up, as well as to fend for themselves. Many, in fact most, died within the first few weeks of leaving the caverns. It was a brutal and merciless winnowing process that ensured only the strongest would survive.

Having stripped the bloody meat from the haunch, Varg snapped the bone in two and sucked out the marrow. His meal was interrupted by a voice.

"We are encamped for the night, Varg." Yip, his second-in-command, stood nearby.

Formalities didn't exist among the Baleful, and all were addressed by a single name. Other than brief couplings between the males and the handful of females, no families existed. Because Marlinda's meld magic produced sterility, surnames were a waste of breath.

Yip waited while the centaur finished his supper. Doglike, and covered in shaggy fur, he stood on two legs and resembled a mastiff except for human hands and feet. A short, shrunken left arm marked his imperfection and thus his expulsion from the Dark Queen's caverns.

"Good. We should reach Markingham within the week," Varg growled. "The outlying areas are empty of human stock. That will be remedied when we reach the city."

Yip grinned to expose sharp canines. "I've sent a spy ahead, but I could also send a *squark*-mounted scout. He could fly there and back with a report in a matter of hours."

Varg considered Yip's proposal. This would be his third trip to Markingham, and each time the city had declined more than the previous visit. If that pattern continued—and he had no reason to believe otherwise—the city would be practically defenseless, and unable to refuse his demands.

The Baleful leader shook his head. "No. Squarks may be spotted, and although I expect no trouble, we don't need to give them advance warning. Let your spy steal in unseen, then report back. When we appear without warning, the terror on those sheep's faces will be all the more satisfying."

Yip raised his muzzle and released an excited howl.

"This time," Varg continued, "we don't negotiate. We take everything."

The earl's audience room was packed.

Tal, with Bozar and Alex beside him, sat around a table carved from the trunk of an enormous tree. The contours allowed for the seating of a dozen or more, and every space was filled with city and army leaders. In addition, Gravelback's sub-commanders of the Imperial Army were crowded around the room.

The atmosphere, thick and heavy, was tense.

Bozar rapped the table for silence. "Tell us again, earl, the significance of the tattoo," he said.

York stood. Haggard, he seemed to have aged years since Boorba brought them his grisly trophy. He cleared his throat.

"The tattoo of the White Eye is the sigil of the Baleful. The symbol is taken from their leader, Varg, a centaur who is blind in one eye. All his followers wear the tattoo."

"What is the Baleful?" Tal asked.

"An army of misfits and melds rejected and expelled from the Dark Queen's caverns."

"Then why all this drama?" Gravelback growled. "What threat does a ragtag group of scavengers pose to us?"

"They are more than that, Lord Gravelback, much more." Morehead stood, a grim look on his face. "In the past, they were a disorganized lot, suffered from constant infighting, and were more a threat to themselves than anyone else. Now, they number in the thousands and are led by Varg. Savage and merciless, he killed dozens of challengers on his way to the leadership of the Baleful. He has forced discipline upon them, and made them into a fearsome army."

Tal leaned forward. "What do they want?"

"Anything, everything. They are like locusts and consume everything in their path," the earl answered.

A disgusted snort came from Maggie. "Yes, you would know about that, wouldn't you, Father? You're good at giving things away to these *locusts*. Why don't you explain that to our imperial saviors?"

The earl's face went red. "Now is not the time, Margaret."

"Tell them—or I will!"

Earl York swallowed. "The last time the Baleful attacked, we were on the verge of being overrun and losing the city. We—we managed to broker an agreement. Besides the scant food we had, Varg also wanted captives he could trade with the Veil Queen. We asked for volunteers from among the city's populace—those willing to give themselves to the Baleful. When this number met Varg's demands, they walked out the gates. We never saw them again, and the Baleful left.

Tears fell freely from his face.

"My wife was among the volunteers."

CHAPTER 25

"**Y**OUR OWN WIFE?" TAL BLINKED. "YOU PERMITTED HER TO BE GIVEN to the Baleful?"

"Yes, you heard right," Maggie spat. "My mother sacrificed herself while my brave father stayed safely behind. I tried to stop her, but Father had me trussed to a chair until the bastards rode away."

The eyes in the room fell on the earl. The creak of leather and clank of weapons filled the sudden silence. A murmur grew among the imperial soldiers and quickly advanced to angry muttering.

"It wasn't like that, Maggie," Lord Morehead objected. "Your mother was dying. She knew she had only a short time left, and rather than preserve the brief time of her own, decided to save someone whose full life was still ahead."

Morehead's chin trembled. "Lady York was the bravest, most selfless person I have ever met."

"What a load of shit," Maggie said, venom dripping from every word. "Rather than fight back, we watched while a sweet, sickly woman and a host of other 'volunteers' carried out this bravery you speak of. I have another word for what was allowed to happen. *Cowardice.*"

Maggie's hard eyes bored into Tal. "Now you know our dark, little secret, and why the Marauders exist. We all lost family to the Baleful because our leaders allowed it. We decided no more. Better to die resisting with honor than become a coward like my father."

"We would have lost!" Earl York cried. "We couldn't stop

them. Varg would have carried off or killed the entire population of Markingham! It was the only way to save lives."

Thump! Bozar's fist struck the table. "Enough! We are here to discuss the present, not the past. And the present has a well-organized force of melds who will be here within days."

The muttering died.

Bozar gestured to Gravelback. "What is our current strength?"

"Six thousand foot soldiers and three hundred flying cavalry."

The First Advisor turned to Lord Morehead. "What are the numbers of Varg's army?"

The veteran soldier rubbed his chin. "Roughly eight thousand. It's been ten years since they last plagued us, so the bastards could have gained more melds."

Loud cursing erupted from Gravelback. "Then they outnumber us! I warned you, Bozar. This is what happens when military decisions are made by the heart instead of the head. Our army would be far larger if we—"

Bozar cut Gravelback off. "Thank you, Lord Commander." He speared him with an icy stare. "I'll be happy to note all your objections to the queen, *after* we have dealt with our current problem."

The two men locked eyes. At last, Gravelback looked away. "No need for that, First Advisor."

"Good." Bozar pushed his chair back and planted both hands on the table. He swept his gaze around the room.

"We have three problems. The first is to defeat a larger army. If history is any indication, size is less important than strategy. There *is* a way to defeat Varg's army, we just need to decide how. The second problem is related to the first. We can't just win this battle, we must destroy Varg's force—the fewer left alive the better. We must depend on the fog and chaos of war to ensure the few who survive report a confused and distorted version of events back to the Veil Queen."

He pointed to Gravelback. "Deception is what's needed now.

From today forward, we no longer wear the livery of the empire or fly the imperial banners. Have our soldiers wear the plain, unmarked livery we brought with us through the Veil. This will add to the jumbled tale any survivor may tell."

Tal listened attentively. "You mentioned three problems, my *Eldred*. What is the third?"

Bozar pinched his lips. "The troll brought us the spy sent by Varg. The meld used the sewers to sneak into Markingham. He could not have stolen past our sentries and over the wall without being noticed. There must be another way into the city that we're not aware of. If the dead meld knew the way, you can be assured Varg knows as well."

Lord Gravelback spread his hands. "I have every confidence in our legions, First Advisor. Even outnumbered, we can defeat the Baleful. But to destroy the meld army as you suggest would take far larger numbers than we possess."

"Not if we surprise them." Lord Morehead, arms folded, wore a triumphant look.

Bozar frowned. "And how would we do that?"

The city watch commander flashed a savage smile. "They don't know an imperial army lies in wait for them. Varg still thinks Markingham is defenseless and ripe for the picking. He'll expect little or no resistance. If we can draw his host onto the open plain before the city gates, they'll be bunched and packed closely together."

Gravelback's eyes lit up. "A killing field! If we can sneak our army behind them, we'll have them trapped. The bastards will have the walls before them and an army at their back. They'll have no place to turn."

"Won't Varg become suspicious when he sees the walls have been repaired?" Tal asked.

Gravelback's face fell. "Aye. He would, Sire."

"I think that problem can be solved," Artemis Thurgood said. "I can cast a glamour which makes it appear Markingham's defenses are still crumbling and in disrepair. But the magic's reach is limited. Varg must be drawn to the city gates so the glamour is restricted to only that single section of the wall."

"I have one more suggestion to even the odds, First Advisor," Morehead said.

"By all means, continue."

"We have an interesting insect, a spider that makes its home in the fields around Markingham. The spider digs an underground burrow and conceals the entrance. Then it hides and waits for prey to blunder by."

Gravelback was the first to grasp Morehead's concept. The veteran soldier crowed, "We can mimic the spider, dig an underground emplacement and fill it with soldiers. Then we camouflage the entry and wait for the Baleful to ride by."

"I'm thinking archers, Lord Commander," Morehead said, the two soldiers sharing a look of glee. "When we emerge from hiding, they'll be so tightly packed, even the greenest recruit can't miss."

"The foul vermin won't know what hit them!" Gravelback exulted. "The confusion it creates will be something even Varg can't control. Then our legions can strike and finish them off."

"*If* the Baleful can be enticed to ride up to the gates, *if* they don't discover the walls have been restored, *if* we can flank the melds by sneaking our legions to their rear, and *if* the hidden archers are successful in springing their trap," Bozar warned. He shook his head. "There is too much uncertainty. We must come up with another plan."

Tal could barely contain himself. "It will work, my *Eldred*! This is the strategy you spoke of. We can rid ourselves of the Baleful in one battle. Are we to wait for them to attack while we cower behind Markingham's walls? Walls which still have gaps and collapsing ramparts? How long before they discover these weak points and attack?"

"I can talk to Boorba and have him keep a closer watch on the sewers," Alex added. "He'll stop any of these creatures trying to sneak into Markingham."

The room erupted as everyone began to talk at once. Bozar held up his hand until there was silence.

"I must give this more thought. But unless a better plan presents itself, our strategy will be to entice Varg into a frontal assault. Once his forces have massed for attack, we will spring our trap.

"And pray to the Creator it works."

CHAPTER 26

THE HOT SUN RODE HIGH IN THE SKY.

A sheen of perspiration covered Tal's face and bare chest as he shoveled dirt onto an oilskin sheet.

Around him, a score of soldiers cursed and grunted as they added to the growing pile. The tarpaulin was located at the bottom of a deepening pit, each corner tied to a rope. When the load was large enough, another group of soldiers lifted the dirt to the surface, dumped it into a wagon, then lowered the sheet back down to be refilled. A parallel excavation was in the works across the field from theirs.

Tal leaned on the shovel's handle and studied their progress. Over twenty feet deep, they were now widening and lengthening the pit to hold a hundred archers. When finished, wooden scaffolds would line the interior walls to allow the archers to pop up and shoot.

"Tal!" a familiar voice called.

He looked up to see Alex motion to him. She held a bladder of water in one hand and a towel in the other. A breeze lifted her golden hair and spilled it about her face and shoulders.

He scrambled up the ladder.

Alex held out the water container. "I brought you some—"

Tal didn't let her finish. He clutched her waist and pressed her lips against his.

Alex pushed him away. "You're all wet!" She used the cloth to dry herself off.

Tal grinned. "And you're a welcome sight." He tried to grab her again, but she dodged away.

"Here." She handed him the water. While Tal drank greedily, she took the towel and sponged the sweat from his body. She started with his back and then moved to his chest, her hand lingering on the flat ridges of his stomach.

He wiped his mouth. "You seem to be enjoying yourself."

She smiled and trailed her fingers across his bare flesh. "More than you know. If we weren't out here in the open in front of scores of soldiers, I'd be tempted to show you how much."

Alex sighed. "But since we are, why don't you tell me how this trap of lord Morehead's is supposed to work?"

Tal took another long drink before answering. "When the Baleful approach Markingham, they'll mass in front of the walls. Varg will demand tribute from Earl York, who'll be standing on the parapet beside the gates. The earl will attempt to negotiate with Varg to give our legions time to maneuver behind the meld army. Once they are in position, Gravelback will give the signal for the hidden archers to spring the trap. They will jump from hiding and start shooting the melds. By the time the Baleful realize where the arrows are coming from, the army will move in and attack."

Alex frowned. "What happens to the hidden archers if Varg doesn't take the bait? Or worse, turns on them before the army can attack?"

Although the day was hot, a cold chill ran through Tal. "Then they will die," he admitted.

Alex shivered. She reached for his hand, concern etched on her face. "What about you? What's your part in all of this?"

"Bozar wants me on the battlements with Artemis. The Baleful have shamans who can cast protective magic. They are not as skilled as the Veil Queen's Dark Brothers and Sisters, but they might be able to stop the arrows we shoot. We can't take that chance, so we are tasked with finding and neutralizing them."

Tal spat on the ground. "It means I won't be able to fight with the army."

"Good! I don't want you to fight."

Tal barked a laugh. "I've wished for many things in my life, most of which never came true."

Alex crossed her arms. "I mean it, Tal. You don't need to be part of every battle. You have professional soldiers such as Lord Gravelback and a host of sub-commanders to lead the army."

Tal arched an eyebrow at Alex. "You expect me to stay behind every time there's combat? Only a spineless cur does that!"

Alex released an exasperated sigh. "Tal, you're the most fearless man I've ever met. No one would ever mistake you for a coward. But you take too many chances."

"Now you sound like Bozar." Anger crept into Tal's voice.

Alex marched up to Tal and pinched his bare skin.

"Ow!"

"Listen to me you block-headed idiot. Do I look like Bozar?"

Tal rubbed his sore flesh. Alex's pantaloons accentuated the curve of her buttocks and small waist. The simple white tunic strained to contain the swell of her breasts. "Thank the Creator, no."

She shook her finger in his face. "Good. I don't want you taking any more unnecessary chances. Understand?"

Afraid she might take the opportunity to pinch him again, Tal stepped back. "Yes...my lady."

Alex whirled and stalked away.

Varg cantered to the top of a rise, stopped, and raised his hand. The meld host behind him—slithering, crawling, hopping, walking on two legs and four—also came to a halt.

Yip scampered up to the Baleful leader. "What is your wish, Varg?"

"We'll stop here for the night. Tomorrow, Markingham will be in sight."

He fixed Yip with a glare. "Have you heard from your spy yet?"

Yip shook his head, his shaggy ears flopping. "No. He should have already reported in."

Varg spat. "The fool probably found a store of ale. If I find out he's lying drunk somewhere, I'll remove his balls and roast them in front of him."

He twisted his lips. "Strange though. First, the Lycans disappear, now this. If I didn't know what a spineless lot the earl and his people are, I'd almost suspect they've grown a backbone."

He looked at Yip and they both burst out laughing.

Tal nuzzled Alex's neck with his lips. Her warm breath caressed his cheek, her hands stroking his back and shoulders. Emboldened, his own hands roamed over her body. Her breathing soon became gasps.

What if, the Creator forbid, you get her pregnant and produce a bastard child?

He cursed his *Eldred* as Bozar's words thundered through his mind. With great effort, he pulled away. Alex, face flushed, drew him back and kissed him deeply.

Evening had fallen, and they were in Alex's room. Tal managed to wrench himself free, and walked out onto the balcony. The night air helped to cool his ardor and clear his head. Alex followed him.

Her husky voice asked, "Are you mad at me for what I said earlier?"

Tal snorted. "It's nothing I haven't heard many times before." He put his arm around her waist. "But coming from you, it seems to ring truer." He squeezed her tight. "And no, I'm not mad at you."

"Then why—"

Her words were interrupted by a loud knocking at her door. Alex threw up her hands. "We're always being interrupted." She went to the door and jerked it open. A young lieutenant stood outside.

He bowed. "Pardon, Lady Alexandria, but the First Advisor has summoned the prince."

Tal approached the young officer. "Why?"

"Scouts have located the Baleful, sire.

"They are less than a day's march from the city."

CHAPTER 27

THE EARL'S RECEIVING ROOM WAS FILLED WHEN TAL ARRIVED.

Artemis Thurgood waved his hand, and a map appeared in the air. The magical chart settled on the large conference table. Perfect in every detail, trees swayed, and leaves rustled in the wind. Water babbled in brooks, birds flew in the air, and white, cotton clouds drifted across the azure blue sky.

Bozar stood at the front of the table, the tension on his face reflected by everyone in the room. He nodded at Tal.

"Now that we're all here, I'll begin. We expect the Baleful to arrive tomorrow. The earl and lord Morehead have assured me if they follow their normal pattern, they will march right up to the city gates. There will be no formalities, no prolonged negotiations. Varg will make his demands, and if we don't agree, he will attack. We won't have much time, so we must be ready."

He motioned to Gravelback.

Gravelback pointed at the map. "The meld army approaches from the north. Lord Tarlbolt has scouts flying out of sight high overhead to follow their every move. So far, there has been no deviation from their path."

He inclined his head toward Morehead. "As we hoped, there is no indication they are aware of our presence. However, in order to flank them, the army must leave the city tonight and march due west. There is no time for complicated maneuvers. Instead, we'll simply lie in wait for the meld army to approach Markingham, then circle back behind them. When they commit to attack, we'll spring the archers from our trap and move to join battle with them. A small force will be left to defend the walls in case Varg ignores the trap and attacks the city anyway. Regardless, these defenders will add their own missiles to those of the hidden archers. The goal is to maximize confusion and give our legions time to close with the bastards."

"Do they have flyers?" Tal asked.

"Aye, mostly squarks, but they also have a handful of wyverns."

Tal closed his eyes in dismay. The presence of wyverns changed the equation. The winged dragon-wyrms were large, dangerous, and armed with rows of saber-like teeth.

"Once our army engages the Baleful, our flying cavalry will take them out, sire," Tarlbolt assured him. "We will not allow any to escape or to attack the city."

"What about my Marauders?" Maggie asked. "Why should you imperials have all the fun?" Hand resting on the hilt of her sword, she wore a determined look.

"*Fun* is not how I would describe our situation, Lady Margaret," Bozar said dryly. "However, there is a series of forested hills south of Markingham. We want you to hide the Marauders within the tree line. Once the battle is joined, your task is to make sure none escape."

"Mop-up. You've given us the job of picking off survivors. That's bullshit!"

"Your Marauders are an irregular force," Gravelback growled, "as apt to get in the way of *real* soldiers as to help."

Maggie's mouth contorted into a snarl. "Listen you—"

"What the commander meant to say is that your task is vital to our success," Bozar quickly interjected. He shot a venomous glance at Gravelback. "Didn't you, Lord Commander?"

"Yes...of course," Gravelback answered stiffly. He and Maggie continued to stare daggers at one another.

"The fewer melds who escape the better," the First Advisor reminded Maggie. "Fewer tongues mean fewer tales."

Maggie waved her hand. "Whatever. All I care about is killing as many of the murdering bastards as possible."

Bozar turned to the grand master standing beside Tal. "Artemis?"

Thurgood clapped Tal on the back. "The lad and I will be on the lookout for the shamans. Once they're located, we'll take them out."

The cheery way the grand master described killing Varg's sorcerers made it seem like they would be off to a picnic. Tal knew it would be considerably more challenging, but Thurgood's enthusiasm was infectious.

He motioned with his fingers. *"Poof,* just like that."

"That's the spirit, lad," Thurgood gushed.

Bozar turned a grim look toward Morehead. "You have the most dangerous task of all. The chaos your archers cause will give our legions time to engage the melds. Are you sure we can't get someone else to spring this trap?"

"My idea, my responsibility," Morehead replied. "Every member of the city watch volunteered for this. My place is with them."

Morehead's courage impressed not only Tal but Gravelback as well. He wore a look Tal had rarely seen on the veteran soldier.

Respect.

Bozar took one last look around the room. "Then it's settled. May the Creator guide us to success."

The meeting broke up and Tal hurried toward Alex's room. Nothing about tomorrow was certain.

And he was going to spend every moment with her.

The sun had barely peeked above the horizon when the Baleful streamed into the open plain before the city.

Tal studied the meld host from under a hooded cloak concealing his features. Beside him, Thurgood wore a similar mantle. Already splotched with spilled ale, the grand master munched on a slice of toasted bread slathered with butter.

He belched and wiped his hands on the cloak. "Got to hand it to you, lad. Since you retrieved me from Waldez, there is never a dull moment."

"I'm sorry, Artemis. I never meant to have your life put in danger."

"Sorry?" Thurgood chuckled. "I'm in your debt! You saved me from the dull university existence of teaching bored students."

Tal cast a wry glance at the grand master. "I seem to recall a conversation where you said how much you enjoy filling those empty minds."

Thurgood's eyes sparkled. "Aye, but think of the tales I'll have to share."

Tal laughed. Only Artemis could wring humor out of their current situation. He quickly sobered and looked back at the city behind them.

"Go on, lad," Thurgood urged. "Varg doesn't seem to be in any hurry. You've got time to see the lass one more time before the fun begins."

Tal nodded and rushed down the nearby steps. A groom handed him the reins of his horse, and leaping into the saddle, he galloped off. A short time later, he crossed the moat into the keep past a group of soldiers guarding the entry. Alex waited in the courtyard with Della. The flying horse was saddled and ready for flight.

Tal dismounted and Alex ran up to him. He caught her in his arms, and held her close. He breathed in her scent and reveled in the feel of her soft curves. With great reluctance, he released her.

"The Baleful are here. Do you remember what we talked about?"

"Yes, but—"

"No buts!" Tal gripped Alex's shoulders. "If the battle goes against us, you are to get on Della and fly for the breach in the Veil. Once there, you'll be taken through the gateway and back to Lodestone Castle."

"I don't want to leave you. Please don't make me."

Tal sighed. "I need to focus on the fight ahead. To do that, I must know you'll be safe. I can't afford to be distracted."

His hands left her shoulders and cupped her face. "If you love me, you'll do as I ask."

Her response, a bare whisper, came with eyes bright with tears. "All right. Don't forget *your* promise," she added, "to not take chances."

Tal smiled. "Don't worry," he pulled her back into his arms, "Why would I do that? I've got you to come back to."

They shared a final kiss before Tal mounted his horse. He clattered across the moat, then paused to look back. Alex stood alone, her hands clasped, a forlorn figure. He turned and galloped back to the ramparts.

The Baleful *would* be defeated. He would do everything in his power to make sure not a single meld survived. But hatred was no longer his motivation.

Not anymore.

Now he was driven to succeed for a different, more powerful reason.

Love.

CHAPTER 28

VARG STUDIED THE WALLS AND RICKETY BATTLEMENTS.

He snorted. "You'd think the fools would learn. Those fortifications couldn't keep a rabbit out."

Yip grinned exposing sharp canines. "They're shitting their pants about now."

Varg's cruel smile matched his lieutenant's. "Let's go hear what that sniveling worm, York, will offer this time."

"I thought we would just take the city."

A chuckle spilled from Varg's lips. "You ever see a young griffin play with its catch?"

Yip shook his head.

"The griffin lets its prey run away thinking it has escaped. Then the griffin tracks down the prey and pounces on it again. I watched one do that with a stag over and over again before it finally tired and ate the deer."

The Baleful leader removed a dagger from a leather sheath strapped to his waist. He tested the sharp point then turned the blade so it glinted in the morning light. "Well, I want to play. Let those cowardly fools huddle in their homes thinking they've cheated us once again. The terror on their faces will be all the sweeter when we strike."

Varg returned the dagger to the sheath. "Then I want all the old men and women, the feeble, and any babes still at the tit killed. Keep a few for sport if you like, but round up everyone else. We will have a rich harvest to present to the Dark Queen. And Yip."

"Yes, Varg?"

"York's wife was a disappointment—not even enough meat on her bones for a decent meal when she died. So, I want the earl alive. By the time I'm finished with him, he'll have wished for death a hundred times over. But before death takes him, I want his last sight to be of his precious city.

"As we burn it to the ground."

Alex watched Tal disappear from sight. As his image grew smaller, a hole opened in her heart. She couldn't help the feeling of dread, her fear for Tal a suffocating weight.

She sat on the steps of the keep and closed her eyes. The memory of their previous night together, still vivid, scrolled through her mind. They both knew the next day would be bloody and filled with killing, and Tal spent most of the night with her. They held hands and sat on the balcony while they gazed at the stars and talked for hours. She lost count of the times Tal said he loved her—probably at least as many times as she told him. She finally led him to her bed. Passionate kissing followed, and soon their clothes ended on the floor. Just as their hunger for each other reached unbearable heights, Tal rolled away and sat on the side of the bed.

Frustrated, Alex scooted next to him. She pushed the disheveled hair from her face and asked, "Did I do something wrong?"

Even in the darkened room, she could tell he was clenching his fists. "I want you so bad, I'm shaking."

"Then take me. I want you too. Why are you waiting?"

"Because it could," he paused and searched for words, "cause unintended consequences."

"Consequences? What do you mean?"

Once again, he struggled to speak. Tal was rarely at a loss for words, and she had never seen him this way.

"Tal, I—"

Then, like a curtain lifting, it dawned on her what he meant. "You're worried I'll get pregnant!"

Miserable, he nodded.

"Tal, there are ways to keep that from happening."

He sat up. "Really? What are they?" he asked eagerly.

We can just jog down to the local drug store and get what we need. Oh, yeah. None of these stores exist on Meredith. How can a planet steeped in magic where horses fly, and enchanted barriers exist not have the means to prevent pregnancies?

She slipped her arm through Tal's. "I'm not sure. Maybe we're just too young."

A sharp laugh erupted from him. "I know a hundred different ways to kill men and beasts, and yet *I'm* too young. I feel like a fool."

She ran her fingers up and down his arm. "We could take a chance."

Tal shook his head. "You don't understand. I will succeed my mother to the throne, and my offspring must have a legitimate claim to succession. Wars have been started because of bastard claimants, and the empire was washed in blood. I won't risk that."

A cold knot formed in Alex's stomach. Since she awakened on Meredith, every day had been filled with danger and intrigue. Thinking days, weeks, or years ahead had been a luxury she couldn't afford. She just assumed their love would bind their lives together. Now, such thinking seemed foolish.

Tal, as if sensing her thoughts, pulled her closer. "First, we have to get through the battle tomorrow. Afterward," he ran a finger down the cleft between her breasts, "we'll plan on what to do next."

Alex shivered at his touch, her desire flaring back to life.

"No," he said when she tried to pull him back onto the bed. "I can't stop myself a second time."

He firmly disengaged, kissed her forehead, and dressed. She followed him to the door, and he held her in a long embrace.

"Don't worry," he assured her. "Once Marlinda's foul creatures are dealt with, I will take care of us. And then we'll no longer need to worry about being together."

Although just last night, the memory seemed a million years ago. And now...now all she could do was wait, each passing second a tortuous experience.

She bolted upright. "I'm will not sit idle while Tal's life is at risk," she barked.

Alex ran to Della, put her foot in the stirrup, and swung into the saddle. She galloped past the surprised guards at the portcullis, toward the west walls facing the Baleful horde.

Her mind churned. She couldn't let Tal, Bozar, or anyone see and recognize her. Guards would immediately escort her back to the keep, this time with orders to prevent her from leaving. She needed a location where she could watch Tal away from prying eyes. Fortunately, she knew just the place. Long walks with Tal had familiarized her with the ramparts, and she knew the wall curved away from the city gates. Since the Baleful were intent on a frontal assault, all of Markingham's defenders, including Tal, would be focused on them.

No one would notice a lone figure far away on the wall.

When she judged the distance from the gates to be enough, she directed Della to a flight of stone steps leading up to the parapets. She ran up the steps and reached the broad walkway along the wall. Crouching, she looked around. Even here, a few soldiers, spaced far apart, kept vigil. None looked her way, however. Their focus was riveted on what lay beyond the battlements.

Alex crept up to the crenellations and peeked through an arrow slit. Her breath caught in her throat. Creatures of feathers, fur, scales, and skin filled the plain.

For as far as she could see.

CHAPTER 29

TAL'S CONCERN GREW AS THE BALEFUL NUMBERS CONTINUED TO increase.

Even at a distance, the cacophony of grunts, chirps, growls, and hisses from thousands of throats was deafening. Dust from the passage of so many creatures formed a cloud drifting like smoke above the meld army.

"That's a lot of melded creatures," Thurgood quipped as if counting tasty apples from a barrel.

They stood on the battlements above the massive gates into Markingham. Their elevated position gave them a clear view of Varg's army.

Tal shook his head. "How are we supposed to locate their shamans among such an enormous host?"

"It makes no difference whether there is one or ten thousand, lad. Magic users emit a signal as clear as a bonfire on a moonless night. We'll have no trouble finding them."

The grand master's cheerful countenance turned serious. "That's the easy part. Once we find them, the hard part comes next. Bozar wants us to kill them quickly before Varg realizes he's walked into a trap. That requires piercing their spells of protection before they raise the alarm—no easy feat. Let's hope there are few Baleful shamans."

He took a deep breath. "You ready, lad?"

Tal nodded.

"Then let's have at it."

Tal closed his eyes and drew on his wellspring of magic. When he opened them, his enchanted vision displayed a plain shrouded in shadow, as if night had fallen. He sharpened his focus, and Thurgood's prediction proved true. Crimson slashes of light, like bloody lacerations, appeared in the gloom. He directed his magic to the nearest one and swooped like a hawk preparing to dive onto a rabbit. Seconds later, the image of a shaman appeared. The melded witch resembled a lynx, her body covered in tawny fur. Necklaces of bone, teeth, feathers, and lodestones swayed from the creature's neck. The shaman sensed Tal's magic and looked up. A yowl whipped past her lips.

Tal struck.

Blue lightning arced around the meld magician. It sizzled like eggs on a hot pan, the shaman encased by a cocoon of magic. Tal felt resistance as the shaman fought back and pushed against the magic. He closed his fist, the web growing smaller and smaller, the shaman's struggles more frantic.

The meld magician burst into flames.

Swiftly, Tal moved on to the next target. Vulture-like with beady red eyes and a curved, cruel beak, black plumage covered the meld's body. He sensed Tal's power immediately, and a raucous squawk erupted from his beak. The mage's resistance also proved futile, and Tal's magic reduced the shaman to charred feathers.

Tal lost track of time. The red pinpricks of light winked out one-by-one as he and the grand master killed each shaman. At last, only one remained. The brightest of all, Tal sensed powerful magic in this shaman.

Thurgood's voice spoke in his ear. "This one won't be easy, lad. We need to work together."

The sorceress's melded form was that of a hyena. Flesh-tearing canines flashed white as she detected their attack and snarled. A shield of magic formed around her. Tal's magic slammed against it, and he hammered against the buffer with little effect.

"Focus, lad. Concentrate on one point and drill into it. That's the only way to rupture her protective barrier."

Tal wiped the sweat dripping from his face and chin. The physical cost of using such an enormous amount of magic left him drained. He felt as if he'd run for leagues. He took a deep breath and targeted a point on the shaman's magical armor. He compressed his power to the diameter of an arrow shaft.

And attacked.

Bozar rode beside Bartholomew through the partially open gates.

Two cavalrymen, one carrying a white parley flag, flanked them. The gates closed as they rode through. Ahead, the meld army spread across the plain, undulating like a single living organism. Hoots and whistles greeted them, the clamor assaulting their ears.

"Try to keep Varg talking," Bozar reminded York. "Have the negotiations go on for as long as possible. We must give Tal and Artemis time to deal with the shamans. Our legions also need time to maneuver into position."

"Varg is expecting Lord Morehead to accompany me. He will be suspicious when he sees you," the earl warned.

"Good. That means he'll ask questions and draw out the parley. Remember, I'm your new advisor. That's all you need to tell Varg. Let him try to piece it together."

They proceeded for a short distance and stopped. The sea of melded creatures parted, and a centaur emerged. In no hurry, Varg sauntered forward, his hooves kicking up small puffs of dust.

Bozar studied Varg as he approached. The giant centaur was even larger than described. Barrel-chested, ridged muscle covered his bare torso. He held a double-bladed axe in one hand that even a strong man would struggle to lift. In the other, he brandished a broadsword. He lifted the weapons high and clashed them together. The clash of metal against metal resounded with bell-like clarity.

He stopped before them and smiled, his filed teeth gleaming shark-like in the morning light. "Where's my tribute?"

No preamble, no opening remark, just a demand. Bozar's uneasiness grew. They needed time, but Varg got right to the point.

"What do you want this time?" York asked the Baleful leader.

Varg studied the edge of his axe and caressed the haft like a lover. He ran his tongue across the flat iron, then looked at the earl and smiled. "Everything."

The promise of violence lay upon Varg like a thick blanket. Bozar had no doubt the negotiations had just ended.

Earl York cleared his throat. "Come, come, Varg. There must be something we can offer."

Varg furrowed his brow. "Perhaps."

York seized upon the comment. "What? Just name it."

"Do you have any more wives? Perhaps children? I was cheated by our last bargain. Your last wife died before I could finish my fun."

York's face turned purple, and Varg chuckled at his reaction.

The situation was slipping out of control. Bozar decided he would need to intervene after all.

"Vulgar savage! Do you always derive your courage from slaughtering helpless women and children?"

Varg impaled Bozar with a merciless gaze. "Who are you? You weren't with this spineless fool before."

"I am the earl's new advisor."

Varg shook with laughter. He waved his hand at the vast army behind him. "And how would you advise him to deal with us?"

A thin smile appeared on Bozar's face. "Oh, my advice is simple."

Varg leered at Bozar. "And what would that be?"

"To kill you. To kill *all* of you."

CHAPTER 30

Bozar waited for Varg's reaction.

Rage scrolled across the Baleful leader's face. "For someone about to become a corpse, you speak brave words."

Bozar remained stoic although inwardly he celebrated. He had succeeded in drawing Varg's ire. Now he needed to keep him talking until Tal and Artemis finished their work. It was a fine line to tread, however. Varg looked ready to attack him at any second.

The Baleful leader studied him with contempt. "Dung-colored skin. I haven't seen your like since we last crossed the southern steppes."

Varg smirked. "I shall enjoy turning your writhing body on a spit. I'll make sure the fire is especially hot. Your skin will be a *crispier* brown by the time I'm finished with you."

"Who speaks bold words now?" Bozar asked. "Your talk reminds me of watered-down ale and just as weak."

They were interrupted by a flash of blue light from among the Baleful. A muffled explosion followed. Varg's head whipped around.

Relief flowed through Bozar. "We're finished here." He signaled York and the soldiers. They backed away, turned, and galloped back to the gates.

◈

Tal and Thurgood continued their assault on Varg's sorceress.

A pinprick opened in the powerful shaman's protective shield.

Tal wormed his magic farther inside the opening. He strained to pull it wider. Slowly, a fissure grew. The shaman pushed back and fought to close the breach. Exhausted, Tal didn't know how long he could continue. Suddenly he felt Thurgood's magical presence.

"Just keep the hole in the shield open a bit longer, lad. I'll take care of the rest."

The grand master's power flowed into the break. Fingers of blue lightning sizzled and popped as they traveled up and down the shaman's body. Seconds later, the buffer ruptured in a brilliant detonation, the shaman's body reduced to dust. When the sparks cleared from Tal's eyes, he found himself slumped against the stone parapet. He tried to push himself up, but his leaden limbs wouldn't cooperate.

Thurgood appeared at his side. "Here. Drink this." He brought a flask to Tal's lips, and a sweet liquid rolled down his throat. Immediately, strength flowed back into Tal's body.

Amazed, Tal sat up. "What's in that?"

The grand master chuckled. "A gnomish brew specifically tailored for magic-users." He took a drink and smacked his lips. "Tasty, eh, lad?"

He handed the flask to Tal. "One more sip, no more. Otherwise, you'll become so restless, you'll chew a hole through that stone wall."

Tal sprang to his feet and turned to study the Baleful. Motion beneath the walls caught his attention. Bozar and York were returning. That could mean only one thing.

The battle was about to begin.

Beneath a thick layer of sod-covered wooden planks, Morehead paced and listened.

So far, everything had gone according to plan. The meld army had passed right over them with no indication their hidden lair had been discovered.

A metal tube hung in front of him. It extended upward and disappeared into the plank-covered ceiling. The end of the tube formed an "L" and contained a lens flanked by a pair of lodestones. He grasped the pipe and eased it up. He put his eye to the lens. The image was blocked, so he pushed it higher and was rewarded with a welcome sight.

The rear of the Baleful army.

The melds had already advanced well past them and were massed before the city gates.

Perfect.

Morehead swiveled the hidden spyglass and studied the tree-line behind them. He caught no movement, no indication Gravelback's legions were in position. Either they were well hidden—or late. He rubbed his face. Varg couldn't be allowed to launch an attack against the city. Only a skeleton force guarded the walls, and they would certainly be overwhelmed. However, if he sprang the trap before Gravelback was in position, then he and all his volunteers were dead men. They would be overcome and killed long before the legions could close with the meld army.

He spun the spyglass back to the melds. A flash of blue light erupted in their midst, and commotion rippled and spread through the creatures. A savage thrill ran through Morehead. *The prince must have killed all their shamans. That'll give the bastards something to chew on.*

That also meant there was no time left. Varg would certainly attack the city now.

He couldn't wait for Gravelback.

A lodestone disk hung from a leather cord draped across his neck. He pressed it once and it pulsed blue, a signal to the commander in the other hidden lair to spring the trap.

"Get ready, boys," Morehead growled. "On my count. One, two, *three!*"

He released a counterweight and the heavy stone plummeted to the floor of the pit. A cable tied to the ballast whined as it raced through pulleys and flipped the hinged planks open. Bright sunlight flooded the hidden den, and the archers sprang up. It took a moment of blinking before Morehead's eyes adjusted. The backs of the mass of meld creatures still faced them. A fierce thrill ran through him. None had noticed them yet.

Time to change that.

Morehead nocked and arrow and pulled the bowstring to his cheek. "Light'em up, lads! Fire at will!" he cried, then released the shaft.

A volley of hundreds of arrows arced through the air and fell among Varg's army. Packed so closely, the tight quarters made it impossible to miss. Within seconds, scores of dead and dying Baleful littered the ground. Chaos erupted. Screeches, barks, and hisses created an earsplitting chorus of pain and fear. The onslaught of arrows continued unabated, each shaft adding to the desperate confusion of the meld army.

***

The explosion of blue light had barely faded when screams and shrieks followed.

"What the hell is going on?" Varg snarled at Yip.

Before his lieutenant could answer, a bloodcurdling roar came from high above. Varg looked up. In the sky, his airborne melds were under attack. The wyverns and squark-mounted fighters were swarmed by hundreds of soldiers on winged horses. The enemy cavalry moved with smooth, military precision. While a dozen or more circled out of reach of his much larger wyverns' teeth and claws, they scored repeatedly with arrows. Others fought individual battles with his squark-mounted melds. A squark and rider, pierced by numerous shafts, plunged to the ground in a shower of feathers.

Varg ripped his attention back to the ground. "Attack the city! Order the—"

The rest of the words died in his mouth. The walls of Markingham wavered and rippled. The crumbling and gap-ridden battlements disappeared to be replaced by unbroken and smooth walls. The menacing images of *scorpions* and other war machines on the battlements gleamed in the morning light.

In a flash, realization dawned on Varg. "It's a trap!"

"What are your orders?" Yip asked.

Varg reared, hooves cleaving the air. "Retreat! We have to fight our way out of here!"

Yip grabbed a standard mounted with a blood-red pennant. He lifted it high over his head and waved it back and forth. Other pennants appeared in response.

The Baleful army turned.

All that stood in Varg's way was Morehead's archers.

When the Baleful army reversed direction to retreat, Morehead knew their lives were now forfeit. A few arrows met the meld creatures, but they had exhausted their supply of shafts. He pulled his sword, hefted his shield, and climbed out of the excavation.

"To me, boys!" he roared.

His men joined him, hundreds against thousands.

Morehead waved his sword. "Let's see how many of these motherless sons of bitches we can kill." As he turned to face the advancing horde, a question continued to puzzle him.

Where is Gravelback's army?

CHAPTER 31

FROM THEIR PERCH HIGH ON THE WALLS, TAL AND THURGOOD WATCHED the meld army reverse direction and retreat.

"They're headed straight for Lord Morehead. He and his men will be wiped out." Tal shook his head bitterly. "Killing the shamans left me spent. I wish I had some magic left to help him."

"All magic comes with a cost," Thurgood reminded him, "and far more soldiers would be at risk if any of the sorcerers had been left alive."

"They knew the risks, especially the commander," a familiar voice added. Tal glanced back. Pulpit stood observing the meld army's sudden retreat.

"Quiet as a wraith. Was sneaking about part of your monk's training as well?"

Pulpit pointed at the Baleful. "A better question is where is the imperial army? If they don't arrive soon, the commander's sacrifice will have been in vain."

Tal scanned the thick forest boundary behind the plain. His sharp eyes detected no movement, no glint of steel or armor to give proof Gravelback's legions lay in wait for the Baleful.

Tal pounded the top of the crenellation. "If we don't do something, these men will be slaughtered, and the Baleful will have slipped through our trap! We have to force Varg to stop his retreat and give Gravelback more time."

He gestured to the grand master. "Give me the gnome's potion."

Reluctantly, Thurgood handed over the flask. "What have you got in mind, lad?"

Tal snatched the flagon and raced down the stone steps. He shouted over his shoulder, "A distraction. One big enough to grab Varg's attention."

Tal hit the ground level and sprinted past the soldiers guarding the gates. He snatched the reins of a nearby horse and leaped into the saddle. He galloped through the gates opened earlier for Bozar's party, and past the surprised faces of his First Advisor and Earl York.

Wind whipped past his face as Tal ripped the cork out of the flask with his teeth and downed the contents. Immediately, euphoria filled every pore of his body. Thoughts raced through his mind with such speed, they blurred into a surging mosaic with no beginning or end. He lifted his face and shouted in exultation at the sky.

He closed on the meld army. Muttering, Tal held the palm of his hand in front of him. The ground rippled and brambles erupted in a shower of dirt and sod. Wicked thorns the length of a man's arm formed a shimmering blue-gold hedge between Morehead's archers and the Baleful. The nearest of the meld creatures ran headlong into the brambles. Impaled, they flopped like fish on a hook, their screams stopping the other Baleful in their tracks.

Tal, eyes a molten cobalt, motioned with his other hand. A cloud formed above the meld army. It expanded, growing darker with flashes of lightning and rumbles of thunder. Hail, covered in a blaze of blue, licking flames, fell in sheets from the storm cloud. Wherever they struck, an explosion of light and fire erupted. Hundreds of melds burst into flame, their shrieks joining the storm's crescendo.

Tal grinned in savage triumph, the gnome's brew racing through his veins.

I'm invincible.

Bozar reacted in horror as Tal raced by him.

"Tal, stop!"

Thurgood and Pulpit dashed down the steps. Breathless, Thurgood pointed at Tal. "The—the lad took the entire flask. Once he drinks it, there's no telling what he'll do. We have to stop him."

Bozar had no idea what flagon Thurgood was talking about, much less its contents. However, he *did* know Tal's impulsive nature.

He pointed to the captain of the guard. "Gather as many men as you can find and follow us."

Moments later, accompanied by fifty soldiers, Thurgood, Pulpit, York, and Bozar galloped after Tal.

Alex, heart in her throat, watched Tal race after the Baleful.

He was alone.

The explosion of magic which erupted from him was so bright it blinded her. When they cleared, the sight she beheld left her numb. A glittering hedge of magic burst from the ground, the thorny brambles protecting Morehead and his men. Storm clouds spit explosive hail on the Baleful.

For the first time, she understood Tal's lineage and what it meant to be a Blood Prince and a direct descendant of Meredith's kings and queens. His power was incredible. She looked past Tal at the retreating meld army.

Their huge centaur leader paused—and turned back toward Tal.

Morehead resigned himself to death. He wanted nothing more than to take as many of the Baleful with him to death's gate as possible.

Then three things happened in rapid succession.

The first was a hedge of iridescent magic which sprang up between his men and the meld army. The Baleful collided with the razor-sharp barbs, skewering melds, and producing screeches of agony.

The second was the sudden appearance of angry, black clouds which rained fire on Varg's army.

The third was the sound of battle horns and the rhythmic pounding of thousands of boots.

Morehead whirled to see rank after rank of legionnaires emerge from the thick forest. They advanced in orderly fashion, shields up, to form battle lines facing the Baleful. He almost wept at the sight.

Ominous thunder continued to rumble, the air thick with magic. Head swimming over the rapid turn of events, Morehead didn't spend a second puzzling over what had happened.

He ran.

"C'mon, boys!" he cried and sprinted toward the imperial army. Their ranks parted to allow Morehead and his men through. He spied Gravelback on horseback and veered for the commander.

"Took you long enough," he growled.

Gravelback motioned to an aide who brought Morehead a horse.

"You ever try to lead an army of over six thousand soldiers through dense woods at night? Then try to keep their movement as quiet as a crypt at midnight? We're damn lucky we didn't wake the entire countryside, much less lose half the legions before we could make for battle."

Morehead flashed a fierce grin. "Good to see you, Gravelback." He swept his hand toward the hundreds of dead Baleful who lay on the plain festooned with shafts. "We pared their numbers a bit, but we left you a few."

A *boom* of thunder reverberated, the shock wave carrying to the men. Fire continued to fall from the sky onto the meld army. Screams and shrieks echoed across the battlefield.

Morehead blinked at the astounding spectacle. "What's happening? Who caused this?"

Gravelback pointed at a horseman galloping from Markingham toward the Baleful.

"Prince Tal."

Varg's ears rang with cries of fear and pain.

The source of the magical assault soon became apparent. A lone figure rode toward them, powerful magic pouring from him like a geyser.

Yip darted up to Varg. He pointed behind them. "Look!"

Varg's towering height gave him a clear view of what concerned Yip.

An army had emerged from the forest. Ranks of soldiers marched to form a crescent-shaped skirmish line. Varg snarled at the sight. His Baleful were flanked, a trap from which there was no escape. The only recourse would be to fight their way out.

"Where did they come from?" Yip asked. "The earl never had an army. He could barely scrape up enough men to guard Markingham's gates."

An obvious question and one Varg planned on having answered—if they survived the battle. "Never mind. Right now we have to find a way out of this trap."

The fiery rain slowed. Varg studied the raging airborne struggle through the gaps in the thinning clouds. The combatants swirled like a giant flock of birds, firing arrows and javelins at one another, the wyverns raking any enemy close enough with claws or impaling them with saber-like teeth. The aerial dance was deadly, and bodies fell like stones to the ground. Too many were Baleful, and

Varg realized his flying corps would soon be defeated. If that happened before they could fight their way free to take refuge in the thick forest, they were doomed. The enemy's flying cavalry would pick them off like flies.

"I want a thousand of the Baleful with me. Since our shamans are dead, I'll have to deal with the wizard raining fire. Once I kill him, order the Baleful to attack the army behind us. We must carve a gap in their ranks to escape."

Yip raised a pennant and signaled Varg's orders. Other banners raised in answer, and the meld army stopped and pivoted. A portion of the melds separated from the main body and joined Varg. He waved them forward.

The mass of creatures surged toward the horseman.

CHAPTER 32

BOZAR CAUGHT UP TO TAL, SNATCHED HIS REINS, AND JERKED THE horse to a stop.

"Let go!" Tal cried. "I've got more of Marlinda's murdering beasts to kill!"

"Where's the flask?" Thurgood demanded.

"Drank it. Now let go."

"You downed the entire flagon? Listen to me, lad, you're going to burn yourself out. *Shut down your magic now!*"

Tal looked as if he if might punch the grand master. Bozar pulled Tal's horse closer. "Listen to Artemis. Withdraw your magic."

Tal's mouth opened and closed several times. He shook his head as if waking from a dream. The thunder and fiery hailstones stopped, and the clouds thinned and dissipated. The murderous brambles withered and collapsed into dust.

He slumped in the saddle and Bozar caught him. "We must get Tal back to Markingham."

The rasp of steel being pulled from a scabbard answered him. York, with a grim look, pointed his sword. "It's too late." A growing cacophony of growls, screeches, and shrieks punctuated his words.

"The Baleful are here."

Afraid he would fall, Bozar kept a firm grip on Tal. "Protect the prince!" Bozar ordered. The soldiers moved their horses to face the melds. Swords and spears formed a prickly ring around the semi-conscious prince.

Bozar shook Tal. "Wake up. Wake up!"

Alex raised the spyglass.

Bozar raced after Tal, along with Pulpit and Artemis Thurgood. Accompanied by a small band of cavalry, they caught up to Tal before he reached the Baleful and formed a wedge around him.

Movement in the distance caught her eye, and she swung the spyglass toward the thick forest bordering the open plain. Legionnaires streamed from the tree line and formed ranks. Gravelback's army had arrived at last.

She returned her attention to Tal.

Within seconds, Varg and his melds surrounded Bozar's little group. The giant centaur taunted them, waving his battle axe and prancing before them. Retreat was no longer possible, nor could Gravelback save them in time. The grim reality weighed on her like a suffocating blanket. She found it hard to breathe.

Varg attacked, his axe shearing the head of a cavalryman's horse completely off. Horse and rider fell to the ground in a shower of blood.

"No!" Alex screamed.

Behind her on the street below, a heavy metal sewer grate flew into the air. With a thunderous *clang*, it landed on the cobblestone avenue. Boorba emerged from the opening, and ran up the steps to join Alex on the parapet.

"Boorba here. What wrong?"

The sudden appearance of the troll, left Alex speechless. Somehow, he had sensed her distress.

Alex quickly found her tongue. She pointed at Tal's defenders and the raging struggle with the melds. Screams, the clash of weapons, and cries of agony reached them even at their distant perch.

"Tal's in trouble, Boorba. He needs help."

The troll hefted his club in a spade-sized hand. Without a word, he vaulted over the battlements and dropped to the ground a hundred feet below. Landing upright on both feet, he barreled toward the conflict.

Alex hurried to the wall's edge and leaned out. Boorba, even nine feet tall with trunk-sized arms and legs, moved with a sprinter's speed. He reached the melds and crashed into them, plowing a path like a giant boulder through a field of corn. Melds flew into the air to land broken and motionless as the troll laid about with his club. For every one he killed or disabled, however, two more took its place.

They swarmed onto Boorba.

Claws, fangs, beaks, and weapons ripped and stabbed at the troll. Boorba shrugged off the attacks like a duck shedding water. While one massive hand plucked off melds and smashed the creatures into the ground, the other laid about with the truncheon. Scores of the Baleful lay in broken, bleeding heaps.

Despite their wounded and dead, Alex realized the melds had managed to slow the troll down. He would never reach Tal in time.

Desperate, she cast about. A flash of metal caught the corner of her eye. She whirled and studied the forested hills south of the city. With the spyglass, Alex scanned the area. A black-clad figure on horseback emerged from the trees.

Maggie.

The Marauders lay in wait to pick off any Baleful trying to flee the battle—a role Alex knew Maggie was still bitter about. Hope sprang into her chest. She raced down the steps and to Della. Grabbing the reins, she swung into the saddle.

"Go, Della, go!" she cried.

With a snort, the winged horse took off. After galloping a short distance, she spread her wings, and they swooped into the air. Alex directed the mare toward the far tree-line. Markingham fell away, and the forest approached.

They flew only a short distance when a reptilian roar rent the air. Alex glanced over her shoulder. Her blood ran cold. A wyvern had left the raging aerial battle high above to pursue her. Fully twenty feet long, the green-scaled reptile was pierced by numerous arrows, the shafts having little effect on the creature. A rider sat astride the dragon between the neck and wings and directed the beast after her. As the pair drew nearer, Alex realized the rider's legs disappeared into the wyvern's trunk.

Man and dragon were fused.

Rows of razor-sharp teeth snapped in anticipation of rending Alex's soft flesh. Terror filled her. "Faster, Della," she cried. The flying horse responded with a burst of speed, her powerful wings a blur. They pulled away and Alex gasped in relief. Then the huge, sail-sized wings of the dragon-lizard began to eat up the distance. Each wing-beat took two for Della to match.

The wyvern closed the distance.

Maggie watched the imperial legions emerge from the thick forest. "About damn time," she muttered. Intent on following the army's progress, she didn't notice the two specks in the sky until a blood-curdling roar grabbed her attention.

"What the—"

She snatched the spyglass from her waist and trained it on the mysterious flyers. The nearest figure was a woman on a flying horse. Golden hair streamed in the wind, and with a start, Maggie realized it was Alexandria. Behind her and closing fast was a huge wyvern.

Maggie jumped off her horse and pulled free a javelin strapped to the saddle. The needle-sharp tip glinted in the morning light. Testing the weight, Maggie judged the angle and distance of the approaching dragon. Alex, however, was in the way. She needed to veer off to give Maggie a clear shot at the wyvern.

Maggie waved frantically with her free hand. "Move!" she screamed. Alexandria shot toward her, the dragon almost on top of her. At the last moment, she sawed the reins and the flying horse veered to the side. The much larger wyvern couldn't maneuver its vast bulk at such a sharp angle, and made a slow turn to continue the pursuit.

That was all Maggie needed.

She took two steps and hurled the javelin. The missile flew unerringly to its target. With a *crunch*, the metal spearpoint punched through the tough scales in the dragon's neck and into its melded rider. The impaled dragon-rider clutched at the spear as the wyvern plummeted. The dragon struck the ground, bounced, and slid to a stop. Its wings beat weakly once, then stilled.

Maggie moved cautiously to the downed wyvern. Taking no chances, she drew her sword and drove the blade through the creature's heart. She did the same to the melded rider.

Relief filled her...then anger. Alexandria wasn't supposed to be anywhere near here. The delicate flower was to stay in Markingham safely away from danger. Yet Alex flew to where Maggie's Marauders waited hidden in the forest, not only risking her life, but possibly giving away their position to the Baleful.

She better have a damn good reason why.

Nancy E. Durham

CHAPTER 33

THE CLASH OF WEAPONS AND THE SCREAMS OF DYING MEN PIERCED Tal's consciousness. Lethargic, his head felt like it was stuffed with wool, his limbs leaden and sluggish.

The coppery reek of blood filled his nostrils, and he shook his head to remove the fuzziness. When his mind cleared at last, a wild struggle appeared. Men and melds hacked and stabbed at one another. In the midst of the battle, a giant centaur wielded an axe with deadly efficiency.

Varg.

Adrenaline coursed through his veins, and his strength slowly began to return.

"Welcome back."

Tal glanced to where a grim-faced Bozar held the reins of his horse. "We're surrounded. Our only chance is to fight our way free and make for the safety of Markingham. Can you defend yourself?" his *Eldred* asked.

In answer, Tal took the reins from Bozar and pulled his sword.

"Why aren't they attacking?" Morehead asked

"Varg's smart," Gravelback answered. "They outnumber us. Better for them if we extend our lines by attacking first. Then he'll pick a place we're stretched thin and clear a path to escape."

"So, we just sit here and stare at each other?"

"Oh, no." A savage smile appeared on Gravelback's face. "I plan to give'em a little motivation."

He motioned to a nearby officer. "Captain, order the archers to the front line."

The officer galloped off to carry out the order. A short time later, over a thousand legionnaires faced the Baleful. Gravelback raised his hand...then chopped it down. A flight of arrows darkened the sky in a graceful arc to fall among the meld army. Many of the creatures held crude shields to deflect the arrows, but enough shafts found gaps to leave a number of the Baleful writhing on the ground.

"Again," Gravelback ordered.

Another deadly round of arrows left more of the Baleful dead. The creatures stirred in panic, their cohesion disintegrating.

"Again!"

The third volley proved decisive. A few of the melds broke, and rushed howling at the Imperial Army. They were soon joined by more. Then, like a broken levee, the rest of the meld army boiled forward. The imperial archers retreated to be replaced by soldiers with shields, swords, and spears. With practiced efficiency, the soldiers locked shields leaving room only for the sharp ends of spears.

Gravelback nodded at Morehead. "Ready to wet your blade?"

Morehead smacked his lips in anticipation. He drew his sword. "Thought you'd never ask."

***

Alex landed a short distance from the dead wyvern. She jumped off Della and ran to the Marauder leader.

"Maggie, I—"

Alex screamed in pain as Maggie grabbed a fistful of her hair and twisted it.

"You stupid bitch! What are you thinking? The prince would blame *me* if you got yourself killed!"

Another savage twist of Alex's hair punctuated Maggie's remark. Alex screamed again, the pain driving her to her knees.

"It's Tal," she sobbed. "The Baleful have him surrounded. They're going to kill him."

"What?" Maggie released her grip on Alex's hair. She spun and studied the battle with the spyglass. "That wasn't part of the plan. Why did Tal leave Markingham?"

Alex got up to stand on shaky legs beside Maggie. "The Imperial Army arrived late. Lord Morehead and his men were about to be overrun."

"And Tal tried to save them," Maggie finished. Her eyes softened. "His courage is matched only by his foolishness."

The two women looked at one another, an unspoken communication passing between them.

"I know how you feel about, Tal," Alex said. "And you're the only one who can save him. Please, I beg you."

"You know nothing about how I feel!" Maggie replied hotly.

Although Maggie quickly turned away, it wasn't fast enough. Alex recognized the look on her face and in her eyes. It displayed an emotion Alex knew well.

She loves him too.

Maggie hurried to her horse and sprang into the saddle. She rode back to Alex. "Fly back to Markingham. Do *not* say a word of this to anyone, especially Tal."

She galloped back to the forest, ripped her sword from the scabbard, and brandished it.

"Marauders! Why should the imperials have all the fun while we mop up their leavings? To hell with that! We are the ones who have suffered at the hands of the Baleful. I say we get our fair share of the melded bastards and we get it now!"

Bradley Sikes trotted his horse out into the open. "Our orders are to stay here and kill the Baleful who try to escape."

"You ever know me to follow orders? Why would I start now?" A chorus of hoots and chuckles rose from the Marauders.

"All who want to obey 'orders' can stay here with Sikes. The rest follow me!"

Maggie charged down the hill toward the distant battle. Five hundred mounted Marauders burst from the trees after her, the rumble of their passage like thunder. Dust rose in a huge cloud. When it cleared, Alex couldn't find a single Marauder. None remained.

Not even Sikes.

Varg blocked the sword thrust of the soldier. He batted aside his opponent's shield with his axe, then used his other arm to ram his sword through the opening. A gurgled scream followed, the blade plunging through the soldier's lungs.

A loud chorus of cries and the unmistakable sounds of battle reverberated behind the centaur. Varg ripped his sword free of the lifeless body and whirled to see what was happening.

His meld army was locked in battle.

"Who gave the order to attack?" he snarled at Yip.

Occupied with a mounted soldier who slashed at his head and shoulders, Yip couldn't answer. He nimbly dodged the blade. When the cavalryman lifted his sword to hack again, Yip darted inside his guard. Two quick stabs with his dagger pierced the soldier's heart. The cavalryman fell off his horse in a spray of blood.

Yip wiped his blade clean on the dead man's tunic. He shrugged, confusion on his furry face. "I don't know. One moment we're fighting the earl's men, the next, I look up, and the Baleful are storming the enemy."

Both melds ignored the ferocious struggle going on around them. Instead, they studied the larger battle at their rear.

Varg's sharp eyes took in every detail. He noted the arrow-pierced bodies of melds strewn across the plain, then the armored ranks of soldiers his melds were engaged with. "We were provoked. They fired arrows hoping to cause a panic."

He spat the next words. "It worked. The fools played right into their hands."

He whirled to face the rapidly diminishing ranks of the earl's men. "We must finish here. I need to regain control of the Baleful... before it's too late."

CHAPTER 34

TAL CHARGED INTO THE MELEE.

A meld with a patchwork of leopard's fur and mottled skin, sprang at him with a snarl. One malformed paw slashed with a saber, the other swiped at him with sharp claws. Tal blocked the blade with his own and caught the creature by the throat. Before the leopard-man could react, Tal plunged his sword through its chest. He lifted the body and hurled it at another attacker, knocking the beast off its feet. "Hup!" Tal cried. His horse reared and crushed the meld.

Tal wielded his sword with murderous efficiency. Dead and dismembered melds lay about him in growing numbers. For every one he killed, however, more took their place. Bozar, Thurgood, and Pulpit fought beside him, along with the earl and the remaining cavalrymen. With each passing minute, their number dwindled, and Tal knew they would soon be overwhelmed.

He spotted Varg. The centaur watched the uneven contest with a cruel smile. Lord Morehead's words about the Baleful leader echoed through Tal's mind. *Varg has forced discipline upon the Baleful and made them into a fearsome army.*

But what if he was dead? The melds would be leaderless, disorganized and easier to defeat.

"*My Eldred,*" he cried. "We need to clear a path to Varg."

Occupied defending himself, Bozar shouted a reply. "Why?"

"So I can kill him. Without Varg, the Baleful will be leaderless. They'll collapse into turmoil."

Bozar barked an order, and Thurgood, Pulpit, and the surviving soldiers swiveled to press toward Varg.

With savage determination, Tal laid about with renewed ferocity. The visages of the melds he slew blurred into a hodge-podge of fur, scales, beaks, and claws. All fell before his furious onslaught, and he inched closer to Varg.

"Fight me!" Tal cried. "Fight me you cowardly scum!"

Varg motioned and the Baleful parted. Tal galloped through the opening. Quickly, the mass of creatures closed, separating him from Bozar and the others.

Varg brandished his blood-drenched axe. "Here I am, lordling."

Although drained, Tal decided to risk using what little magic remained within him to kill the centaur. He motioned with his fingers, and the air shimmered before him. A blue, luminescent spear appeared. Tal flicked his wrist and the sharp lance flew toward Varg. The Baleful leader made no attempt to dodge away. Instead, he calmly watched the weapon sail toward his broad chest. Just before it reached him, the spear bounced harmlessly away and dissipated in a shower of azure sparks.

Varg chuckled, an evil resonance filled with malice. "You'll have to do better than that. My first task as leader of the Baleful was to find a powerful shaman and gain a ward against enchantments. I'm afraid only ordinary weapons work against me...not that they will do you any good."

His forehead wrinkled. "*Hmm.* What shall I cleave from you first? An arm? Leg? I think I'll save your head for last. I want you to see every piece I carve from you."

The centaur flashed an icy smile. "Then tonight, I shall feast on your remains."

Tal spat on the ground. "Speaking of heads, yours will decorate a pike. However, I do plan to cut off your tail and save it.

Every time I use it to swat at pests, I'll be reminded that it covered the best part of your worthless flesh."

Varg's face darkened. "Prepare to die."

Tal tightened his grip on the hilt.

They rushed at one another.

Maggie raced across the plain, her focus on Tal.

He wasn't hard to spot. At the center of the battle, he faced a huge centaur. The Baleful leader stood out like an island amidst an ocean of smaller melds.

A heaving mound covered with biting, stabbing melds, appeared a short distance away. A guttural roar shook the air, then a massive hand shot through the squirming mass, snatched one creature after another, and crushed them. Other melds took flight, batted into the air by an enormous club.

She blinked. *The troll.*

Distracted by Boorba and battling the small force with Tal, the melds didn't realize the threat from her Marauders until they were on top of them. With a thunderous crash, they bowled into the Baleful, plowing a bloody furrow.

The deeper her Marauders drove into the Baleful, the less organized the struggle became. Frenetic, furious battles raged all around Maggie, and she became separated from the main body of the Marauders. Attackers came from all sides, and her breastplate of tough, boiled leather saved her more than once from sharp weapons and claws. Although not skilled fighters, the Baleful more than made up for their deficiency with ferocity and numbers. No matter how many she killed or maimed, there seemed to be an endless supply of them.

The deafening noise level climbed the farther she waded into the battle. The cacophony of curses, shouts, and growls, competed with the sharp clash of weapons. Through it all, Maggie never lost sight of Tal. With relentless determination, she drove her mount forward, her sword cutting a path through the melds.

Melds rushed past her to fight the Marauders, leaving fewer to block her path to Tal. She had almost broken through, when a goat-legged meld thrust a rusty pike into her mount. The horse stumbled and fell to its knees, blood gushing from the wound in its chest. Maggie jumped free to keep from being pinned by her stricken mount. The Baleful surrounded her, snarling and snapping.

Maggie crouched. She motioned with her hand.

"Which of you ugly bastards wants to be the next to die?"

Tal swung his sword to block the battle axe wielded by Varg.

The sharp axe descended on him in a pendulum-like arc. Before Varg's weapon could cut him in two, Tal's blade met the haft in midair. The steel separated the axe-head, and it spun harmlessly away. Varg was left holding a piece of wood.

Tal reversed his swing and scored a bloody line across the centaur's ribs. Varg roared in pain. He reared, iron-shod hooves aimed at Tal's head and chest.

At the nudge of Tal's knees, his horse, an experienced battle mount, quickly moved out of range of the deadly hooves. Space opened between the two combatants, and with it, a brief lull in the fighting.

Tal—sweat dripping from him in a steady stream, his breath a series of heaving gasps—waited for the centaur to make his next move. Although fatigued from his profligate use of magic, he forced himself to remain alert. To let his guard slip even for an instant meant certain death.

Varg whirled to face Tal. He hurled the useless axe handle away and switched to his sword. Hand pressed to his dripping wound, he laughed. Raising the bloody palm to his mouth, one-by-one, he licked the blood off each finger.

"A tickle, nothing more," he sneered. "Sharpens the appetite." Brandishing his sword, he sped towards Tal.

They met with a clash of weapons, each attempting to beat down the other's guard and score a fatal blow. Tal's lightning quick strokes wove a deadly web, but Varg blocked each strike. The centaur used his greater size to push relentlessly against Tal's horse. His mount stumbled, and Tal barely dodged a blow whistling a hair's breadth from his head. The next time the giant centaur used his bulk, Tal was ready. At his cue, his horse danced away, and he easily blocked the sword stroke. But the action brought Varg within arm's length. Tal's fist shot out and connected with the centaur's jaw.

Crunch. Tal put the full force of his strength behind the punch. Stunned, the Baleful leader stumbled and fell to his forelegs. Tal's hand went numb from the impact—it felt like he had struck an anvil—and he was forced to pause and get the feeling back before he could press his advantage.

The hesitation gave Varg time to recover. With a shake to clear his head, he lunged to his hooves and charged.

Making no attempt to parry any blow, the giant centaur made straight for Tal's horse. Caught by surprise, Tal couldn't move his mount out of the way in time. His horse was bowled over, and Tal thrown off.

He landed hard and rolled, his sword sailing away. Before he could get to his feet, Varg tried to run him down. Hooves pounded at him, and Tal desperately rolled out from under Varg, barely escaping death. Scrabbling away on his hands and knees, he jumped to his feet and spun to face the giant centaur.

Weaponless and alone.

CHAPTER 35

TAL SEARCHED FOR ANYTHING HE COULD USE AS A WEAPON.

His sword lay on the grass behind the centaur, so close but it might as well have been a thousand leagues away. Varg was between him and the weapon. Worse, he had left his dagger embedded in the body of a meld.

The severed haft of the axe Varg had thrown away lay only a short distance away. It was better than nothing—and nothing was all he had now.

Tal feinted like he was going to dash in the opposite direction, and Varg leaped to cut him off. In a flash, Tal pivoted and raced to the haft. He plucked it up, sensed motion, and ducked. Varg's blade whisked by his head. As large as the centaur was, he moved with uncanny speed.

Varg's momentum carried him past Tal. As the centaur's hindquarter flashed by, Tal took a two-handed grip on the wooden haft and swung.

Thwack!

The stave struck Varg's meaty rump with a blow that shook Tal's arms. Varg cursed as he bucked from the painful wallop.

"Bad pony. Did that hurt?" Tal quipped with a fierce smile.

The smile quickly left his face as the melds surrounding Tal moved in to attack.

"No!" Varg screamed. "He's mine. The first one who lays a paw on him dies!"

The melds backed away.

Berserk with rage, the giant centaur howled, his long, braided hair swinging back and forth like a rope. Tal eyed the cord of hair, a desperate plan forming in his mind. To work, however, he needed to stoke Varg's fury even more. The Baleful leader needed to be so consumed with anger, that he became careless and allow Tal to get closer—much closer.

And of course, Tal had to stay alive long enough for his plan to work.

Maggie prepared to die. Surrounded, she had no hope of fighting her way free. Strangely, she felt no fear, no regret, only sorrow she wouldn't see Tal's face again.

A commotion came from her left, and she whirled, ready to defend herself.

Bradley Sikes and Terrell Simmons burst through the mass of melds. Horseless, blades dripping gore, they joined her.

"Looks like you're having so much fun, we just had to join in," Sikes quipped.

Relief coursed through Maggie. "The ale's on me when we get back to Markingham.

She glanced over her shoulder. Varg and Tal, locked in battle, hacked at each other.

"Go on," Simmons said. "We'll take care of these shit-spawned bastards."

Maggie nodded, then spun and ran. A few melds turned to meet her, and she quickly dispatched them. Breathing hard, she stopped to assess the struggle between Tal and the centaur. Varg, focused on his frenzied attacks against the prince, didn't notice her.

She braced herself to attack the centaur when pain blossomed below her ribs. A hot rush of blood followed and she looked down to find a blade buried in her side.

Tal kept hammering Varg with the axe handle.

The blows did little damage, but they did madden the centaur. As Varg's anger grew, so did his recklessness. Each sword swing became more rage-fueled and less precise. His strokes looped wider and wider.

Tal measured Varg's quickness and the timing of each swing. He dodged a vicious blow, and the miss left Varg's sword-arm extended across his chest. The force of the wild swing turned the Baleful leader's head so that Tal was on the same side as the centaur's blind eye.

It was the mistake Tal had been waiting for.

Varg never saw Tal dart toward him and grab his dangling braid of hair. Tal used it to swing himself onto the centaur's back. In a blink, he looped the thick rope of hair around Varg's neck, then rolled the remaining braid round and round the axe handle. Tal jerked the haft, and the cord of hair tightened, garroting the Baleful leader.

A choked cry erupted from Varg. After a few fruitless attempts to slash back at Tal, Varg dropped his sword and tried to pry the braid loose. His powerful muscles bulged, but with little success. Tal's strength and leverage was more than a match for the giant centaur. Changing tactics, Varg bucked in a frantic attempt to unseat Tal, but Tal pressed his knees tighter against the centaur's barrel. Varg's breathing became strangled, the cord digging deeper into his neck. Desperately, he tried to jab Tal in the ribs with his elbows, but Tal's position behind his broad back made a direct hit impossible.

Tal pulled harder on the axe handle, the tendons in his neck etched like cords of steel. Varg's lips turned blue.

The centaur fell to his forelegs.

Maggie cried out in pain.

She whirled and slashed with her sword. A meld holding a bloody dagger dodged away. The creature resembled a dog covered in red-brown fur. The hand wielding the dagger was covered in normal flesh, but the meld's other arm flopped useless at his side.

Maggie's fingers probed her wound. They came away wet with blood. Her tough breastplate had slowed but not stopped the blade. Another inch and she would have been lying dead on the ground.

The dog-meld darted in, his blade a flash of motion. Maggie lunged to the side, the knife sliding along the breastplate. Scrambling to her feet, she instinctively raised her sword. The meld's dagger skittered along the blade catching at the guard. She jerked her sword free, and in the process, wrenched the dagger away from the meld. It flew into the air to land near her feet. She snatched it up.

Breathing hard, she eyed the meld. He moved with a quickness unlike any opponent she had ever faced. Behind him, she spied two of the Baleful creeping toward Varg and Tal. A snake meld slithered to Tal's right into an attack position. A bird meld with sharp talons and feathers, closed in from his left. Both carried lances. Occupied with throttling the giant centaur, Tal had no idea he was in danger. The creatures moved closer and raised their spears.

With no time to shout a warning, Maggie hurled the meld's knife. The blade flew past her canine opponent and buried itself in the snake-man's chest. He dropped the lance and clutched the knife, his serpentine body thrashing in death throes. In the next breath, Maggie snatched another dagger from her belt, and threw it at the other meld. The sharp blade pierced its throat. Feathers flew, and blood spewed from the mortal wound.

Her dog opponent howled in rage and attacked. She tried to parry the assault with her sword, but once again, she underestimated the creature's quickness. He leaped inside her blow and knocked her down, sharp teeth biting her wrist. With a cry she dropped the sword. The dog meld pinned her to the ground, ivory fangs snapping at her.

"You're weaponless," the creature snarled. Hot breath washed over her face. "I'm going to tear out your throat and lap up your blood!" Maggie struggled to hold the slavering jaws from her neck with her injured hand. Her other hand groped desperately at her boot. The meld's spittle-flecked canines neared her throat.

"Good thing I always carry a spare," Maggie gasped.

The dog-meld's eyes widened. "What—"

The comment died in a wet gurgle, her boot knife buried in the creature's neck. He grabbed weakly at the blade, blood gushing from the wound to spatter on her. The light faded from his eyes, and the meld collapsed on Maggie. She shoved him off, retrieved her sword, and spun to a crouch, ready to defend herself.

The larger battle around her had transformed while she fought the dog-meld. The combination of her Marauders and the imperial legions turned the pitched battle into a rout. Leaderless, the Baleful fought as individuals and in small groups, not as a cohesive unit. Legionnaires cut down melds all around her, the survivors ridden down and dispatched by Marauders. Having won their aerial fight, the flying cavalry glided among the Baleful, their arrows, swords, and javelins reaping a terrible harvest.

Maggie returned her attention to Tal and Varg. She hefted her sword, moved to help the prince, then stopped. Her aid was no longer necessary in the titanic struggle.

Varg was on his forelegs. Face blue, his swollen tongue protruding, the centaur's hands plucked impotently at the braid of hair buried in his neck. Tal, hard muscles etched in the bright sunlight, strained to keep pressure on the improvised garrote. Varg's arms dropped, his tongue now as blue as his face. The centaur fell over on his side, and Tal leapt off.

He quickly locked his arms in a viselike hold around the Baleful leader's head. He twisted, and Varg's neck broke with a sharp *crack*. The centaur's hindlegs kicked in death spasms...then stilled.

Varg dead and the battle won, the adrenaline fueling Maggie in the wild struggle ebbed away. Her bitten wrist throbbed, but it was nothing compared to the pain of the knife wound in her side. Worse, the loss of blood left her dizzy. She dropped her sword. Shaky, knees no longer able to support her, she pitched forward— only to be caught by a pair of strong arms.

Tal cradled her to his chest. Head nestled on his shoulder, Maggie inhaled his pungent smell of blood and sweat.

Blackness overtook her.

Three figures on horseback watched the battle wind down. Hidden within a thick grove of trees, their perch on top of a hill gave them an unimpeded view of the battle. Each wore a forest-green cloak making them all but invisible to any observer. Two of the riders towered over the third, a diminutive form on a smaller mount.

"The Baleful have been defeated," one of the riders commented in a voice tinged with incredulity. "Who would have ever thought that possible?"

A feminine voice came from the smaller figure. "The melds finally faced a disciplined army."

"Where did they come from?" asked the last member of the trio.

"I don't know, but he," she replied gesturing to the victor beside the prone form of Varg, "is who interests me. His magic helped turn the tide of the battle. Even from this distance, I sensed his power." She turned to the others. "We need more information."

"Agreed," the first speaker said. "We'll wait a few days to let things settle down.

"Then we'll sneak into Markingham and see for ourselves."

CHAPTER 36

TAL FOLLOWED THE SOUND OF WEEPING.

The *clicking* of his bootheels echoed from the walls of the cavernous warehouse. The defeat of the Baleful, although a tremendous victory, had come at a dreadful cost, and the warehouse had been needed to store the dead. Necessity required the bodies to be burned, the ashes scattered on the battlefield, and each fallen soldier's name entered onto a list for family notification. Haze from the numerous funeral pyres still hung over the city.

The building now lay empty—except for one massive form.

Boorba's body rested on several tables pushed together. Alex held one of the troll's huge hands. Her heart-wrenching sobs touched a raw cord within Tal.

He reached her side. "I brought the tapestry Boorba gave you."

With tears dripping down her face, Alex arranged the fabric on the troll's broad chest.

"It was his favorite treasure, the one he valued above all else," she whispered. Body shaking with grief, she buried her face in Tal's shoulder. He put his arms around her, the lump in his throat a hard knot.

The sense of helplessness within Tal left him hollow, and he found it hard to breathe. He would give anything, move mountains if he could, to ease Alex's pain. Yet all he could do was hold her and wait for time to somehow ease the sting of Boorba's death—a death he was partially responsible for.

"I'm sorry," he said. "It's my fault. If I hadn't drunk the gnome's potion and charged off like an idiot, Boorba would still be alive."

Alex pushed away and wiped her eyes with the heel of her hand. "You saved the lives of Lord Morehead and countless others. Bozar told me you turned the tide of battle against the Baleful."

She touched his face, her thumb caressing his cheek. "The most important thing now is that you're alive and unharmed."

Her face hardened. "But you lied to me. You promised to be careful and instead, you were reckless and almost got yourself killed. And I don't care why you did it, Tal. Do you hear me? I don't care! The reasons don't matter to me. I'm so angry with you, so numb over Boorba's death, I can barely get through the day."

She punched him hard in the chest. Then again and again until her fists beat a staccato. Breathless, she wheezed, "Don't you *ever* lie to me again!"

Tal tried to speak but Alex shoved her hand over his mouth. "No! You don't get to talk. You don't get to say a damn thing!"

Alex pivoted—then burrowed back into Tal. She grabbed his arms and wrapped them around her like a blanket. Tal swallowed… and made sure his lips remained clamped shut.

Silence descended, Alex's muffled sniffles the only sound. Tal held her tight and studied the troll's large form. There wasn't an inch on Boorba's body not marked by an injury of some sort. Teeth, claws, beaks, and sharp weapons had scored his flesh countless times. That the troll managed to keep fighting, despite numerous mortal wounds was miraculous.

"I want you to do something for me, Tal."

"Anything."

Alex pushed away. "When you become king, I want you to declare an edict."

Tal frowned. "Ah, what do you have in mind?"

"I want a decree protecting trolls and other faerie creatures. I don't want them killed, harmed or harassed in any way."

"But some are dangerous!" Tal protested.

"Dangerous…or just different? Don't you remember? You were going to kill Boorba."

Heat rushed to Tal's face. "I—I remember."

"I'm different too. There are things you still don't know about me."

Alex reached down and tenderly ran a hand over Boorba's hairless head. "You see, I know what it's like to be afraid, to be alone, to want to hide so no one will pick on me or hurt me. Maybe Boorba sensed that. Maybe that's why he trusted me when he wouldn't trust anyone else. When I told him you were going to be killed, he leaped over the wall and tried to save you."

Alex crossed her arms and faced Tal. "I'm not stupid. I know why men look at me, how *you* look at me. But this," she gestured at herself, "is just flesh. It's not who I really am. I keep telling myself you love me because I *am* different just like Boorba. But I don't know anymore. How can you love me when you foolishly risk your life and put me through so much pain? Every second you were surrounded by the Baleful felt like hours. It was excruciating."

Alex looked ready to collapse, and Tal moved to catch her, but she waved him away. She pressed her fist to her heart, breathing in sharp gasps. "And Boorba's death isn't your fault, but mine. I asked him to help you, and it got him killed." A fresh round of sobs shook her.

Afraid to say anything or even move, Tal remained rooted in place. He knew Alex was right. The line between his duty and his impulsiveness was easy to see. He simply chose to remain blind. He never bothered to consider how his actions affected those who loved him. Not his mother, Bozar…and not Alexandria.

He found his voice. "When I become King, I'll make sure faerie creatures are protected and revered. You're right, Alex. Different doesn't mean evil or vile—it just means *different*."

Tal moved to Alex. She stiffened as he pulled her close. "You are indeed a beautiful woman, Alexandria Duvalier. Statues in a park are moved by your passage, and there are few men on Meredith who can resist you. But that's not why I love you. You have a kind and gentle spirit, and you care about others. There's a purity about you that is both rare and intoxicating. When I'm with you, you have a way of making me feel like a better man. If that's how you define different, then I am and will always be, hopelessly in love with you."

Alex sighed—then punched him again in the chest.

"*Ow.* What's that for?"

"Because you ruined it. I wanted to stay mad at you."

Tal grinned. "Then I'm forgiven?"

Alex looped her arm through Tal's. "Shut up, Prince Talmund. I want to go for a walk in the bright sunshine and fresh air, and you're going to escort me."

Side-by-side, they left the warehouse.

Maggie brooded over her tankard of ale.

After a night of drinking and revelry, the tavern was empty except for her and a sleepy barkeep. Although late morning, it was still too early for many of her Marauders. With every shift of her weight, the creak of the wooden planks beneath her chair was a reminder of just how alone she was.

Celebrations throughout the city had been nonstop the past two weeks. Defeat of Varg and the Baleful was a momentous event, the most glorious thing to have happened to Markingham in generations.

But all she could think about was Tal.

After she passed out in his grasp, when she came to, he was carrying her back to the city. Although weak from blood loss, she still recalled the thrill to be cradled in his arms. When he lifted her to his horse and swung up behind her, he held her to his chest all the way back through the city gates. The play of his muscles, the sound of his heart as she lay against his chest, and the feel of his arm around her waist, all indelibly etched in her mind.

Unfortunately, she passed out again, and the next time she regained consciousness, she was in her room at the keep, lying in bed. Tal was nowhere to be seen. Her recuperation was swift, and she soon moved back to the tavern.

Since then, she rebuffed all attempts by Sikes, Simmons, and other Marauders to join them in celebrating. She ate alone, drank alone, and slept alone.

A harsh laugh bubbled up in her throat. All she ever wanted out of life was to be free to exact her revenge against the monsters who killed her mother and carried off countless others. Now the meld army was destroyed and Varg dead. She should be giddy, but instead, a gaping hole had opened in her—all because she loved the one man she could never have.

The doors to the tavern rasped open followed by the tread of footsteps. Maggie looked up and almost dropped the tankard she was holding.

Tal and Alex approached her.

They came to her table and stopped. Alex cleared her throat. "You've been hard to track down, Maggie. But I wanted to thank you. The Marauders not only helped win the battle against the Baleful, but you also saved Tal's life."

"No thanks necessary," Maggie growled. "Killing melds is always a pleasure."

An uncomfortable silence silenced followed. Alex touched Tal's arm. "I'll wait outside."

Maggie waited until Alex disappeared, then turned to Tal. "She wasn't supposed to tell you."

"She didn't," he replied. "But others did. Most of them Marauders."

"Damn fools," she groused.

Tal took a seat next to her. "The two dead melds next to Varg had daggers in them." He placed his hand on hers. "There's only one person I know who could have made throws like that. I owe you my life."

Tal's touch disconcerted Maggie. "It was nothing." She willed her hand to pull away without success.

Tal took her injured wrist and eyed it critically. "Looks to be healing well. What about your side?"

Reluctantly, Maggie stood and pulled up her tunic, partially exposing the swell of her breast. Tal squatted and gently probed the bandaged area with his fingers. His touch lit a fire inside her.

Maggie swallowed. "Tal, please. That's enough."

Tal stood. "Of course. But I do have something for you. Come on."

Curious, Maggie followed Tal outside. She stopped and took in a sharp breath. There beside Alex stood a bay flying horse.

Tal rubbed the horse's snout. "This is Hanley. He's a gelding and a strong flyer. I know your horse was killed in the charge against the Baleful, so I'd like to replace him."

"He's magnificent," Maggie breathed. She ran a hand across his neck. Hanley snorted and flapped his wings. "But aren't flying horses restricted only for imperial soldiers?"

Tal's eyes twinkled. "Being a prince has some advantages." He pointed at a satchel hanging from the saddle. "That contains cavalry pants. You'll need to wear them to keep from being unseated."

Before Maggie could answer, a woman ran up to them. Breathless, tears streamed from her face.

"My son's been taken. Please help me!"

CHAPTER 37

THE YOUNG MOTHER'S HYSTERIA MADE HER DIFFICULT TO UNDERSTAND. Alex gently gripped her shoulders. "Take a moment and breathe. Then tell us what happened."

Calmed by Alex's touch, the woman's panicked babbling began to make sense. "I was at the central market with my little boy. It was crowded, but I noticed a woman in a gray cloak giving sweets to all of the children. Everyone's been celebrating for weeks, so I didn't pay her much attention. I traded a basket of dandelion greens for bread from a baker, and when I turned back, I couldn't find my son. He was gone and so was the woman in the gray cloak."

The mother looked vaguely familiar to Alex. "What is your son's name?"

"Don't you remember him, mistress? You gave us food and water."

Alex closed her eyes in dismay. *Of course. Little Brighton and his mother.*

"You said the market was crowded. Couldn't he have become separated and wandered off?" Tal asked.

"No, Sire. My friend Alana's girl is missing too. We were both at the market. She thinks the woman passing out sweets took her too."

Tal shook his head. "I know you're upset, but two children becoming separated in a busy bazaar seems easy enough to explain. They're probably just lost and a thorough search will find them."

Panic crept back into the mother's voice. "But we've looked, sire. Everywhere! And my son and Alana's daughter aren't the first to disappear. Other children have also gone missing."

Tal's eyes narrowed. "I've heard no word of this. Why hasn't it been reported?"

The woman's shoulders slumped. "We tried, Sire. But life has been so…desperate. Every day is another struggle. No one cares about a few misplaced children."

Alex knew exactly what the young mother referred to. Until Thaddeus Finkle appeared with the offer to swap her life for another, she'd been prepared to down an entire bottle of pills. Whether by starvation, fear, or cruel bullying, at some point life became too hard, and the will to live slipped away. When Tal and the Imperial Army appeared at Markingham's gates, a lifeline had been thrown to the citizenry with the most precious commodity of all—hope.

She gripped Tal's shoulder. "We need to do something!"

Tal's rigid stance signaled Alex his anger. "I'll organize a search party immediately."

Their horses were nearby, and Tal vaulted into the saddle. He pointed at Brighton's mother. "Meet us at the market with your friend. I'll be back within the hour."

"Thank you, Sire." She ran off.

Alex hurried to her horse. Before they could leave, Maggie shouted, "Wait! I'm coming with you."

Tal frowned. "You've never ridden a flying horse before. You need time to get used to your mount."

Maggie kicked off her boots and stripped off her pants, her bare skin a pale contrast to the bright sunlight. She grinned at Alex's shocked expression, then snatched the pantaloons from the satchel and put them. Jamming her feet back in the boots, she untied the reins from the hitch and mounted Hanley.

"I've been riding since I was a girl. The day I need lessons to ride *any* horse is the day I shit gold turds," she retorted.

Tal nodded. "Then let's go."

An hour later, they returned with Pulpit and fifty mounted soldiers.

Upon learning about the missing children, the monk requested to take part in the hunt. After an exhaustive search of the area proved fruitless, Pulpit suggested they clear the still busy bazaar. It took the better part of another hour to remove the grumbling vendors and disappointed customers, and then the monk took a position in the middle of the deserted marketplace. With eyes closed, he slowly spun clockwise until he had made a complete circle.

"What's he doing?" Maggie asked Tal.

"Monks of the White Order are sensitive to dark magic," Tal explained. "If these children were ensnared by an enchantment, he may be able to detect the scent."

Pulpit reversed direction, and like a weathervane, pivoted counterclockwise. He stopped, and his eyes snapped open.

"Witch."

The word hung in the air like a dagger of ice.

Brighton's mother fell to her knees and began to sob. "No!" she wailed.

Alex slipped off her horse and rushed to her side. With an arm around the distraught mother, she glanced at Tal. "Can we find them?"

The look on his face answered her question before his words did. "Markingham is surrounded by league after league of wilderness, and the city is a warren of deserted buildings. We could search for years and never find these children."

Fresh sobs of despair erupted from Brighton's mother.

"I believe I can follow the witch's trail," Pulpit said.

Tal blinked. "How?"

"Because this witch's magic has a particular potency, a sharp evil which even now cloys my senses. I suspect she is not used to covering her tracks or being followed."

Pulpit, face pinched in concentration, raised a hand. He moved it like a compass searching for an orientation. He stopped and pointed. "The enchantment leads southeast out of the city."

The monk pursed his lips. "If more children have gone missing over a period of time, the witch must need a steady supply. She wouldn't stray far. I'm certain this vile creature must take her victims to a hidden place close by."

Tal's eyes blazed. "So what do we do now?"

Pulpit started for his horse. "You follow me."

Tal and Pulpit trotted along at a steady pace. High in the air, a mere pinprick, flew Maggie on her new steed.

Because stealth was a necessity to catch the witch unawares, the accompanying soldiers trailed a quarter league behind them. They escorted a wagon to transport the children—if they found any still alive. Bozar directed the wagon's team of horses with Alex in the seat beside him. The First Advisor, made aware of the disappearances, insisted upon going along.

Tal glanced at the sun's position in the sky. "How close are we? There's only three hours of light left."

"The scent grows stronger. We are near."

They traveled another quarter hour when Pulpit stopped and dismounted. "We should proceed on foot. The evil stench is so strong it sickens me."

Tal hopped off, and they tied their horses to a nearby tree. Cautiously, they slipped through the forest gloom. A clearing opened in the midst of the thick woodland. A thatched cottage with a stout door and shuttered windows sprouted from the middle of the glade. Smoke drifted from a chimney of flagstone, the roof and sides of the hut a blend with the trees and vegetation. A small corral next to the cottage contained a dray horse. Next to the corral stood a four-wheeled covered cart.

Tal's magical senses tingled. Although not attuned to evil like Pulpit and members of his order, the proximity to what was in the cottage caused an uncomfortable itch. He clenched his jaw.

We found the witch.

CHAPTER 38

DRUSULLA HUMMED TO HERSELF AS SHE STIRRED A BUBBLING POT. The witch sniffed the concoction in the black iron kettle and wrinkled her nose. She searched the table behind her crowded with a collection of vials, bottles, and glass jars of potions and powders. She selected the ingredient she wanted from a slender vial filled with a green, viscous fluid. Drusulla uncorked the liquid, then poured a single drop into the simmering brew. A shrill shriek like steam from a tea kettle resounded throughout the cottage. The mixture heaved and moved as if with a life of its own.

Drusulla sniffed again. "Ah, just right." She smiled in satisfaction and hung the ladle on a hook above the pot.

She tapped her foot impatiently. The brew couldn't cure fast enough. With the ingredients from the four children she enchanted, she could at last complete the aging potion. For the hundredth time, she checked her appearance on the mirror mounted on the wall. An ancient crone gazed back at her. She looked every bit of her two-hundred and fifty years. Silver-white hair crowned her head, and deep wrinkles fissured her face. Rheumy, watery-blue eyes stared back at her stooped posture and liver-spotted skin.

Angrily, the witch turned away. *What a fine state I find myself in.*

Once upon a time, she had been young and beautiful. Back then, enticing men to her cottage was child's play, enchanting them even less so. They supplied all her needs and more. When her lovers outlived their usefulness, she had them dig a grave, stand in it, then slit their own throats. She long ago lost count of the number of men bewitched by her feminine, magical charms.

Drusulla sighed. *Those were the days.* Bitterly, she shook her head. Her prolific use of magic had exacted a price upon her body. Over time, her beauty faded. The transition from a fresh-faced woman to a hag with wrinkled skin and sagging breasts seemed to take place overnight. Desperate, she turned to an age-defying potion that used children's youthful essence as the main element. After some experimentation, she refined the potion to deliver the results she desired. At first, the brew worked beautifully, and she returned to the vitality and appearance of her youth. Even better, the effects were long-lasting, and years passed before she had to concoct another dose.

Unfortunately, Drusulla discovered each time she took the tonic, it lasted a shorter time than the last. This forced her to increase the potency of the brew, which required even more children. Although this returned the potion to its former strength, repeated use caused the same thing to happen—the potency faded to shorter and shorter periods. Now she needed four children to distill enough essence to make the potion last for years.

When the mysterious army showed up at Markingham's gates, the days of easily slipping into the city and capturing children evaporated. She despaired she might die before she could return and seize the children she needed.

Then the Baleful appeared. And with them came opportunity.

The aftermath of the bloody battle created chaos, and in the days that followed, Drusulla managed to enchant two children. Caged in her cottage, they were joined by the two she captured today. Now all she had to do was wait for the potion to cure so she could add their essence.

Satisfied, Drusulla took a pipe from her pocket, stuffed it with a savory herb, and lit it. She collapsed in a chair, puffed away, and looked forward to the return of her youth and beauty.

Just a bit longer and all will be ready.

Tal chaffed while he waited for Bozar and the soldiers.

Pulpit left him to watch the cottage while he rode back to tell them the witch had been found. The sound of a twig snapping caused him to snatch his sword from its sheath and pivot. He relaxed his grip on the weapon at the sight of Pulpit. Bozar followed, leading the legionnaires.

Alex emerged from the brush right behind them.

Distracted by the graceful sway of her hips, he didn't notice Bozar slip up beside him. "Any sign of the children or the witch?"

"Eh? No. What's Alex doing here? I told her to stay behind."

"Apparently, you've rubbed off on Alexandria. She can be as stubborn as you when it comes to following plain instructions."

Further banter halted when Pulpit joined them. "We need to examine the cottage and immediate area," the monk said. "The witch may have warded the dwelling. If so, she'll be warned when we try to force our way in. We don't need to give her any time to react."

Tal nodded. "I'll take care of any wards."

Bozar shook his head. "That's what I'm afraid of. Subtlety is needed, not brute force. Use your magic to unlock the wards, not blast them—and the hut—into pieces."

Tal grinned. "Of course, my *Eldred*."

Joined by Pulpit, Tal ran to the cottage. They froze beside the door and listened for movement. Hearing none, Tal nodded to the monk, and they went in opposite directions around the abode. Letting his magical senses expand, Tal examined the house. Soon he met Pulpit and they compared results.

"Only the door and windows contain wards," Tal whispered.

"I agree, but they appear potent. Can you disable them?"

Tal thought for a minute, then nodded. "Yes…although the process may not be as delicate as my *Eldred* prefers."

"Very well, but if you can't disable the wards quietly, then you must be quick about it," the monk warned.

Tal flashed a fierce smile. "One way or the other, the wards will be gone."

He moved back to the front of the cottage. His focus on the entrance, he let his power flow. The wards, situated at each corner of the doorframe, glowed red like beacons. After a few moments, he had the measure of their strength. A savage thrill ran through him.

No subtleness needed here.

The magical pressure built on each ward. He strained to keep it in check until the last minute. The air hummed and crackled, growing in intensity with each passing second. He judged the pressure sufficient and released his magic. *Boom!*

The door catapulted backward, torn from its hinges.

Drusulla's pleasant musings were abruptly interrupted.

A prickling sensation signaled the use of magic nearby. Before she could take a breath, her door flew inward and ricocheted off the wall with a loud *bang*. A strapping young man rushed in with a drawn sword.

Drusulla reacted with a quickness that belied her age. She pulled a glass vial from the folds of her dress and hurled it to the floor. Greasy, green smoke rose from the contents of the shattered flask. It drifted upward, undulating before the vapor coalesced into an enormous, green serpent. Mouth open to expose poisonous fangs, the hissing snake struck at the invader.

The young man made no effort to dodge the serpent's strike.

With a movement so quick it appeared as a blur, the intruder caught the snake by the neck. Magic erupted from the attacker, and the serpent disintegrated before her eyes. A thin shriek signaled the creature's end. Before Drusulla could move a step, the intruder was beside her in a flash.

Dagger at her throat, he hissed, "Move, and I'll open a new mouth for you from ear-to-ear!"

CHAPTER 39

AL LED SEVERAL SOLDIERS IN A SEARCH OF THE WITCH'S COTTAGE. They quickly located a back room containing a large cage. Made of stout iron bars, the cage had a hinged gate secured by a padlock. It held four small children: two girls and two boys. Half-naked, filthy, and scared, they clung to each other, eyes wide with fear. The sharp smell of urine and the fetid reek of feces gagged Tal, an indication the children had never been allowed out. Two of the children, perhaps a brother and sister, looked to have been held captive longer and were malnourished. Distended stomachs contrasted with the hard lines of their ribs against their skin. All the children shared the same gaunt cheekbones and haunted eyes. The sight of the dirty, hungry children caused red rage to explode inside Tal.

"Find a way to break the lock and free them!" Tal ordered the soldiers. Then he rushed outside to where the witch was held prisoner. He whipped out his dagger and held it to the witch's jugular, his hand trembling in fury.

"Your life ends now!" he snarled. The witch wailed and struggled to pull away from Tal's blade. A trickle of blood ran down her neck where the knife's sharp edge sliced her skin.

"Mercy, master, mercy!" she cried.

"Mercy for one who shows none? I think not!"

"Tal!" Bozar's sharp cry pierced Tal's burning rage.

Bozar approached Tal. "Stay your hand. Would you cheat the executioner? We need a trial to show the people of Markingham that imperial justice has returned to their city. Then the witch will hang."

"Trial?" A harsh laugh erupted from Tal. "You must be joking."

"Put the knife away," Bozar repeated.

Torn between his desire to kill the witch and obey his *Eldred*, Tal stood quivering with anger. Finally, he spat on the witch and stepped away. "I will be the one to put the noose around your neck."

A sudden breeze brushed Tal's face. He raised his hands against the swirl of dust and leaves. Moments later, with a buffeting of wings, Hanley landed nimbly in the clearing. Maggie slipped off the horse, chuckling at Tal's surprised expression.

"I told you I've been riding since I was a girl. Wings or not, a horse is still a horse." She looked around, her eyes hardening at the sight of the captured witch. "Did you find the stolen children?"

Tal gave a grim nod. "Still alive in the cottage. The witch held them in a pen."

Maggie pointed at the ancient hag. "Then why's that bitch still breathing?"

Before Tal could answer, Pulpit stumbled around the corner of the cottage. He approached them on unsteady feet, his face pale and drawn.

Tal's hand flew to the hilt of his sword. "What is it? What's wrong?"

Pulpit took a moment to collect himself. "There are shallow pits behind the cottage. They're filled with the remains of so many I couldn't count them all. Scavengers have been at them, and the bones are scattered everywhere."

Tal whirled on Bozar. "And you wanted a trial." He gestured to the soldiers holding the witch. "Stand her up!" He snatched the dagger from his belt.

The wrinkled crone wailed, "No! Mercy, master. Have mercy."

As Tal raised the knife to plunge it into the witch's heart, Alex emerged from the cottage. Their eyes locked. The look on her face—similar to the day the dark lord's men burned to death at the abandoned farmhouse—caused shame to blossom inside him.

Alex rushed to his side. She pushed him away from the enchantress. "No! Leave her alone."

At her touch, the anger left him in a rush. Chagrined, he sheathed the knife.

"Bullshit!" Maggie snarled. "That murderous bitch has killed who knows how many children. I say she dies now, and we leave her body to the vultures."

"Lady Margaret, let me remind you that my decision holds sway here, *not* yours," Bozar snapped. "There *will* be a trial and then judgment."

Alex pushed harder, pulling Tal away from the witch. "Listen to me. She is Bozar's responsibility now. We need to take care of these poor children. They're hungry and frightened."

Maggie's jaw dropped. "You mean to preserve this piece of shit's life just so you can take it later?" Harsh laughter spewed from her. "Now I've heard everything." She stalked to Hanley and jumped into the saddle. The horse broke into a canter, and with wings pumping, soared into the air. Maggie circled the clearing, then flew off.

Bozar motioned to a pair of soldiers. "Bind the witch. Make sure no harm comes to her."

"Thank you, kind mistress, thank you," the witch whimpered.

Alex turned and walked up to her. "What is your name?"

"Drusulla, mistress."

Alex's hand flashed, the sharp crack of her palm against Drusulla's cheek jolting the air. "You're a cruel monster. I'll be *very* sure to be there when you hang."

Alex led the children out of the cage.

She ignored the filth caked to them as they clung to her. She hugged each one and whispered calm assurances. When one of the soldiers returned with a bucket of water and clean rags, she began to wash each of them.

"You are so pretty," she purred to a little girl with disheveled, honey-brown hair. Gently, she scrubbed dirt from the girl's face.

Another soldier brought bread, cheese, and cool water in a canteen. Alex gave each of the children small portions so the food wouldn't overwhelm their shrunken stomachs. After they wolfed the food down, she let them take sips of water before giving them more of the bread and cheese. As they ate, she continued to clean them.

A small hand gripped her finger. "Can we go home now?"

Alex turned her head and Brighton looked up at her. She hugged him. "Yes. Yes we can."

An hour later, the sun low in the sky, Alex sat beside Bozar as he drove the wagon team back to Markingham. Two children flanked her on either side, her arms around them like the wings of a mother hen. Fast asleep, their small heads filled her lap.

In the back of the wagon, gagged and trussed from head to toe, lay the witch. Every time Bozar trundled across a rut or depression, Drusulla's bound body rolled around on the hard wooden bed of the wagon. This produced a constant stream of muffled curses and moans.

They ignored the witch's protestations. After what they had seen at the hag's cottage, Alex thought even Bozar took no small pleasure at Drusulla's discomfort.

"Thank you," he said.

Alex arched an eyebrow. "For what?"

"You kept Tal from killing the witch. A trial has benefits beyond judgment and execution. The people of Markingham need a return to normalcy. More importantly, they need to know that justice has been restored."

Alex smiled and waved her hand. "You give me too much credit. Tal just needed a little…help. He can be impulsive—"

"—And hot-tempered."

"Yes, all that," Alex said laughing, "but he has grown so much. I'm proud of him."

Bozar shook his head. "No, I don't think I give you credit enough. You have managed to do more to settle him than anything I've ever been able to accomplish. Fate crossed your path with Tal's, and I thank the Creator for His infinite wisdom in doing so."

Bozar chuckled. "To think I once believed it a wise choice to send you back through the Veil so you and Tal would be separated."

They rode in silence for a short distance before Bozar spoke up again. "I think it's time for a grand celebration. There is much to rejoice. What do you think?"

"You mean like a—a party?"

"Actually, something larger. A city-wide festival with food, wine, music and dancing."

Alex clapped. "I think it's a splendid idea."

They planned the celebration all the way back to Markingham.

CHAPTER 40

EARL YORK GLOWED WITH CHEERFULNESS.

"The First Advisor's suggestion for a holiday to commemorate the defeat of the Baleful, is a wonderful idea."

He thought for a moment. "We have a number of parks scattered throughout the city. All are neglected and overgrown. However, it's possible to clean them up and restore them, starting with the largest park near the central square."

Bozar chuckled at the earl's eagerness. "Consider it done." He gestured at Tal and the other senior advisors sitting around the table in the earl's conference room. "Are we in agreement?"

All thumped the tabletop in enthusiastic response.

"I can spare soldiers to help with clean-up and construction," growled Gravelback. "It will be good for morale after such a hard-fought battle."

"I'll make sure plenty of ale is on hand for our celebration," Thurgood added. He winked at Bozar. "No festivity is complete without it."

The First Advisor smiled. "I have no doubt you are up to the task, Grand Master."

"The first of the summer crops are stored and harvested," Tal said. "There should be plenty of fresh vegetables and food."

Earl York rapped the table. "Then it's decided. Best to get to work since we only have a week to prepare." Cheers and clapping greeted his announcement.

Bozar's countenance turned grim. "Now, about the witch. I

would like to have her trial *after* the celebration. No sense casting a pall upon an otherwise happy occasion. At her trial, evidence will be presented, summary judgment pronounced, then her swift death on the gallows. Comments or disagreements?"

Icy silence greeted Bozar's question.

"Although a hanging is a cruel public spectacle, in this case, I think we must allow the citizens of Markingham to witness the execution. Too many families have lost loved ones at her hands. Again, are there any who disagree?"

No one spoke except Tal.

"I swore I would put the noose around that black-hearted hag's neck." He stood and placed both hands on the table. "I mean to keep that oath."

Bozar shook his head. "Revenge is a meal that never completely satisfies. But if you must, then place the rope on the witch's neck."

The meeting ended.

A week later, Tal and Bozar observed the final arrangements for the night's big celebration.

They stood in the newly revitalized park that ran through the middle of the city. Once an overgrown, trash-filled eyesore, a small army of volunteers had cleaned it up, the grass and shrubbery trimmed to display a brighter, healthier greenery. The park was already filled with revelers, the merrymakers clustered around the spring-fed ponds and fountains spaced throughout the green.

Long strings of bunting and light crystals festooned the park. A newly constructed stage stood in the middle of the green. Tables, groaning under the weight of food and drink, stretched in long lines near the platform. An eclectic group of musicians practiced on the stage, the notes of their music afloat on the soft breeze. The impromptu ensemble, a mix of imperial soldiers and city residents, more than made up for their lack of skill with energetic effort.

Tal winced at a series of sour notes. "I hope our musicians improve before tonight's performance."

Bozar chuckled. "I don't think we need to worry. Artemis made good on his promise to have plenty of ale available." The First Advisor pointed at a group of partygoers already stumbling about the commons. "Even the most discordant note will soon sound sweet."

Tal grinned. "I understand the grand master managed to find some pyro-crystals in that enchanted trunk of his."

"Yes, he's planning quite a display. I haven't seen him this excited since we showed him the open portal." They shared a laugh and continued their trek through the park. When they reached their horses, they mounted them and made their way back to the keep.

"The earl gave Alex some of his wife's old dresses," Tal said. "The grand master claims his enchanted trunk can act like a seamstress and transform them to fit her. She wants to try them on, then get my opinion." The thought of seeing Alex caused his heart to beat faster.

Tal sighed and stopped his horse. He shook his head.

"I can't wait any longer, my *Eldred*. I thought I could, but I can't."

Bozar turned in the saddle and studied Tal. "Explain yourself."

"I ache for Alex. I can't wait until we win the war against the Veil Queen. I love her and each day my feelings grow deeper. I know you and mother think we're too young, that I'm too impulsive and hot-tempered to even know what love feels like. But I don't care what you, mother, or anyone else in the empire says or thinks. She *is* for me, and I will have no other but her. I've restrained myself long enough, and if Alex becomes pregnant, I will claim any issue as my legitimate son or daughter."

Bozar's gaze bored into Tal. "I see. Are you certain about this?"

Tal met his Eldred's eyes. "Yes."

"Then you give me no choice." Bozar urged his horse toward the keep.

After a moment's hesitation, Tal caught up with him. "Wait. What are you going to do?"

Bozar turned to Tal, a hint of a smile on his face.

"Arrange a betrothal."

"And you're sure this will work?"

Alex eyed Daisy skeptically. The enchanted trunk waggled her tasseled end so vigorously, her contents rattled the air with *clinks* and *clanks*.

Artemis Thurgood stood beside Alex, a gown draped over his arm. "Oh, I'm certain it will." He leaned closer. "I spilled an entire bottle of excellent red wine on my formal robes at one of the university's stuffy functions. I had a class to teach next, and despite my, uh, *gregarious* reputation, I couldn't appear in such a wine-besotted state before my students. So, I put my robe into Daisy, and a short time later, it shot out of one of her drawers. Before, the robe was a bit snug, but not only was it spotless, it fit me perfectly!"

"An enchanted chest that alters garments? You constantly amaze me, Grand Master."

Thurgood chuckled. "So I have been told—many times. Now, here's how Daisy's magic works. First, you place the dress firmly against your figure. Be sure to press tightly. The, ah, fewer clothes you have on, the easier it will be for the magic to adhere to the material. When you're finished, place the dress inside Daisy. Then wait. It shouldn't be long, and you'll have a gown properly cleaned and sized."

Alex took the dress from Thurgood and thanked him.

"Send Daisy on her way when you're finished. She's very taken with you, so you might need to be firm with her. Just push her into the corridor and she'll get the message."

A knock came at the door, and Tal walked in. He grinned at the sight of Thurgood. "I can't wait for your demonstration tonight."

The grand master rubbed his hands. "It will be unforgettable, my young prince. Especially when viewed after imbibing copious amounts of ale." Chuckling, he left and closed the door behind him.

Tal kissed Alex. "What do you want me to do?"

Alex pointed at the bed. "For now, sit."

Alex slipped out of her pants and tunic. She turned to Tal. "Can you unlace my bodice?" Wide-eyed, he nodded, his fingers fumbling with the laces and stays. A short time later, she pulled off the bodice and sighed with relief.

"I can't tell you how much I hate this thing."

Mute, Tal could only manage a nod. The thin undergarment Alex wore barely reached her thighs and did little to mask her lush figure underneath.

Alex held the formal gown against her figure. "I need you to help me with this."

Transfixed, Tal stared.

"Did you hear me?"

When she still received no response, Alex raised her voice. "Tal!"

Blinking, Tal swallowed. "Huh? What?"

"Press the fabric of the gown so it's molded against me. Start by my feet and work your way up."

While Alex held the dress up, Tal knelt and pushed the hem against her legs. His hands traveled up the material to her waist and abdomen. He paused at her chest, then firmly squeezed the material against her breasts. He lingered, holding the fabric in place far longer than necessary.

Alex giggled. "Thank you. I think that's probably enough."

Tal frowned. "It never hurts to be thorough. Perhaps we should start again. In fact, I'm available to help with *all* of your clothes."

Laughing, Alex tried to push away, but Tal pulled her closer and started to plant kisses on her neck and shoulders. Resistance crumbling, Alex felt the volcanic rise of desire inside her. Soon they fell onto the bed, the gown forgotten. Alex pulled off her undergarment and flung it away. While Tal tugged off his tunic, she fumbled with unfastening his belt and trousers.

The bed quivered.

Alex turned...and stifled a scream. The top of the enchanted trunk was perched just inches from her face! Propped up by her stubby feet, Daisy waggled back and forth rattling the bed frame.

Alex snatched the bedsheets and covered herself. "We forgot about Daisy."

Tal tried to pry the bedsheet off Alex. "So? You've seen one magical trunk, you've seen them all."

"She's watching!"

"Who's she going to tell? All the other enchanted chests?"

"I am *not* making love in front of Daisy!"

Tal groaned and rolled off the bed. "Then what do you want me to do?"

Alex quickly dressed before answering. "Nothing else right now. All I have to do is give Daisy the gown." She pushed Tal toward the door. "Pick me up this evening."

Tal wrapped his arm around her waist and plucked at her hastily fastened bodice. "Sure I can't help you in other ways?" he murmured.

Alex kissed him—then firmly pushed him away. "No. See you tonight."

With a sigh, Tal left.

The three strangers stood on the commons and watched revelers straggle by.

"Amazing," one said. "A fortnight ago, Markingham was besieged by the Baleful. Now they are throwing a festival."

"Yes, remarkable," agreed the smaller female. "But the festivities allow us to mingle with the citizens tonight. We can discover more about these newcomers."

"What do we do until then?" asked the third member of the group.

The woman gestured at the tables holding the food and ale.

"Eat and drink like everyone else."

CHAPTER 41

MAGGIE STOOD BEFORE A MIRROR IN HER ROOM AT THE TAVERN, AND inspected her appearance.

She tugged at the black dress she had chosen from among her late mother's clothing. Thin straps held the gown on her bare shoulders, and she struggled to adjust them. In unfamiliar territory, Maggie had last worn a formal gown more than a dozen years earlier. She found the entire process exhausting, from changing into appropriate underclothes, to choosing jewelry to match the gown.

She took a step back and turned to observe her profile. The dress hugged her contours. It fit snugly around her trim waist, and displayed her full breasts to their best advantage. Parading in front of the mirror like an ornament on display made her self-conscious, a new feeling for Maggie. Then, of course, there was the question of how to arrange her hair. After numerous curses, she gave up and let it cascade about her shoulders.

Why am I going to all this trouble?

The answer, of course, was Tal. Maggie knew it unlikely, but maybe if he saw her as a woman, not the hard-bitten leader of the Marauders, she might be able to ignite a spark of desire within him.

Though it wouldn't come close to the firestorm he produced in her.

When she first saw him outside the gates of Markingham, the attraction was immediate. Like a magnet, she found him irresistible. In spite of every effort to fight these feelings, they only grew stronger. What others viewed as Tal's flaws, she found to be strengths.

His recklessness she saw as courage. His impulsive behavior, bold-ness. She'd been surrounded her entire life by whimpering cowards, while Tal feared nothing.

And he was *so* easy to look at.

She'd spent many a restless, sweaty night, tossing and turn-ing over thoughts of Tal unclothed, his bare skin against hers. He was a curse she could not get rid of, her feelings an endless loop of hopeless, doomed dreams. She would never have a chance as long as Alexandria held his heart.

Alexandria's beauty, a thing to behold, made other women no matter how fair, ordinary by comparison—including Maggie. She could try on a hundred different gowns, have perfectly coiffed hair, jewelry, and make-up, and it would make no difference. Alexandria's beauty would always shine brighter.

It's not fair. Not fair! I saved Tal's life while Alex stood and watched. She can offer him nothing beyond her body. He needs me, not her!

Maggie hurled the brush that she'd been attempting to tame her hair with. It bounced off the wall and clattered to the floor. "This is a fool's errand, and I'm the biggest fool of all." She stormed out of the room, slamming the door behind her.

The sooner she started drinking the better.

Alex did a pirouette.

"What do you think?"

"Are we talking about the gown or what lies beneath it?" Tal asked with a grin.

Alex rolled her eyes. "I should have known better than to ask."

She examined herself in the mirror. The blue material of the gown, soft and silky, fit her figure perfectly. Daisy's magic also added a fresh crispness to the gown, as though straight from a seamstress. The dress left her shoulders bare, the scalloped neckline exposing a fair amount of cleavage. She chose a necklace and earrings composed of blue gems from the earl's late wife's jewelry, a flawless complement to the dress.

"You don't think the neckline is too daring, do you?" she asked Tal.

He chuckled. "Everyone in Markingham will comment on what a lucky man I am, so the answer is no."

Tal's eyes twinkled. "I have a surprise for you when we leave the keep."

Alex paused. *What's he up to?* He'd been acting strangely for days as if keyed up about something. Whatever it was, he remained tight-lipped and gave her no clues.

Hands on hips, she asked, "Are you going to tell me?"

He smiled. "I told you, it's a surprise."

"I'm not talking about that. You're a bundle of barely restrained energy, like you might burst. What's going on?"

Tal draped his arms around her waist. "So you think you know me that well?"

Alex pushed him away. "Yes. Just like I know you're trying to distract me. No touching or kissing until you answer me."

"You have me, m'lady." Tal held up his hands in mock surrender. "My surprise awaits us if you're ready."

Her curiosity aroused, Alex grabbed Tal's hand. "Then let's go."

They'd taken only a few steps past the keep's doors and into the courtyard when Alex came to an abrupt stop.

A covered carriage with gilded trim, waited for them. High wheels lifted the coach above the cobblestones, a pair of lanterns flanking each side. The exterior was composed of gold leaf and paneled in wood and burgundy leather. The carriage's carpeted interior contained seats made of stitched cushions covered in crushed, red velvet. A matched pair of silver flying horses waited to pull the carriage with a coachman seated on the driver's bench.

Alex clapped with delight. "It's beautiful," she breathed, "like a scene from a fairy tale. Is this your surprise?"

Tal smiled. "Part of it. I found this old coach in the earl's stables. It needed a lot of restoration, and I've been working on it for several days."

A crowd of servants gathered to witness the send-off. They cheered when Tal opened the carriage door and helped Alex in. Once both were inside, he signaled the coachman, and they rolled toward the park.

The horses gathered speed. Wings flapping, muscles taunt against their harness, they soared into the night. When the coach lurched and became airborne, Alex gasped and clutched Tal's arm in alarm.

He chuckled. "Don't worry. The carriage is enchanted. All I had to do was recharge the lodestones."

The city fell away into a glitter of lights. The triple moons, in full phase, cast a soft glow on the ground far below. Still clutching Tal, Alex peered out the coach window. She sighed.

Magical.

No painting or picture could ever have captured the moment. The soft *whish* of the wind, the beautiful city lights, the moons' ethereal glow, and the creak of wood and leather, all indelibly etched in her mind forever. But the most important part of all was that she shared it with Tal.

She turned to him. "Thank you. I'll never forget this night."

They shared a long kiss. When they broke away, Tal's face wore an uncharacteristic nervousness.

"The other part of tonight's surprise involves a question."

Alex sat up straighter. "Oh. What do you want to ask?"

Tal took a deep breath. "Before I rescued you from the gargoyles, I lived only to kill the Veil scum. My goal was to keep on killing until none were left." He shook his head. "My rage and hate left little room for anything else. I didn't realize it then, but my life was an empty and lonely existence, each passing day just as gray and featureless as the one before."

He cupped her face in his hands. "Then I met you, a bright and beautiful light, and everything changed. The hatred I had so carefully nurtured seeped away, and in its place flowed a warmth and compassion. You saved me. You saved me from myself, and I can't imagine a single day of my life that doesn't include you. I love you, Alexandria Duvalier, and I want you for my wife, to stand beside me as my princess and, one day, my queen."

Alex's breath came so rapidly, she feared she might hyperventilate. "You—you're asking me to marry you?"

Tal nodded.

"Yes!" Alex jumped into Tal's lap. "Yes, yes, yes, yes, *YES!*" She smothered his lips, not giving him a chance to say a word. He lifted her and laid her on the plush seat. Even then, Alex didn't stop, pulling Tal atop her and raining kisses on him.

Tal struggled to speak. "My mother still needs to approve our betrothal. She can be as stubborn as me at times—"

The rest of what Tal tried to say became jumbled as Alex continued to crush her mouth against his. Breathless, Alex reluctantly broke away. She stroked Tal's face.

"If I could take every dream I've ever had since I was a little girl, put them all in a bottle, and with a word, fulfill them, they would still pale in comparison with the happiness I have now."

Tal gently ran his thumb along the ridge of her chin. "Then it would match my joy as well." His expression turned sober. "My *Eldred* promised he would set up our betrothal. It won't be easy, but he has laid out a case for our marriage that even my mother will have a hard time objecting to."

Alex felt a chill creep up her spine. "You mean she might not approve?"

Tal exhaled. "She is the queen as well as my mother. My wishes often do not take precedence."

He helped Alex up, and they sat quietly for a few moments. *What if Queen Celestria forbids our marriage?* A vise clenched her heart. "But what—"

Tal placed a finger on her lips. "I can be very persuasive, and so can Bozar. Besides, our union makes sense politically. The empire needs cooperation to reintegrate Dalfur, and what better way to start than with my marriage to the Duke of Wheel's daughter?"

It seemed a lifetime ago that Alex had fled betrothal to a man she loathed and straight into the arms of Tal. It was a not so subtle reminder of Diana and the threads of time, each a possible future that could provide doom or joy. She shivered. *If I had made just one wrong choice—*

"Are you cold?" Tal put an arm around her. "Is something wrong?"

I'm not going to let my fears ruin the happiest night of my life. I can be strong too.

Alex turned and kissed Tal. "No. In fact, everything is perfect."

A panel was recessed in the carriage's roof. Alex pushed it back to expose an opening to let in fresh air and light. She grasped Tal, and they stood, their heads and shoulders protruding from the coach. The wind streamed by, the warm night air caressing their faces. Alex raised her arms and cried out in jubilation. Tal placed his hands on her hips, and turning, she leaned into him.

They remained wrapped in each other's embrace all the way back to the city.

CHAPTER 42

A MIX OF THOUSANDS OF CITIZENS AND OFF-DUTY SOLDIERS FILLED the old, city park.

The make-shift ensemble played with enthusiastic vigor, the occasional sour and off-key notes either ignored or unnoticed by the festivalgoers. The babble of cheerful voices mixed with the musical notes to create a gala atmosphere. Ale flowed, food was consumed, and couples swayed and danced to the music.

Alex and Tal stood on the edge of the commons watching the throngs of celebrants stream by. "Oh, Tal, this is so wonderful," Alex breathed. "When we first came here, Markingham was filled with starved, desperate people. Everything seemed so hopeless. Now, look at all the happy faces."

Tal nodded. "This is how it should be, how it *will* be when we destroy the Veil and kill the Veil Queen and King."

Alex recognized the hard glint in Tal's eyes and the tautness in his muscles. She thumped his chest. "No thoughts of the Veil tonight. We are here to celebrate." She nuzzled his neck to distract him, and his tension melted away.

"You're right," he admitted. "Besides, look." Tal pointed. "Artemis is about to start his light show."

The City Watch had cleared a wide area around the largest pond on the commons, and the grand master stood on a platform near the water's edge. He fished into his pouch, retrieved an orange crystal, and tossed it into the water.

The surface of the pond rippled and moved as if with a life of its own. A mist rose from the water's surface to form a cloud of fog. It twitched and stretched, tiny sparkles of light flashing on and off within the cloud. Without warning, the mist coalesced into the image of a giant stag. With a shower of iridescent, multicolored light, the stag bounded up and into the night sky. Like the tail of a comet, an arc of shimmering radiance trailed behind the glittering beast. Finally, with a mighty leap, the stag-image exploded with a *boom!* Glittering sparks sprayed in all directions, followed by a fine, watery mist which floated down onto the transfixed spectators below. Wild clapping and cheers erupted at the astonishing display. Alex found herself applauding as energetically as everyone else.

Alex hugged Tal. "That's the most amazing thing I've ever seen!"

Laughing, Tal said, "The grand master certainly knows how to put on a show."

Arm-in-arm, they watched Thurgood continue to delight and amaze them all with his collection of pyro-crystals.

Alex groaned in disappointment when the dazzling spectacle came to an end. Tal tapped her shoulder. "I'm going to find Artemis and congratulate him on such an impressive display. Be back soon." He trotted off and disappeared into the throng of spectators.

Alex closed her eyes and hugged herself. She felt her lips stretch into a wide smile. *This is the most wonderful night of my life. Could it get any better—*

"Well, well, if it isn't the delicate flower. Thinking happy, warm thoughts?"

Alex snapped her eyes open at the familiar voice. Maggie stood beside her, a bottle of wine in her hand. The earl's daughter wore an elegant gown rather than her usual black pants and tunic.

Maggie leaned closer. "If I had him under the sheets with me, I'd have such thoughts too." Her breath carried the thick odor of wine, and Maggie staggered slightly. She snickered, "Although I imagine I could be much more creative with Tal than you."

Alex ignored Maggie's attempt to bait her, and instead, said, "You look very nice, Maggie."

"Yes, I decided to dress up tonight." Maggie twirled, almost falling in the process. "What do you think, *Lady* Alexandria?"

"As I said, you look nice," Alex repeated, uncomfortable with the encounter.

"Why, thank you. Believe it or not, I was asked many times for a dance, some by members of my own Marauders."

Maggie wobbled closer. "Guess what? Many of them didn't even recognize me." She tittered and took another drink from the flask. "What do you think of that?"

It was clear Maggie was drunk and rapidly becoming drunker. Alex wished Tal would return and rescue her from further conversation. "You're very pretty, Maggie," she managed to reply. "Of course men would want to dance with you."

"Oh, what a wonderful compliment. I shall be sure to remember it," Maggie chortled.

She raised the bottle to her lips and drained the last of its contents. Disappointed, she tossed the bottle away and swayed on unsteady feet.

"But I'm not as beautiful as you," Maggie said, her voice filled with bitterness. "And isn't that what it comes down to? Men, including Tal, ruled by lust and blinded by your beauty?"

Heat crept up Alex's neck. "I don't know what you're talking about," she retorted, "Tal loves me for who I am, not because of what I look like."

Maggie laughed so hard, she tripped and almost fell. "You fool. Are you that naïve? Tell that to the men who, when you walk by, follow every sway of your ass with mesmerized devotion."

She wiped the tears of mirth from her eyes. "Why did you leave Wheel, Alexandria? I've never heard that story. Could it be that another loved you first? One you didn't love in return? Is that why you're here?"

Alex's cheeks flushed with anger. "It's none of your business!"

"Oh, I'm afraid I've made it my business. I asked myself why a duke's daughter would leave such a comfortable and privileged position in Wheel. So many answers come to mind." She wagged a finger at Alex. "Have you been a *bad* girl?"

"You're drunk, and I won't answer any more of your stupid questions!"

Harsh laughter spilled from Maggie. "Not half as drunk as I intend to be."

Maggie lunged and caught Alex's hand. She jerked Alex to just inches from her face. "What does Tal see in you besides a pretty face and big tits? I mean, what are you good for? Just an object of his desire, or do you actually possess a useful skill or talent?"

Maggie hissed in her ear. "I saved his life and, come to think of it, yours as well. Tal needs *me,* not you, a woman whose head is as soft as her breasts. You nearly got him killed once. You remember your little trip into the country and the trio of werewolves, don't you? Maybe the next time, he won't be so lucky."

Anger and jealousy surged through Alex. "You—you stay away from Tal."

"A threat? From you?" Maggie snorted in disbelief. "Oh, this *is* a night of wonders."

Maggie tightened her grip and squeezed until Alex cried out. "Why don't you make me, *Lady* Alexandria?"

Alex bit her lip and refused to answer. Maggie shoved Alex roughly away.

"Just as I thought. You won't even contest me for Tal. You're not worthy of him," Maggie spat.

Jealous rage grew within Alex to the point she thought she might explode. A now familiar *click* resonated in her mind, heralding the release of her wild power. Her skin tingled, the glow of hot magic filling her palms. Pulpit's voice floated through her mind. *The release of magic is triggered by your emotions.* Alex clenched her fists, willing herself to regain control before the magic burst from her and obliterated Maggie.

"Oh, look. Here comes Tal!" Maggie cried. She smirked at Alex. "I think I'll ask him for a dance."

Maggie stumbled over to Tal. She ignored his surprised expression and grabbed his hand. "Let's dance."

She held him tight, and they swayed to a slow waltz. Maggie giggled. "Why, Prince Tal, you are a marvelous dancer."

"Uh, thanks," Tal answered.

"Can I ask you a question?" When Tal nodded, Maggie continued. "I decided I needed an image change—of the softer, more feminine kind." She arrayed her arms around Tal's neck and pulled him closer. Her lips close to his, she murmured, "What do you think?"

Alex's angry stare drilled a hole through Tal. Bewildered, he looked back and forth between the two women and stammered, "You, uh, are lovely."

"That's what a girl wants to hear from a handsome prince," Maggie slurred. "I have another question." She kissed him. "Do I taste like a woman?" She took Tal's hand and cupped her breast. "Do I feel like a woman?"

"Stop it!" Alex cried. She ripped Tal away from Maggie.

Irate, Tal barked, "What's going on? What's wrong with you, Maggie?"

"She's drunk and throwing herself at you!" Alex whirled on Tal. "Tell her. Tell Maggie we're to be betrothed."

Tal's eyes widened. "I haven't even told my *Eldred* yet."

"*Tell her!*"

Tal held up his hands. "Look, I don't know what's happened here, but all right. Just calm down, Alex."

He turned to Maggie. "It's true. I asked Alex to be my wife."

Maggie's lip quivered. "You're going to be married?"

"Yes. As soon as it can be arranged with my mother, Queen Celestria."

Nancy E. Durham

"See? I told—"

Alex stopped as Maggie stumbled away and fell. Tal rushed to help, but she pushed him away.

"No! Don't touch me. I don't need your help." Tears streamed down her face. "I don't need anyone's help."

She picked herself up and disappeared into the crowd.

CHAPTER 43

MAGGIE WANDERED ABOUT IN AN ALCOHOLIC FOG.

Her resentment toward Alex smoldered like a fire. She stumbled to a bench and fell heavily onto it. Mumbling curses, she drew stares from passing revelers. Her stomach chose that moment to rebel against the contents of too much alcohol and too little food. Maggie lurched to her feet and vomited. Gasping, she collapsed on the ground, her head in her hands. The nausea slowly ebbed away, and her dizziness passed.

Maggie picked herself up and staggered away. Her feet took her along no discernable path down random streets and alleys. She lost track of time, and when at last she stopped, she found herself beside the dungeon not far from the keep. A thought pierced her ale-dulled mind.

The witch is kept here.

Her anger rekindled at Alex. If she hadn't intervened, there would be no need for a trial. Tal would have killed the murdering bitch. Now the families who lost children to the witch's youth potion would have to relive their pain.

Potion.

The word floated in her mind. *The witch makes potions…and there are all kinds of potions.* A ripple of excitement rolled through her.

Maggie took stock of her appearance. Crusts of dried vomit lined the front of her gown. She hurried back to one of the fountains she passed earlier. She pulled the hem of her skirt up, and ripped a piece of her undergown off. She dipped it in the water and cleaned the spew from the fabric. Then she splashed the cold water on her face. It revived her somewhat and helped to lift the curtain of alcohol still clouding her thoughts.

Smoothing her skirts, she backtracked to the dungeon. A pair of imposing doors marked the entrance. Reinforced with stout bands of iron bolted to the wood, once locked, nothing short of a dozen men and a heavy battering ram had any hope of forcing an entry.

Maggie took a deep breath, then knocked. After a moment or two, the door opened, and a sentry wearing a lapel of the imperial crest peered out. Maggie didn't give him time to ask a question and brushed by. The guard room was brightly lit, the light piercing her aching brain like a dagger.

The sentry quickly recovered and moved to block her way. "What can I do for you, miss?" Another sentry appeared, and both eyed her warily.

"I wish to speak with the prisoner."

"No visitors. Unless you have a pass signed by the earl or the First Advisor, our orders are to keep the witch isolated." The guards fingered their weapons.

Maggie tossed her hair. "Do you know to whom you're speaking? I am Lady Margaret, the earl's daughter."

After a moment's hesitation, the sentries burst out laughing. The first guard spluttered, "You're Maggie, the leader of the Marauders? I heard she slew so many of the Baleful, she should be called Maggie the Meld-Killer." He wiped his eyes. "And no offense, m'lady, but you look like you would have trouble swatting a fly." A fresh round of laughter shook the guards.

Tired of their insolence, Maggie snatched the soldier's dagger and pressed the tip under his chin. "Rather than a fly, why don't I stab a fat toad instead?"

The sentry froze, his eyes the size of platters. "Now, miss, don't do anything foolish."

"The name's Maggie, you fool, and if your friend moves another step, I'll carve you a new asshole."

The other guard halted and relaxed his grip on his sword.

Maggie expertly flipped the dagger in the air, caught it, and handed it hilt first to the still motionless sentry. "What's your name?"

"Lester, miss—I mean Lady Margaret," the guard hastily amended. "And this here's Bolin," he said with a gesture at the other sentry.

"Call me Maggie," she snapped. "Now, Lester, do I get to see the prisoner or not?"

Lester shifted uneasily from one foot to the other. "Our orders are specific. No one is to approach the witch without the earl or First Advisor's permission."

She speared both sentries with a fierce glare. "Well, there you have it. Since I'm Bartholomew York's daughter, by extension, I speak for him. You have a problem with that?"

Both guards looked at each other, uncertainty on their pale faces.

"Very well." Maggie whirled to leave. "I'll tell my father how uncooperative you were. Further, I'll make sure he reports the same to the First Advisor."

"Wait!" Lester cried. He fumbled for the keys at his belt. "Follow me."

He led them to another stout door and unlocked it. A moist breeze wafted out, and carried with it the odor of mildew and dust. They took a short flight of stone steps down to the dungeons. Light crystals mounted in sconces revealed a dozen cells on either side of a wide stone walkway. Heavy iron bars framed each cell, the back wall and floor made of the same quarried stone as the walkway.

In the last cell sat the huddled form of the witch. She watched them approach, her eyes a mix of fear and wariness. When they stopped at her cell, she cowered, her back grinding against the hard masonry.

"Leave us," Maggie commanded the guards.

"But—but, the witch is dangerous," Lester stuttered.

"If I can handle an army of melds, do you think this wrinkled bitch poses any problem?" Maggie snapped. She pulled her dress up to expose a stiletto fastened to her tanned, muscular leg. "Wait for me by the door," she added.

Lester and Bolin hurried away.

"Have you come to kill me?" Drusulla's quavering voice asked.

The crone crept closer until she reached the bars. Her eyes, large and piercing, gazed at Maggie. "A quick death would be a mercy."

The witch's stare was hypnotic, her eyes deep, blue pools. Maggie leaned closer, drawn to Drusulla's gaze. A harsh laugh spilled from her lips. "Although magic has been absent these long years from Markingham, I am of noble birth. That gives me a natural resistance to charms like a bewitching."

She whipped the stiletto from her leg and pressed it against Drusulla's bony chest. "Try that again, and I'll slice pieces off you one at a time."

Drusulla wailed and wrenched herself away. She fled to the cell's corner and out of reach. A bowl of bread and cheese lay untouched beside her.

"Not eating?" Maggie observed. She pressed her face against the bars. "How fortunate. I'm giving three to one odds your neck doesn't snap when the hangman drops you. You'll just swing, slowly strangling while you shit and piss yourself. *Hmm.* Now that I think of it, I need to raise my odds to four to one. I'm sure to make a fortune."

She stepped back and paced in front of the cell. "Of course, there is another option. One which might save your miserable life."

Drusulla sat up. She scurried closer. "Yes, mistress? Tell me, please!"

Maggie turned to face the witch. "Can you make a love potion? One which makes me the most beautiful woman on Meredith to the one who drinks it?"

Drusulla grabbed the iron rods of her cell and rattled them. "Yes, mistress, yes! I can create a potion that fills any man with unquenchable desire."

Maggie tapped her lips. "Describe how this elixir would work."

"You slip it into any liquid a man drinks. Wine or ale works best, although even water will do. A thimbleful will make you irresistible, a vial and you become an object of such seductive desire, your lover would follow you barefoot across burning coals. Best of all, once the potion wears off, your lover falls asleep and awakens with no memory of what has happened. The brew can be used over and over with no one the wiser."

The thought of a night alone with Tal caused a shiver to grip Maggie. Her mouth dry, she asked, "What would you need?"

"I just need to return to my cottage—"

"You think me a fool?" Maggie spat. "You're not leaving this dungeon! Just tell me what you need and I'll get it."

Drusulla slumped. "Then either kill me now or let me hang. The ingredients are varied and specific and must be carefully mixed. All my implements are also at the cottage, and without them I couldn't make even a simple brew."

Maggie's every instinct within warned her to turn around and leave. The witch was a cunning, cold-blooded killer. That she would try to deceive her and attempt to escape was a foregone conclusion. But the prospect of Tal making love to her was too much of a lure.

And the witch wasn't the only dangerous killer in the room.

"Be ready tomorrow night."

CHAPTER 44

The rattle of a key woke Drusulla.

Heart pounding, she sat up and rubbed her eyes. *Has the woman from the night before returned?* Drusulla had waited long into the night until at last, sleep took her.

The click of boot-heels told her someone was descending the stairs. She rushed to the metal bars of her prison to see. It was her! The sight brought the witch equal parts fear and rejoicing. *Will I be freed if I make the potion? Or killed afterward?*

Drusulla had cheated death many times over her long life, but her only chance now was to get back to her cottage and her potions and powders. She didn't trust this woman to keep her promise, but only there did she have the possibility to escape death once again.

The woman stopped at her cell. "I suppose we need to be properly introduced," she snapped. "Name's Maggie. Now that we have that nicety out of the way, let me show you something."

She lifted a small crossbow and pointed it at Drusulla. "I can hold this wonderful toy in one hand all day. But don't let the size fool you. It holds a dozen bolts, each with an embedded lodestone. The lodestones cause the shafts to be released in a rapid-fire fashion, and with enough force to punch through flesh and bone. I think a demonstration is in order, don't you?"

She angled the weapon down and fired. A bolt streaked inches past Drusulla, so close the fletching brushed her skirt. With a *thump*, it struck her straw-filled pallet hard enough to drive through the thick planks beneath.

Maggie smiled, baring her teeth. "I can fill your body with all twelve darts before you can draw a second breath. But perhaps you're such a skilled witch you know a few quick incantations you'd be tempted to try."

Maggie centered the crossbow on the witch's chest. "Shall we see which is faster? Your spells or my shafts?"

"No, mistress, no!" Drusulla shrieked. She collapsed to the floor, her arms held up to shield herself.

Maggie snorted. "Good. Because if you try to escape or use magic in any method other than to make my potion, I will kill you on the spot."

Drusulla's thin shoulders trembled. "Yes, mistress."

"Now get up. We've got a trip to make."

Maggie was convinced her demonstration instilled fear in the witch. The prospect of painful death was a remarkable motivator, and as long as the witch thought she could win her freedom, she would do anything Maggie asked. Regardless, she still intended to treat the witch like a dangerous snake. Any wrong move and she would kill her, potion or not.

"Show me your hands."

The witch thrust her hands through the gap in the bars, and Maggie bound them securely with rope. She unlocked the door and motioned. Drusulla stepped out of her cell.

"Move!"

The witch trudged along the dungeon walkway and up the steps. She stopped at the door and looked back. "What about the guards?"

"Taken care of. Go!"

They entered the guard room. The same two sentries, Lester

and Bolin, lay sprawled, snoring, across a table. Two empty tankards rested near them.

Maggie grinned at the expression on the witch's face. "You're not the only one with knowledge of potions. The sap of Nightweed mixed with ale causes a deep sleep."

She cracked the door and looked out. "Good. No one's stirring."

She grabbed Drusulla by the arm and opened the door wider. After another quick scan, she yanked the witch outside and kicked the door shut.

Hanley was tied to a nearby post and snorted as they approached. "Get in the saddle," Maggie ordered.

The witch eyed the horse with apprehension. "I've never ridden a flying horse before, mistress."

"That's too damn bad." Maggie helped the witch onto Hanley. "You better hope I don't let go of you."

Maggie swung into the saddle behind Drusulla. With a nudge of her heels, Hanley broke into a trot, spread his wings, and they soared up into the air.

The city below fell away, and soon they left Markingham's lights behind. The triple moons supplied enough ambient illumination for Maggie to easily navigate the path back to the witch's cottage. They circled the small clearing once, then with a buffeting of wings, Hanley alighted near the cottage. Maggie jumped off and dragged Drusulla from the saddle. She retrieved the crossbow and pointed it at the witch.

"Go. Remember what happens if you try any trickery."

Drusulla stumbled to the hut. Maggie grabbed her and pulled her back before she could enter. Because Tal had blasted the door off, the opening into the cottage appeared as a dark maw. After a quick peek at the gloomy interior, she took a light crystal from her pocket, activated it, then tossed it inside. The crystal skittered across the floor, illuminating the room.

Nothing stirred.

Maggie jerked the witch into the cottage and shoved her into a chair. "Don't move!"

With the crossbow aimed at Drusulla, Maggie made a cursory inspection of the abode. Satisfied, she returned to the witch and used her dagger to cut the rope from her wrists. When Drusulla tried to rise, Maggie pushed her back down. She ran the blade across the witch's cheek and stopped, the tip just below her eye.

"Careful," she whispered in her ear.

The witch quaked. "Y-yes, mistress."

Drusulla stood and staggered to a large table in the middle of the room. Stoppered vials, flasks, and ampules covered the surface. Some contained dry powders, crushed herbs, and the desiccated remains of insects, reptiles, birds, and other dead creatures. Additional containers were filled with fluids ranging in color from red to purple. The witch selected several of the vials and carefully poured precise amounts into an empty flask. She then took a mortar and pestle, sprinkled dry herbs, bones, and a piece from the shriveled remains of a bat-winged creature into the mortar. She ground them up into a fine powder and poured the contents into the flask with the rest of the mix.

Drusulla pointed at the cold hearth. "May I?"

Maggie nodded and the witch gathered kindling from a nearby basket. She placed it in the hearth, mouthed a word, and the kindling caught fire. The witch threw on more wood, and flames began to lick upward toward a blackened cauldron. Drusulla then added a cup of water and the flask's ingredients to the pot. She mumbled an incantation while stirring the brew. Soon the mixture began to bubble.

Drusulla returned to the table, selected a vial filled with a blood-red liquid, and returned to the hearth. Carefully, she added two drops from the vial to the cauldron and stirred. The brew hissed like water thrown onto a hot fire. The witch let it simmer for a few moments more, then dipped a ladle into the pot. She poured the contents of the ladle into an empty vial, stoppered it with a cork, and held it before her. The potion was clear and colorless.

"You must add this to water, wine, or ale. Make sure you are alone with the one you have chosen when he drinks the potion. If another woman is in the room and is seen first, she will be the one who drives his desire."

Maggie nodded, fixated on the vial of potion. She licked her lips, heart hammering at the prospect of Tal enthralled to her by the elixir.

She pointed. "Give it to me." The witch handed her the vial, and Maggie slipped it in her tunic.

Momentarily distracted, she missed the flicker of the witch's wrist. Out of sight beneath the table, a drawer slid open. At another twitch of the witch's finger, a vial rose from the drawer and shot into Drusulla's hand. She palmed the ampule and dropped it in her pocket.

Maggie gestured at the ruined doorway. "Let's go."

"Where are we going?"

"Back to Markingham."

"But you promised my freedom!" Drusulla cried.

"Do you really think I'd leave you here with everything you need to murder other children?" Maggie snarled. "Your choice, witch. Either back to the city to hang, or I take you deep into the wilderness where you'll never find your way back."

"But I'll perish, mistress! I'll die in the wilds."

"To the city and the hangman it is then."

"No!" Drusulla screeched. "I-I choose the wilderness."

Maggie suppressed a smile. She never intended to take Drusulla back...not alive anyway. She bound the witch's hands, then roughly helped her into the saddle. A much shorter trip than the witch realized lay ahead. But Maggie planned to make it up to Drusulla.

Because it would be followed by a long drop.

CHAPTER 45

A THOUGHT STRUCK MAGGIE AS SHE HELD THE REINS AND STOOD beside Hanley.

She glanced up at the witch. "Will the potion work on a magic-user?"

Puzzled, Drusulla frowned. "What do you mean, mistress?"

"Will the elixir produce the desired effect on someone of noble birth? Would he be immune to the effects of the potion?"

A gleam of recognition dawned on the witch's face. "You mean the fierce young man who captured me, don't you?" Drusulla shivered. "He wanted to kill me."

"Yes, who would have thought? Just answer the question, witch!" Maggie snapped.

"May I ask the strength of his magic, mistress?"

Maggie recalled the fiery hail and the bramble forest Tal caused in the battle against the Baleful. "There are few who can match his power."

"He loves another doesn't he? The woman who was with him when I was taken."

Drusulla screeched as Maggie dragged her from Hanley and threw her to the ground. Knees on the witch's chest, Maggie bent within inches of her face. "You stupid bitch!" she screamed. "Tal only thinks he loves Alexandria! Her beauty has blinded him. The potion is to make him see he needs *me!*"

Maggie stood and yanked Drusulla to her feet. "Now answer me! Will the potion work on Tal?"

Gibbering in fear, Drusulla cried, "Yes, yes, it will work! Just add more of the potion to his drink."

"How much more?"

Drusulla took a shaky breath. "A few drops will do. To be sure, you could add a half-dozen drops. Even the most powerful sorcerer would be unable to resist such a dosage."

Maggie thought of another question. "How long will the effects of the potion last?"

"Most of a day or night, mistress. You can prolong the enthrallment by having your victim—I mean lover—continue to take the potion. Before the effects wear off, have him drink water or ale mixed with a drop or two of potion. You can keep him enthralled for days, weeks even. Just remember the potion works best in isolation."

Maggie scowled, "You already told me to make sure no other woman is present."

"But you need a place with no distractions or worse, other folk. Even the sound of another voice will weaken the potion's effect. An isolated farmhouse or abandoned homestead would be ideal."

The story of how Tal saved Alexandria's life from the dark lord had been re-told so many times at the tavern, Maggie threatened to kick any Marauder in the balls who mentioned it again. But... the deserted farmstead where Tal destroyed the dark lord's forces sounded perfect. Even by flying horse, the abandoned farm was days away. Once Tal was enthralled, she could take him there for days of uninterrupted lovemaking.

But first, I have in mind a much closer place to test the potion.

The anticipation lay so thick upon Maggie, she found it hard to breathe.

"Have you ever heard of Traver's Crossing, witch?"

Drusulla shook her head.

"It's a long-abandoned village several day's ride from here by flying horse. That's where I'm going to take Tal."

"It sounds perfect, mistress."

Maggie suppressed a savage grin. *So glad you approve. But since you won't be alive to share this with anyone, why not let you in on my little secret?*

She hauled Drusulla back into the saddle then seated herself behind the witch. She nudged Hanley with her heels, and the flying horse took off. A short time later, they were high in the sky. Maggie directed Hanley away from Markingham, and over the trackless forest far below. The leagues passed by, their passage marked by the swish of Hanley's wings and the brush of streaming wind.

Maggie judged they had traveled far enough and let the flying horse glide. "Here's your stop, witch."

The moons' light displayed an unbroken march of the forest beneath them. "But, mistress, I see no place to land—"

Drusulla's comment ended in a shriek as Maggie shoved her from the saddle.

The witch plummeted toward the treetops far below.

<hr/>

The rush of air ripped Drusulla's raw screams from her mouth.

She pawed at her gown for the pocket that held the vial. Only moments remained before she struck the trees, and her body would be broken and shattered. Desperate fingers closed on a smooth cylinder. She ripped the ampule from the pocket, tore the cork from the top, and downed the contents.

A green, oily cloud exploded. From the midst of the fog came a *caw*, and a huge raven emerged, powerful wings carrying the bird above the forest. It streaked away, black feathers ruffling in the wind.

Maggie watched as Drusulla plunged to her death. *That foul bitch is finally getting what she—*

Maggie's mouth fell open at the sight of a mushrooming green cloud. She blinked in disbelief as a raven shot out of the roiling mist. By the time her stunned mind processed what had happened, the raven was a mere speck.

Maggie spat curses as she urged Hanley in pursuit of the bird. Somehow, the witch must have obtained a potion. But how? She watched her the entire—

Maggie closed her eyes in dismay. *It happened when I took the elixir from Drusulla.* So focused on the vial of potion, she'd let her attention waver. Only a mere moment to be sure, but it was all the witch had needed.

It soon became clear she would not catch up with the transmuted witch. Voice hoarse from screaming oaths, Maggie admitted defeat. The raven's lead was too large to overcome, and the bird had disappeared into the night. The witch could have gone in any direction, could even now be roosted on a tree branch laughing at her. Maggie took a deep breath, closed her eyes, and tried to think. Alone and without any of her potions or powders, what would she do if she were Drusulla?

Her eyes flashed open.

"Go, Hanley, go!" she shouted. The flying horse surged forward, mighty wings beating the air.

Back to the witch's cottage.

With a raucous *caw*, the raven flew into the hut and alighted on the floor.

Whoosh. Drusulla emerged from a cloud of emerald smoke. She hurried around the hut, hidden drawers and compartments opening at the wave of her hand. She grabbed a cloth bag and filled it with potions and powders. Maggie clearly wanted her dead, and the woman was as cunning as she was vicious. Even now, she might have reasoned Drusulla had returned to the cottage and was charging back. Drusulla didn't have time to be choosy, so she selected only the most important of her magical unguents and materials.

Drusulla paused at one hidden compartment and removed two vials, the last of her youth elixir. Saved for only the most dire of circumstances, they were all that stood between her and the rapid death of old age. Unfortunately, she would need to use one to transform back into a raven.

That would leave only a single dose.

Another concealed bin revealed a leather cylinder. She ripped the cap off and removed a rolled piece of parchment. She swept a portion of the table clear, flasks and vials flying to shatter on the floor. Drusulla spread the parchment flat and murmured an incantation. A map appeared. Another hastily chanted spell produced a glow of light from the palm of her hand. The magical glow revealed the map's details—mountains, rivers, and the locations of numerous abandoned villages. Drusulla ignored all of them, and instead, her finger traced a path to a range of mountains north of Markingham.

"Here," she whispered, "here is where the dark lord's fortress must be."

Many years earlier, one of her lovers claimed to have been a courier for a sorcerer of great power. He said the dark lord lived in a mountainous stronghold, and was served by an eyrie of gargoyles. At the time, she viewed his claim as nonsense, and after he outlived his usefulness, his remains joined her other victims' in a shallow grave. But now, she was convinced he must have been telling the truth.

She tapped the map. *And this is the nearest mountain range to Traver's Crossing, the place Tal killed the dark lord's gargoyles.*

A fierce thrill ran through Drusulla. She had information she could offer as trade to the sorcerer. *I'll be richly rewarded!* She could tell him that Markingham was now occupied by a mysterious army, and that the Baleful had been defeated. Most valuable of all, she could reveal that the pair he sought, this Tal and Alexandria, could be found in Markingham.

A bitter sigh escaped Drusulla. She had a general location but not a specific one. The mountains were some distance to the north, and undoubtedly, she would have a long search for the fortress. It might take months, a year even, before she could find it. In the meantime, not only were the sands emptying from the hourglass of her life, but she would have to remain a raven while she searched. That meant surviving attacks from eagles, owls, and a host of other predators while on a diet of seeds, berries, and insects.

She rolled up the parchment and jammed it into the cloth pouch. She mouthed a spell and the pouch contracted to the size of a thimble. She dropped it in the map cylinder, repeated the spell, and the tube shrank to the size of her little finger. Drusulla pulled up her skirt and placed the cylinder against the bare flesh of her leg. She mouthed a final incantation, and her skin bubbled and frothed. A hiss of pain escaped her lips, as her flesh, like melting wax, dripped and puddled around the tube, encasing it.

She thought she heard the buffeting of wings outside the cottage. Whether real or imagined, terror coursed through her. Quickly, she took one of the two vials of precious potion and drank it. With a *poof*, she transmuted back into a raven.

Wings a blur, Drusulla shot out of the cottage.

CHAPTER 46

THE RAVEN STREAKED FROM THE WITCH'S HUT LIKE AN ARROW.

Caught by surprise, Maggie barely had time to snatch her crossbow from the saddle. The soft light of the triple moons lit up the clearing, backdropping the bird against the dark tree-line. She took hasty aim and fired. The bolts left the weapon in a blur, each tracking closer and closer to the bird. Just as the raven reached the treetops, the last dart appeared to make a strike. Feathers flew, followed by a blood-curdling screech.

"Got you!" Maggie cried. "I got—"

The words died on her lips. The dark shape of the raven continued to rise above the forest and disappeared into the night. *Only an indirect hit, not a fatal one.* Maggie swallowed her bitter disappointment. Cursing, she whirled and stalked into the cottage.

Moonlight filtered through the splintered doorway to reveal that the witch had been busy. Drawers and bins were open everywhere, vials and flasks upended and shattered on the floor. A foul, acrid odor filled the place, evidence alchemy had been in play. Furious, Maggie gathered the remaining kindling and arranged the dry wood about the cottage. With a flint, she sparked each mound to life. Soon, smoke and flame filled the interior.

Maggie retreated outside and watched fire consume the witch's hut. "At least I can deny you this," she hissed. "Whatever's left of your potions and powders is now lost to you forever."

She jumped on Hanley, and the flying horse took to the sky. From Maggie's vantage point high above, the blazing cottage appeared like a bright, fiery bloom. Her hand crept to the pocket she placed the potion in. *But I got what I wanted…and soon, I'll have Tal as well.*

She turned Hanley and headed back to Markingham.

***

A crease of agony burned across Drusulla's feathery back. The cross-bow bolt had struck only a glancing blow, but even that had almost dropped her to the ground. The witch landed out of sight, on a leafy bough high in a tree. While she recovered, her sharp avian vision watched the flying horse and rider wing back to Markingham.

The witch launched herself into the air. An angry *caw* escaped her beak at the scene of the flaming remains of her home far below. Black hatred filled Drusulla. Maggie would pay. They would *all* pay. Turning, she flew north.

The sooner she found the dark lord, the sooner she could exact her revenge.

***

Bozar steeled himself.

What he was about to do—present Tal's betrothal to the queen—had only a handful of possible outcomes. This included his immediate removal as Tal's First Advisor, followed by his recall and imprisonment at Lodestone Castle. If the queen felt generous, rather than the dungeon, she might banish him to his ancestral home in the Kazir Islands. There, he would live the rest of his life in exile.

And then there was the small possibility he could get Celestria to agree to their union.

He chose an obscure room in a corner of the keep for his meeting with the queen. If Celestria ordered his arrest, he preferred to suffer the indignity in front of as few pairs of eyes as possible. A knock came from the ornate wooden door.

"Enter."

Tal rushed in pulling Alex along with him. "Well?"

Bozar sighed. "I told you to wait outside." He pointed at a large communication ring which hung motionless in the middle of the room. "Magical transmissions through the open portal take some time. Be patient. I'll call you when I'm ready."

Tal shook his head. "But—"

Alex pushed him back to the doorway. "Stop arguing and just do what Bozar asked. He doesn't need your help."

She propelled him into the corridor. Before she closed the door, Alex flashed Bozar a smile.

The First Advisor clasped his hands and cast his eyes upward. *Tal actually listens to Alexandria! Somehow, I must convince Celestria to approve their marriage.*

As if in answer to his silent plea, the area within the magical ring clouded over. Moments later, the image of Queen Celestria appeared. Dressed in a gown of gold brocade, she sat in a sumptuous, cushioned chair. A pair of advisors flanked her on either side.

Piercing blue eyes appraised Bozar. "What news, First Advisor?" She peered past him. "You are alone?"

"All is well, my queen. Since the defeat of the Baleful, we have completed repair of the walls and fortifications. Our army continues to grow, and Markingham is close to self-sufficiency."

Celestria crossed her arms. "That answers my first question but not the second."

Bozar cleared his throat. "May I speak to you...privately?"

The queen studied Bozar for several moments. "Very well." She waved her hand and dismissed her advisors.

Celestria speared Bozar with a hard gaze. "Now, what is it?"

Bozar decided the best approach with Celestria was to be simple and direct. As the busy ruler of an empire, she valued frankness far more than subtlety.

"I would like to propose Tal's betrothal and marriage to the Duke of Wheel's daughter, Alexandria Duvalier."

The queen's expression hardened. "I seem to recall you told me the duke had betrothed her to another. Has this changed?"

Bozar cleared his throat. "No. But Lady Alexandria has told us the duke has been beguiled by her stepmother. The duke doesn't realize the man he has chosen for her is a dark lord, possibly the son of the Veil Queen."

"Has it occurred to you, First Advisor, that a young woman in her position might say anything to avoid an unwanted marriage?"

"Of course, but—"

"And that we must avoid any act that threatens an alliance with the Duke of Wheel and reintegration of the dukedom to the empire?"

"I agree. But what better way to seal this alliance than by Tal's marriage to Alexandria? The duke will welcome—"

Incredulous, the queen snapped, "Have you taken leave of your senses that you should spout such nonsense? You are supposed to guide my son, not indulge his foolish fantasies!"

Bozar calmly held Celestria's angry gaze. "Tal loves her. And Alexandria loves him. He will not give her up."

The queen dismissed his comment with a wave of her hand. "He will do whatever I command. Tal has seen only twenty summers. He knows nothing of love and will soon forget her."

"No. He will not."

Celestria stood. "Are you defying my wishes, Bozar? Do you think your friendship with my late husband or your high position at court somehow insulates you from my wrath?"

Bozar sighed. "No, my queen. I'm simply telling you the truth. And the truth is that Alexandria is the best thing that has ever happened to Tal. She has smoothed his jagged edges, tempered his anger, caused him to see what has long blinded him. It's hard to put into words, but she has found a way to cool his volcanic rage. Alexandria *is* his missing piece."

The time for temerity was past. Boldly, he stepped forward. "Mathias was my friend, a brother in all ways save by blood. When he died, his son became my son, and I gave up all thought of having my own family. Although a poor substitute, I gladly stood in my beloved friend's place for Tal. From a small boy of five to the young man he is now, I have been with him every step of his life. I know him and know him well, so heed me on this, Celestria. If you deny Tal's betrothal to Alexandria, it *will* destroy him."

The silence lay thick between them.

"Is he truly happy?" she whispered.

Bozar smiled. "I have never seen him happier."

A tear ran down her cheek and Celestria wiped the moisture away. "Then she has given him a gift I never could. I'm afraid you're wrong, however."

Uncertainty gripped Bozar at the comment.

"You were never a poor substitute. Send in my son and Alexandria."

Relief flooded Bozar. He hurried to the door and let the young couple in. He led them to Celestria's image within the communication ring. She reached out as if to touch Tal.

"I have worried so much about you. Now I see my concerns are unfounded." She turned to Alex. "And you must be Alexandria. The descriptions do not do you justice. You are far more beautiful."

Alex blushed. "Th-thank you, Your Highness."

"Do you love my son?"

Alex looked at Tal. "Yes. With all my heart."

"Do you understand the enormous responsibility that goes with this marriage? You will be a princess, and one day, a queen. Your prodigy will be heirs to a powerful empire. Millions of lives will be in your hands."

Alex shook her head. "No, I don't understand it all. But I know I love Tal, and I will always support him, a partner to help in all things good or bad."

Celestria smiled. "I didn't understand either. I cared only for Mathias, and in my reasoning, since we loved each other, that was all that mattered. Looking back, it seems so foolish now, yet it was our love that sustained us during the best and worst of times."

She nodded at Alex. "As it will for you."

A long pause followed. Bozar replayed the queen's words in his mind, convinced he hadn't heard her correctly. Then Tal's jubilant shout shook the room.

"Thank you, mother, thank you!" With a whoop of joy, he caught Alex up in his arms.

Laughing, Celestria clasped her hands to her chest. She nodded at Bozar. "You had better get busy. We have a marriage to plan."

CHAPTER 47

MAGGIE WATCHED THE DOORS TO THE TAVERN.

"Think he'll come?"

She turned her attention to the Marauder next to her at the table. "Huh? Who are you talking about?"

"The prince," Bradley Sikes said. "That's who you're waiting for, right?"

"Mind your own business, Sikes."

"So it *is* the prince."

Maggie's fist struck the table with an angry *thump*. "Remind me, when did you become such a smartass?"

Sikes grinned. "I had a good teacher."

Maggie couldn't hold back a chuckle. "I guess you did."

"So what does Prince Tal have to do with any Marauder business?"

"What is it with you and all these questions?" Maggie quipped. "If I tell you, will you go away?"

Sikes scooted his chair closer. "Let's hear it."

"I'm going to take Tal, uh, I mean the prince, to where we train new Marauder recruits."

Sikes frowned. "That old estate? Why?"

Maggie threw up her hands. "Do I need a good reason? The Imperial Army has outgrown the city barracks. Maybe it can be used to house more soldiers."

Sikes expression remained doubtful. "The whole place would

have to be rebuilt and even then, wouldn't hold more than a few score of men—"

"Enough! No more questions. Get the hell out of here!"

Sikes held up his hands and pushed away from the table. "I'm going, I'm going."

Bradley finished the last of his ale, wiped his mouth, and made his way to the doors. Just as he pushed them open, Tal brushed by. Maggie's heart fluttered, and her mouth went dry. He walked up to the table and sat.

"Did you bring your flying horse?" she asked.

"Yes, but your message only said you wanted to show me something. It didn't explain where or why."

Maggie forced herself to rein in the anticipation of being alone with Tal. "I want to show you where we train Marauders. It's my family's old summer estate, and it may have military value for the empire. It's a few leagues from Markingham, so we'll get there much faster on flying horses."

Thoughtful, Tal rubbed his chin. He nodded. "Why not? Any help defeating the foul Veil Queen and King is appreciated."

Maggie stood. "Good. Let's go."

Sikes watched from the shadow of a nearby alley as Maggie and Prince Tal emerged from the tavern. His eyes narrowed as they mounted flying horses and became airborne.

Maggie tried to hide it from him, but Sikes knew she was keyed up about something...and that something was the prince. Since that bastard showed up with his army, everything had changed. The Marauders became less important with each passing day. Soon, they wouldn't be needed at all. But the worst part was Maggie. He'd never seen her like this, panting after Prince Tal like a lovestruck lass.

When Bradley first met her, he was only a lad. Cold, starving, and afraid of his own shadow, Maggie convinced him and scores of others that they could be part of something far grander and better. Although no older than her fledgling Marauders, her fierce spirit and determination buoyed them through the difficult early years. But when she finished molding them, they were sheep no longer.

They were wolves.

Although Sikes knew it was hopeless, he loved her. He could have continued to live with loving her from afar, but then the cursed prince showed up. Now she practically salivated each time she saw him. The hurt produced within Sikes was a persistent ache that wouldn't go away.

Sikes tapped his lips as he watched Maggie and Tal disappear from sight. *She's got something planned.* He didn't know what, but there was one sure way to find out. He ran deeper into the alley to retrieve his horse. They galloped out onto the road and toward the nearest gate. It would take him longer to get to the Marauder training site, but his horse was a strong mount.

He would get there soon enough.

***

The day was clear and cloudless, and Tal had no trouble following Maggie's horse. Soon, a large estate in the middle of a clearing appeared below. The manor was a crescent-shaped structure with servants quarters, a barn, and a paddock behind it. Arranged outside the perimeter of the estate was a field which included an archery range and another corral. The overgrown nature of the area around the manor became evident as they drew nearer. Small trees, bushes, and brambles had overtaken grass in many areas.

A sizable courtyard fronted the manor, and Maggie circled

once before landing onto its gravel surface. With a final beat of wings, Tal's horse settled beside hers. Curious, Tal studied the surroundings.

A brick and mortar wall encircled the entire estate. Rusty spikes the height of a man were embedded in the top of the wall and spaced at intervals. The gravel drive circled the estate and led from an opening in the brick partition. The heavy iron gate that once guarded the entry into the courtyard, lay rusting on the ground. Grand flowerbeds, now weed-choked, filled the courtyard.

Tal turned his attention to the manor. One glance told him it was sturdily built, and no expense had been spared in its construction. Two stories in height, a pair of turrets rose from each corner to tower over the courtyard. Windows lined the façade of the first floor. At one time, they must have allowed abundant sunlight to stream in. Now, however, they were all boarded over. A single oaken door led inside. Broad and tall, its surface was carved with intricate scenes of birds and other woodland creatures.

"I thought you said the Marauders trained here?" he said. "I don't see any evidence of that."

Maggie shrugged. "The training ground and equipment are outside the walls. We use this place as a muster site for recruits before we start their training. We'll go there after I show you the inside."

Maggie gestured to Tal, and they walked up crumbling stone steps to the portico. She took a large brass key from her pocket, unlocked the door, and they walked in.

Once Tal's eyes adjusted to the dim interior, he saw a thick layer of dust everywhere. Furniture, much of it overturned, lay on the floor also coated in dust. A grand staircase led to the second floor. Maggie caught Tal by the hand and led him up the steps. They traveled a short distance and stopped before a closed door.

She opened it and they went in.

Maggie led Tal to the middle of the room and stopped.

She could tell he was puzzled. Unlike the rest of the manor, she had made sure this room was free of dust and neglect. She had also carefully arranged the room's contents. A large, canopied bed lay against the back wall, and the floor was thickly carpeted with rugs. A table sat not far from the bed and was flanked by a pair of chairs. A large bottle of wine and two goblets and rested on its surface. Maggie walked over to the table and motioned for Tal to sit.

"This was my parents' bedroom," she explained. "As a small child, I used to play here. I don't have many fond memories, but the few I have are found here." Wistful, she waved her arm. "So, I try to keep it as I remember. That's why it's in better condition than the rest of the manor."

Tal nodded. "I understand."

"I've never invited anyone here before, not even my Marauders." A nervous laugh escaped Maggie. "Do you mind sharing a drink with me?"

Tal didn't answer immediately. Wild thoughts galloped through her mind. *He's suspicious. What if he refuses to—*

"Of course," he said.

Maggie quickly turned away before Tal could see the relief on her face. She pulled the cork from the bottle and poured the wine. Her back to Tal, she palmed the vial and added six drops to his goblet. When she handed him the wine, he wore a strange look. Again, her worst fears gripped her.

He must have seen me!

"Are you well?" Tal asked. "You seem on edge."

"No, no, everything is fine," Maggie quickly assured him. She poured wine into her own goblet, hoping he didn't notice the jittery shake of her hands.

Maggie lifted her cup. "A toast! To a better future." She gulped the wine down without tasting it. Her heart beat faster as Tal raised the cup to his lips...then swallowed. Hurriedly, she refilled their goblets, and they drank again.

Tal studied his cup. "Of what vintage is this wine? It has an odd aftertaste."

Maggie raised an eyebrow. "Oh? I taste nothing amiss. Here, let me pour you some more. This time drink it slowly and savor the palate." Tal nodded and held his goblet out to Maggie. She filled it and watched as Tal slowly sipped the wine.

Tal smacked his lips. "*Hmm*. You're right. I can't detect an aftertaste now." He placed the goblet on the table and stood. "Now, can you show me your training facilities?" He swayed and placed a hand on the chair to catch himself.

Tal chuckled. "I think I've had enough wine. It's gone straight to my head." He loosened the buttons on his tunic. "When did this room become so insufferably hot?"

His breath began to come in quick gasps. "My blood feels like it's on fire. It roars in my ears."

Tal picked at his tunic. Impatient, he gripped the fabric and stripped it off. Maggie stared at his ribbed muscles, desire rising within her. She tugged at her own clothing, and soon stood naked. Tal growled, fevered eyes traveling from her curved hips and flat abdomen to her full breasts.

With a roar, he sprang toward her.

Sikes left his horse hidden outside the estate walls.

He spied the two flying horses in the courtyard and nodded.

They're still here. He darted to the manor's front door, cracked it open, and peered inside. He detected no movement, so he cracked the door wider and slipped inside. Puzzled, he looked around. *Where are they?*

Then he heard it. Floorboards creaking, the scrape of furniture, and odd cries from the second floor. He hurried up the stairway following the sounds. Soon he came to the source and stopped at the door. A cacophony of grunts and growls assaulted his ears. He turned the handle and edged the door open.

"No," he whispered. Naked, Maggie and the prince rolled back and forth on a bed, their bodies locked together. Bestial noises issued nonstop from the prince and were answered by Maggie's own groans and cries. Tears sprang into Sikes' eyes. His heart felt like it would explode.

He turned and fled down the stairs. He rushed out the door and sprinted for his horse. Leaping into the saddle, he galloped away, intent on putting as much distance between himself and the manor as possible.

But no matter how fast he went, he couldn't outrun the memory burned into his mind.

CHAPTER 48

NAKED, MAGGIE SAT ON THE EDGE OF THE BED. NEXT TO HER, TAL LAY unconscious.

She stared blankly at the floor. Her breasts were scratched, and her back bruised and chafed. When she stood on wobbly legs, a thin line of blood trickled from between her thighs. The physical pain, however, was a trifle compared to the wounds in her mind and heart. The potion had worked as the witch claimed it would.

All too well.

Tal had savagely joined with her over and over again with frightening and painful ferocity. There was no tenderness, no soft caress, no evidence of anything other than unslakable lust. After the first time, she tried to resist but Tal's strength was incredible. She couldn't stop him. Mercifully, he passed out after their last tryst. Whether it was from the effects of the potion wearing off or from his frenzied exertions, she didn't know or care.

A sob caught in Maggie's throat. Not once did Tal gaze at her with the adoration he held for Alex. Not once did he hold her with any semblance of gentle affection. But the most crushing blow of all—the one that cut the deepest—was that Tal viewed her as little more than a vessel to satisfy his raging desire. The witch's treachery and her own stupidity were clear. Magic, no matter how powerful, could ever create love. It couldn't be distilled, mixed up in a pot, and served like a favorite ale. Love could only come from the heart.

And Tal's heart belonged to Alexandria.

Maggie buried her face in her hands. Sobs racked her body,

tears streaming down her cheeks in a deluge. When she could take a breath without weeping, her bleary eyes found the vial of potion on the floor. In the haste to shed her clothes, it had fallen out of her pocket. With a shriek, she grabbed it and ran out of the room. She sprinted down the stairs, threw open the manor's door, and darted outside. Ignoring the pain of the sharp gravel on her bare feet, she hurled the vial to the ground. It shattered, the liquid seeping through the rocky grit and into the soil. Not satisfied, she looked left and right, searching. A branch as thick as her wrist lay nearby. She seized the limb with both hands and pounded the broken vial again and again.

Lifting her face to the sky, she screamed, *"No, no, no, no!"*

Chest heaving, she tossed the makeshift club away and slowly made her way back to the manor. There was one more task to complete.

Remove all evidence of her deceit.

Tal's eyes fluttered open and he attempted to sit up.

A headache so intense he almost retched, pounded within his skull. Moaning, he fell back. He took deep, even breaths, and the pain faded a bit. With great caution, he tried again. This time the pounding was only a dull ache. His blurry vision took in his surroundings and he discovered he was sitting on a bed.

How did I get here?

Tal shook his head to clear it. The last thing he remembered was having a drink with Maggie. After that…nothing. A bitter, metallic aftertaste filled his mouth, and he smelled wine. Examining himself, he discovered damp blotches of spilled wine on his clothing.

He carefully got to his feet. Fatigue weighed so heavily on him, he almost collapsed back onto the bed. Instead, he took a few tentative steps on shaky legs. As he did so, Maggie walked into the room.

"What happened to me?" he croaked.

She pointed at three empty bottles on the floor. "You can't hold your wine, that's what happened," she snapped. Gone was the warm and pleasant Maggie his foggy memory recalled from earlier. Now she was all steel.

Tal rubbed his forehead. Nothing made sense. He knew he wasn't much of a drinker, but he had never been *this* drunk.

"It's late and we need to head back. Can you ride?" Maggie asked tersely.

He nodded. "I think so."

He followed Maggie outside, the bright sunlight like daggers in his eyes. Staggering to his horse, he tried twice to mount before Maggie was forced to help him. When she swung up onto her own horse, a hiss of pain escaped from her lips as she settled into the saddle.

They flew back to Markingham in silence.

※

Alex stood patiently while the earl's sister, Patrice, made alterations to her marriage dress.

Patrice finished, took a step back, and ran a critical eye over her work. "It fits perfectly." Delighted, she clasped her hands to her chest. "You will be such a beautiful bride. I can't wait."

Alex examined herself in the oval mirror fixed to the wall. The dress of ivory silk, was floor-length with a train that ran several paces behind her. Delicate lace trimmed the sleeves and bodice, and a thin silver chain encircled her waist.

"Thank you, Patrice. You've been so kind, and the gown is stunning."

Patrice dismissed the comment with a wave of her hand. "I should be thanking you. Seeing you in my old dress brings back such fond memories. Besides, it's been so long since we've had a wedding, I'd forgotten how much fun they can be." Alex hugged her, and they both giggled.

Alex twirled. "What do you think, Pulpit?"

The monk stood near the balcony observing the process. "I would say Lady York's wizardry with a needle and thread is impressive…and that I agree. You will be a lovely bride."

Alex studied herself again in the mirror. "I hope Tal likes it." She turned away with a frown. "He hasn't been himself since he returned from the earl's old summer estate. Do you know what's wrong with him? He won't tell me anything other than he drank too much wine."

Pulpit shook his head. "I'm sorry, m'lady. The prince hasn't shared with me anything he hasn't already told you."

Alex released an exasperated sigh. "And now Tal has taken off to go who knows where? All he would say was that it was a surprise and he'd be gone a few days. Why must things be so complicated?"

The monk shrugged. "I imagine that many ask the same question. But such is life." He gazed out past the open balcony and broke into a chuckle. He motioned to her. "Why don't you ask the prince yourself."

Alex hesitated, then hurried to the balcony and looked out. In the sky, dark specks approached the keep. Soon they were close enough, she could see it was Tal and a detachment of flying cavalry. They had returned!

Alex pulled up her skirt and rushed for the door.

"M'lady!" Patrice's scandalized cry stopped her.

"You can't let Prince Tal see you in the marriage gown before the wedding!" She grasped Alex by the arm and pulled her back. "Let's change into another gown, then you can go to the prince."

Pulpit made his way out. "I'll wait for you downstairs."

Alex quickly slipped into a different dress. She rushed down the stairs and out into the courtyard. Tal's horse had just settled with folded wings on the cobblestones when she reached him. Impatient, she helped him off the saddle and hugged him.

"*Ooof.*" The breath left his lungs from the rib-cracking embrace. "You must have missed me," Tal coughed.

"More than you know." She pushed away and shook a finger at him. "I want to know where you've been the past the past three days."

"I told you—"

"I know, I know, it's a surprise." Hands on hips, Alex shook her head. "But you've been acting oddly, and I want to know what's going on."

Tal reached out and took her hands in his. "I've been preparing a gift to surprise you with on our marriage day. Now you know my secret."

Alex cocked an eye at Tal. "And that's it? There's not something else bothering you?"

Tal groaned. "No! I admit I've been a bit weary of late, but I feel much better now." A hungry glint appeared in his eye. "In fact, I think we're due for some catching up." He led her into the keep, and they headed for his room. A happy glow warmed Alex's heart.

My old Tal is back.

CHAPTER 49

MAGGIE WATCHED THE RIDER APPROACH.

She sat in the soft grass on the same hill where she had killed the wyvern and led the charge against the Baleful. Hanley grazed nearby while birds chirped in the trees. No clouds marred the azure sky, and a warm breeze caressed her face. All was right. All was peaceful.

Or should be.

Maggie's days were anything but peaceful. Guilt, regret, and shame had turned them dismal and gray. In the two months since luring Tal to the old manor, she had been unable to capture even a single night of untroubled sleep. Despite efforts to distract her thoughts by drinking, hunting, and training till near collapse, nothing worked. The stain on her soul wouldn't go away.

And just when she thought things couldn't get any worse, her life took another cruel twist.

In the preceding months, she had twice missed her maiden's blood. This was followed by tender breasts and a general feeling of lethargy—all clear signs that could mean only one thing. Her hand crept to her belly.

I'm pregnant.

A harsh laugh escaped her lips. *Hmm. I wonder who the father is?* This time the laughter that rushed from her rolled on and on until she was left breathless.

She wiped the mirthless tears from her eyes. Tal could never know he was the cause of her pregnancy. What would she say? *Oh,*

I hope you don't mind, but since arriving at Markingham, you've raised such desire within me, I struck a bargain with a child-killing witch. In return for her life, she made a potion for me. You drank it, she escaped, and now I'm pregnant. That's worth a few jokes over ale at the tavern, don't you think?

With a growl, she ripped the dagger from her belt and stabbed it into the soft loam. The blackest moment of her life was the day she made the bargain with Drusulla. She should have killed the witch. Instead, her foolishness had left her dangling like a fly, trapped in a web of her own making.

The drum of hooves drew her from her thoughts. The rider was close enough she recognized him immediately.

Bradley.

He stopped and dismounted, his horse joining Maggie's to browse on the rich grass. "You're a hard one to catch up to. Thought you might like some company."

"If I wanted someone to talk to, I would've stayed in Markingham," Maggie scoffed.

Sikes shrugged and sat beside her. "You've been like a ghost the past couple of months. You flit here and there, don't talk much, and you stay to yourself. What's going on?"

"Go to hell."

"C'mon, Maggie!" Bradley blurted. "We all miss you. The Marauders need their leader back."

A bitter chuckle left Maggie. "You don't get it, do you?"

"What?"

"We've been replaced. The empire is in charge now, and we're not needed. Within another month or two, those Marauders who haven't already enlisted with the imperial army will take up a different life. Maybe they'll become farmers, blacksmiths, who the hell knows?"

"Well, I'm sticking with you!" Sikes vowed.

Maggie stood and brushed off the grass and dirt. "It's no good,

Bradley. When winter comes, I'm moving out of the tavern and to my family's country estate. I just want to be left alone."

Sikes leapt to his feet. "This is all the prince's fault!" He clenched his fists. "If it wasn't for him, you wouldn't be doing any of this."

Maggie studied Sikes' angry face. "I don't know what you know or think you know, but Tal risked his life for you, me, and everyone in Markingham. He is—"

Overcome with emotion, her breath caught in her throat.

"He is the bravest, most honorable man I have ever known," she managed to finish.

"Bullshit! I saw you. I saw what he did to you!" Sikes cried.

"What?" Maggie grabbed his tunic. "Talk! What did you see?" She shook him when he was slow to answer.

His teeth rattled from Maggie's angry shaking, and the words flew from Sikes' lips. "I—I followed you to the old manor. I heard noises and went upstairs. When I opened the door, I saw you and Prince Tal. You were both together and, and..."

His voice trailed off, unable to continue.

Maggie whipped out her knife and held it at Sikes' throat. "If you say a word of this to anyone, I swear I'll kill you."

Sikes, paralyzed with fear, could only nod.

Maggie shoved him away. "Get out of here before I change my mind and kill you anyway."

Sikes moved to retrieve his horse. He paused and looked back, pleading. "Please, Maggie. I love you. I always have. Take me with you when you decide to leave Markingham."

Maggie turned so Bradley couldn't see the tears that suddenly sprang to her eyes. "Go. Leave now," she rasped. Reluctantly, Sikes put his foot in the stirrup and swung into the saddle.

Maggie watched him ride away. "Don't waste your time on me, Bradley," she whispered.

"I don't deserve anyone's love."

Alex looked out the balcony windows at the courtyard below.

A large pavilion had been erected and chairs occupied every available space. The seats—

arranged into two halves with a passageway down the middle—were already filled with guests. A thick, red carpet covered in red and white flower petals, had been laid through this path, and led to an arch. The arch, decorated with gold bunting and colorful lodestones, sat on a platform within the pavilion where Pulpit would officiate the marriage ceremony. A communication ring was in place on the platform to allow the queen to view the ceremony. Compared to the splendor and spectacle if their royal marriage had occurred at Lodestone Castle, their ceremony would be rather ordinary. But not to Alex. Nothing about this day would ever be ordinary.

Goosebumps covered her skin. *It's happening. It's really happening. I'm going to marry Tal.*

He stood at the base of the rotunda dressed in the royal colors of the Meredithian monarchy. An embroidered red cape rested on his shoulders. A blue tunic with gold braid covered his broad chest, and his breeches disappeared into gleaming, knee-high black boots. A thin crown of gold rested on his head. Encrusted with precious gems, the golden circlet held Tal's thick, long hair away from his face.

Alex closed her eyes and sighed. *In less than an hour, we'll be wed.*

She thought this day would never arrive. She would have happily married Tal in a barn if it sped things along, but Queen Celestria insisted that certain protocols be met. These included the ceremonial crowns and the exchange of marriage bracelets crafted by the royal jeweler. They had to be transported through the breach in the Veil to Markingham, a long and arduous process. When at last these items arrived, the date of their marriage was set.

And now was here.

Earl York would stand as witness in place of her father, the Duke of Wheel, while Bozar would do the same for Tal. A knock came at the door.

"Enter."

The earl stood at the threshold, a broad smile on his face. "Are you ready, Lady Alexandria?"

Alex beamed. "Yes."

He offered his arm, and Alex eagerly took it. Together they made the trip down the stairs and out to the courtyard. The audience was small, a select group of men and women from Markingham, and officers from the army. But what they lacked in numbers, they more than made up for with enthusiastic cheers and applause. The ovation followed Tal and Alex down the carpeted path, through the pavilion, and at last, to the platform.

Pulpit, resplendent in his formal white robes, raised his arms for silence. He asked, "Who presents the Lady Alexandria Duvalier?"

"I, Bartholomew York, the Earl of Markingham, do." With that, he took Alex by the arm, and they stepped up under the wedding arch. He then retreated several steps behind her.

"Who presents Prince Talmund Edward Meredith?"

"I, First Advisor Bozar Ali Shaheem, do." With a broad smile, Bozar guided Tal to his place beside Alex. Tal took her hand in his. The formal presentation of the betrothed couple now complete, Pulpit began.

"We are gathered before the Creator to join…"

Unable to take her eyes off Tal, Alex barely heard Pulpit, and his words faded into the background. Happiness filled her heart with such fullness, she thought it might burst. When Tal nudged her, she forced her attention to a small boy approaching them. Brighton carried a satin pillow with two objects resting on top. The little boy bore the marriage bracelets, his small hands balancing the cushion upon which they rested.

When Brighton reached them, Tal took one and turned to face her. "If I could have but one wish, it would be to describe the breadth and depth of the love I hold for you. But words fail me, because no matter how eloquently I could craft them, they would still be inadequate. So instead, I say to you before every witness of this ceremony that I will always, now and forever, love you." He placed the bracelet on her left wrist. Chased in silver and gold, the metal band moved like a living thing. Flowing like water, it encircled her wrist to form a perfect fit.

Alex took the remaining bracelet. She couldn't help herself and reached up to stroke Tal's cheek. "I have loved you since the moment I awoke in the enchanted cabin and first saw you. Every day since my love has grown and in ways I never thought possible. You are an inseparable part of me, Talmund Edward Meredith, now and forever."

She placed her bracelet on Tal's wrist and the band morphed to snugly fit around his flesh.

"Come forward," Pulpit ordered. Alex and Tal took a step and knelt. The monk placed a crown on Alex's head, a twin to the one Tal wore. With a broad smile, he helped them up and turned them to face the assemblage.

"By the authority given me by the Creator and the Empire of Meredith, I present Prince Talmund and Princess Alexandria. May the Creator keep and bless them."

Wild cheers shook the pavilion.

Celestria stood, her gown a shimmering blue, the bejeweled crown of an imperial monarch on her head. She held a scepter whose length matched her own height. A sapphire the size of a large egg was mounted on the scepter's tip. The ovation died away. All eyes riveted on her image displayed within the communication ring.

Boom, boom. Celestria pounded the base of the scepter onto the marble floor of the palace. "Hail to my son, Prince Talmund,

Heir to the Imperial throne, and to my new daughter, Princess Alexandria. All hail!"

Behind the Queen, her advisors cried, "Long live Prince Talmund and Princess Alexandria!" They were joined by the marriage audience whose shouts added to the tumultuous ovation.

Tal reached for Alex and they kissed. The act caused the enthusiastic cries to rise to an even higher pitch. Arms around each other's waist, they walked down the carpeted path.

Alex's breath caught in her throat as she saw the enchanted carriage and team of flying horses waiting for them. The coachman sat atop, their baggage stored behind him. Tal helped her into the coach and slid in beside her. With a snap of reins, the coachman got the carriage moving. A short time later, a slight bump indicated the carriage had become airborne.

Curious, Alex asked, "Where are we going?"

Tal chuckled. "To my wedding gift." He stretched his long legs, then put his arm around her shoulders. "Get comfortable.

"It's going to be a long trip.

CHAPTER 50

ALEX AND TAL TRAVELED SOUTH FOR MOST OF THE REST OF THE DAY. A score of flying legionnaires escorted the enchanted carriage, and easily kept pace with the magical coach. Alex and Tal busied themselves kissing, cuddling, and talking. From time-to-time, Alex parted the curtains in the coach to observe the landscape below. It was a sea of endless green, a wilderness that spread unrelieved into the horizon.

After hours of nonstop travel, impatience began to creep into Alex. "Are we ever going to get there? Wherever *there* is?"

Tal laughed, his mirth an infectious vibrancy that caused Alec to smile despite her exasperation. He slipped an arm around her shoulder. "I told you we have a great distance to travel, but I promise, you will not be disappointed."

Alex moved into Tal's lap. "Then I guess I must amuse myself in other ways until then."

"M'lady, I am your humble servant," Tal said. "Whatever you need of me, you have but to ask."

Alex giggled, and he laid her down on the soft cushioned seat. His mouth tracked a course from her lips to the sensitive nape of her neck. From there his kiss traveled to the deep cleft of her breasts. Wherever he touched produced a fevered heat, and her gasps echoed within the small confines of the coach. Impatient, Tal tugged on her dress to loosen her bodice. When the undergarment refused to cooperate, he redoubled his efforts. Alex groaned and forced herself to push him away. Breathing hard, she sat up.

"Stop. You're going to rip my gown."

"I'll have another commissioned for you." Tal gripped the fabric again.

Alex kissed him, then firmly removed his hands. "I was married in this dress, and I don't want another one."

He flashed a lascivious grin. "Fortunately, it's only cloth. The real treasure is underneath."

Alex laughed and scooted away. "You may claim your prize *after* we reach our destination. I don't—"

She blinked. Through the gap in the curtain, a line of dark shapes appeared like jagged teeth in the horizon. She pushed the curtain open wider for a better look. Snow-capped peaks appeared.

"Mountains," Alex breathed.

Tal joined Alex and peered out. "The Sherrington Range. The steppes and the Sea of Sand begin at their southern slope and stretch to the Ocean of Dreams."

Alex tilted her head. "Why are we going there?"

Tal sat back. "You remember the enchanted cabin where you recovered from the scorpion dog's sting?"

She nodded. "How could I ever forget?"

"The magic infused in the cottage was ancient but still potent. I learned from the earl that the fabled kings and queens of old had built a royal retreat called Eagle's Croft in the Sherrington's. I hoped, like the cabin, the magic of Eagle's Croft might have survived the passage of years as well. So, I traveled there to see for myself. That's where I'd been and why I couldn't tell you. I wanted to surprise you."

Excited, Alex gripped Tal's arm. "Well? Does the magic still exist?"

Tal grinned. "It does."

Alex clapped. "Is it grand as what you thought it would be?"

"Beyond my wildest dreams. But I don't want to describe it to you. You need to see for yourself."

From that point on, Alex found her attention glued to the carriage's windows. The mountains grew in size and detail. The forested slopes became steeper and transitioned from hardwoods to evergreens. Sunlight glinted off snow clinging to high, rocky peaks. Rushing rivers roared down boulder-filled gorges, and summits thrust stony fingers skyward. Updrafts rocked the carriage, and forced Alex to sit back and hang on to Tal.

After another hour of travel, the carriage circled a flat, rocky escarpment. The promontory jutted outward, the cliff facing dropping precipitously to a ravine below. Clumps of pine grew like tufts of hair in the scree and thin soil, their roots relentlessly seeking purchase in the unyielding rock. A swift stream ran down the mountain, the water so clear the rounded stones of the streambed were visible. Small waterfalls formed deep pools before transitioning to boiling rapids.

By the time the carriage landed on the flat ledge, the sun was low on the horizon, and long shadows covered the area. Tal climbed out of the coach, retrieved their baggage, then helped Alex out. He signaled the coachman and the carriage joined their escort circling above. They flew over a ridge and disappeared.

Puzzled, Alex asked, "Where are they going? Back to Markingham?"

Tal shook his head. "No. The only way Bozar would allow us to travel here is with an armed escort. There are servants' quarters and stables just over the ridge. I don't expect trouble, but if need arises, they can be here at a moment's notice."

He put his arms around Alex and drew her close. "So, it will be just the two of us."

Alex looked around. "That's nice, but, uh, there's nothing here. We're standing on a cliff."

Tal laughed, grabbed her hand, and led her to a part of the ridge that looked no different than the rest of the ledge. His eyes glowed blue as he drew magic. He placed his hands palms down, and the air shimmered with pulses of magic. Alex yelped and jumped back when a section of rock rumbled aside to reveal a flight of steps descending deep into the bowels of the mountain. Tal swept Alex up into his arms, and carried her down the passage. Brackets holding light crystals were mounted every twenty paces. They blazed to life to light their way.

They came to a large chamber carved from the mountain's living rock. Light crystals fixed to the stone ceiling flickered on. Arranged strategically throughout the spacious room were couches, tables, and chairs. Paintings hung from the wall and sculptures decorated tables. A curved, smooth wall encompassed the entire area.

The amazing sight astonished Alex. She placed her hand Tal's chest. "Oh, Tal. This is so wonderful."

"Watch this." Tal put Alex down and walked up to a section of the wall. He placed his hand on it. Once again, magic flowed from him. The rock facing clouded—then became transparent as glass.

Alex gasped in surprise at the panoramic view. She could see everything, mountain slopes, the valley floor, the stream, even the sky. She ran her hand over the translucent stone. The surface was hard and abrasive, evidence it was hewn from mountain rock, yet she could see right through it.

Tal chuckled at her reaction. "Magic made this section of solid rock clear and colorless as the air. The enchantments creating Eagle's Croft were powerful indeed."

Mesmerized, Alex stared until Tal called to her. "Let me show you our bedroom." He led her up a short flight of stone steps. They entered another room, and light crystals winked on.

The illumination revealed thick rugs on the floor and a large four-poster bed. Fluffy pillows occupied the front of the bedstead, and a thick quilt, embroidered with beautiful scenes of forest and mountain, was spread atop the bed. A table paired with richly upholstered chairs filled one corner, a plush couch with thick cushions in another. A walk-in closet larger than her room at the keep completed the picture.

An open doorway led to another chamber. When Alex investigated, she discovered a privy of epic size. The bath was so large she would have to step down into it, much like a swimming pool. Gilded fixtures jutted from the tub's edge, and a vanity of rose-colored marble sat beside the bath. A mirror with precious gems inset into the frame was mounted above the vanity.

Alex finished her inspection and returned to the bedroom. She sat on the bed and ran her hand over the quilt, marveling at the feel of the rich fabric. She inspected her fingertips, then shook her head.

Not a speck of dust.

"How long has Eagle's Croft been empty?" she asked.

He sat beside her. "Since the formation of the accursed Veil a thousand years ago."

"Everything is so clean and perfectly preserved…like it was only yesterday a royal king or queen was here."

Tal nodded. "The magic hasn't faded."

They retrieved their baggage and arranged their belongings in the room-sized closet. Tal had already restocked the pantry, so all they brought with them was clothing.

Tracing her steps back to the large common room, Alex discovered a long couch alongside the transparent wall. Carved from solid rock, its seat and backrest was furnished with plush cushions. Alex sat on it and watched the setting sun, a beautiful palate of reddish-gold color. High in the air, an eagle soared, while below, the stream's rushing water glinted in the dying light.

Tal came up behind her and placed his hands on her shoulders. "Do you like my marriage gift?"

Alex squeezed his hand. "It's so beautiful and so perfect."

She stood and walked around the bench. Hugging Tal, she said, "I never thought you could top the ride in the enchanted carriage, but you did." She placed her arms around Tal's neck and stood on her toes to kiss him.

"I wonder…"

Tal frowned. *"Hmm?* What do you wonder?"

Alex pulled him closer.

"What should we do now?"

CHAPTER 51

A LEX LAY NEXT TO TAL, UNABLE TO SLEEP.

She replayed every moment of their first night together, unwilling to let even a single moment slip from her memory.

They had eaten a cold supper of cheese, ham, and bread, then sat together on the observation couch with glasses of wine. There they watched the day turn into night. They talked very little, content to just be with each other. With Tal's arm around her and her head nestled against his shoulder, she felt a peace that had eluded her for most of her twenty years of life. Hours passed, and they were deep into the night before they finally stirred and retreated to their bedroom.

She smiled at their first bout of lovemaking. It didn't turn out the way either of them expected. Despite their previous near-misses—breathless experiences filled with scorching, spontaneous passion—their intimacy was awkward. Lacking spontaneity, they overthought everything, like planning the next move on a chessboard.

The second time was completely different.

After sleeping a bit, Alex rolled over and began kissing Tal. What followed was wild, frenetic lovemaking, every inhibition from their first time gone. Alex's body responded to Tal as if all the nerve cells in her body had been laid bare. By the time they finished, she was so exhausted she couldn't move. Her heart hammered, her breath a series of explosive wheezes, and her limbs limp as if boneless. Even Tal lay unmoving, as drained as she was. She didn't think they could possibly make love again any time soon.

But she was wrong.

After several hours of sleep, she awoke to Tal running his fingers up and down her bare flesh. That was all it took to reignite her passion. This time, however, they were unhurried, their passion leisurely. They explored each other with slow caresses, long kisses, and soft embraces. With Tal's warm weight against her, she felt so close to him, it was like they occupied the same body. Her focus so fiercely on him, she lost track of time. The experience was, well…*magical*.

And then it happened.

A *click* in her mind heralded the unlocking of her power. However, it didn't rush out in a mad explosion. Instead, it flowed from her in a calm, unhurried fashion. Her eyes rolled back into her head, but she never lost consciousness or her vision. If anything, her senses became enhanced. Her magical sight displayed her power as smokey tendrils that moved and undulated. Fingerlike, they seeped from her pores to and traveled over Tal. She could measure every beat of his heart, every breath he took. Her magic made everything about Tal quantifiable, every physical attribute and emotion.

This is what pure, untainted love looks like.

She could feel his love for her. Like an endless sea, it was unfathomable in width and depth, a match for her love for him. The power continued to pour from her, and a soft aura of light enveloped them. It lifted their intertwined bodies, and they floated. Tal never reacted or gave any sign he was aware of what was happening. At last, passions spent, they drifted back onto the bed.

Tal fell asleep immediately, but Alex remained awake ever since.

She turned and kissed his bare shoulder, then caressed his broad back, her fingertips tingling from his warm flesh. A few scars marred the smooth perfection of his skin, evidence of the violence of war so much a part of Tal's life. It saddened her to think of how little happiness he had experienced, and she vowed to do all she could to return joy to his life.

He murmured, rolled over, and draped a muscular arm over her. Soon, his breath returned to the regular cadence of sleep. Alex took his large hand and intertwined his fingers with her own. He never ceased to amaze her. She had seen him battle werewolves, night walkers, and a giant centaur. Yet despite his astonishing strength, when he touched her, he always did so with a tender gentleness. That a man of such stark contrasts could manage such a feat made her love him all the more.

Restless, she gently disengaged Tal's arm and slid out from under the sheets. She padded to the end of the bed and put on her robe. Then she moved to stand beside Tal. She didn't worry about disturbing him. She knew he slept like a cat and would notice the moment she got out of bed. Had there been anything wrong, he would have already been on his feet, reaching for a weapon.

A stray lock of hair fell across his face, and she brushed it away. In the dim light, he looked so young, his face a picture of serenity. She leaned down and kissed him, then made her way to the observation couch. Pulling her robe tight, she sat.

The triple moons, crescent slivers of light, cast a weak glow. The stars at this high altitude and thin air were brilliant. Scattered in their innumerable millions and billions, it looked like a giant had taken a fistful of faerie dust and hurled it in all directions. Below the night sky, the mountainous ridges and slopes were gray shadows, the trees tall silhouettes.

Beautiful. It was all so beautiful.

She was tempted to reflect on her journey from scared, bullied Mona Parker, to her new life as Alexandria and where it had taken her. But she decided it didn't matter. She would do it all a hundred, no, a million times, again. She could live a thousand lifetimes and never find the kind of love she shared with Tal.

Alex chuckled. All along, she had harbored simmering anger

at Thaddeus Finkle, her guardian angel, for deceiving her. Yet if he appeared to her now, this very second, she would thank him over and over again for making her the luckiest woman on two worlds.

A nagging guilt nibbled at her thoughts. She couldn't keep her secret from Tal forever. One day, she would have to tell him she started her life as Mona Parker of earth, a skinny, plain-featured, and suicidal teenager. But not tonight...and probably not for many nights to come.

She sighed and ran her hands over her lower abdomen. A pleasant ache lingered from muscles long unused, and thoughts of her former life immediately faded.

A pair of hands slid onto her shoulders. Startled, Alex jumped.

"The bed grows cold without you."

She recovered and stroked Tal's arms. Another of his catlike qualities was the ability to move silently. "Have you missed me already?" she teased.

She squealed as he picked her up and cradled her. "I'll let you decide." He carried her back to the bedroom.

Alex quickly discovered he *did* miss her.

A lot.

***

Alex and Tal stood on the escarpment, their baggage gathered about their feet. High above, the carriage circled lower in preparation to land.

The week had passed all too quickly. A tear slid down Alex's cheek at the realization their wedding trip was at an end. It was time to return to Markingham.

Tal, sensing her sadness, pulled her closer. "There will be other opportunities to return here."

She patted his arm. "I know. It was such fun, just the two of us...."

Alex's voice trailed off. Unspoken was her uncertainty of when a return would be possible. The coming war against the Veil Queen and King loomed, a promise of more violence and death. Their week at Eagle's Croft—like a quiet eddy in a swift river—was a respite from events that were coming whether she liked it or not. In the meantime, she would have to make do with her memories. But that didn't mean she intended to stand idly by and look demure and pretty. Tal and the other members of his inner circle were in for a shock.

She planned to be a princess in more than name only.

Alex knew she could never be a warrioress like Maggie, an expert in sword and spear. But she had something far more powerful—Tal's love. And she would wield that as her weapon of choice whenever and wherever needed. Mercy and compassion were always the first to disappear in war, and she would not allow Tal to lose this essential part of himself. Nor would she permit him to make reckless decisions like charging into battle against overwhelming odds. Whether he realized it or not, those days were over. He *would* listen to her.

The last thing she determined to do was to develop control over her magic. She thought that impossible, but her wedding night changed everything. For the first time, the power didn't burst from her in an uncontrolled eruption. Instead, it flowed from her steadily, and she didn't lose consciousness. That meant there must be a means to harness and control it. Making love to Tal to trigger the release of her power, while appealing, was impractical. There had to be another way.

The carriage landed and brought her musings to an end. Tal helped her into the coach, then slid in beside her. A short time later, they left the ground and flew north. Alex pushed the curtain aside and watched Eagle's Croft grow smaller and smaller.

She watched until it disappeared.

CHAPTER 52

THUNK.

The impact of the arrow in the straw-stuffed target dislodged a drift of snow. It fell from the human-shaped dummy to join the carpet of white below. Maggie chose another arrow. Careful to hold the bowstring a safe distance from her protruding belly, she released the shaft.

Thunk. The missile struck the crude outline of a heart sewn onto the mannequin. *A perfect hit.*

She released a sigh of satisfaction, her breath a billow of white in the crisp, cold air. She drew her thick woolen coat tighter and absently rubbed her swollen stomach. At least her pregnancy hadn't affected her aim. At seven months now, even the heavy coat couldn't completely hide her advanced pregnancy.

Maggie slogged through the snow to a tall metal basket. It held a variety of javelins. She selected one, hefted it, then turned and trudged to face another target. The crude mannequin wore patches sewn on all the vital areas: head, heart, groin, and neck. She moved twenty paces back, held the javelin balanced in her right hand, then took a quick step and hurled it. The spear flew true, and the stuffed figure shook, its straw chest impaled.

This time, Maggie frowned. A mortal hit, but she had been aiming for the neck, not the chest. Angrily, she spun and stalked away from the Marauder training site. As far as she was concerned, her throw, although a near miss, was evidence her skills were finally being affected by her gravid condition. *I've stayed as long as*

I can. It was time to travel to the abandoned farmstead at Travers Crossing—while she still could.

It started to snow, a few fat flakes at first, then a swirling curtain of white. She lifted her face to the gray sky, the snowflakes brushing against her skin like the whisper of butterfly wings. Maggie liked snow. It softened everything, blurred sharp edges, and transformed the landscape into a quiet peacefulness. With a sigh, she started for the manor.

While she walked, her mind returned to the day five months earlier when Tal and Alex returned from their wedding trip. Maggie had been retrieving the last of her belongings from the keep, when the carriage landed and the happy couple exited. Although Maggie tried to get out before they saw her, she ran right into Alex at the foot of the staircase. Alexandria fairly glowed with contentment.

Black jealousy filled Maggie with such intensity, she had to force her hands to stay at her side lest she wrap them around Alex's throat. With a brusque nod, she flew out the door—only to collide headlong into Tal. He tried to help her up, but she shoved his hands off and ran for Hanley. Fortunately, she was winging away before he could see her burst into tears. She hadn't been back to Markingham since.

Shaking her head to be rid of the unwanted memory, she stopped at the sight of a familiar form waiting outside the manor.

Bradley.

A bulging canvas bag lay at his feet. He lifted a hand to greet her, then dropped it when she swept right by him. After a moment's hesitation, he picked up the sack and followed her through the door.

"Maggie, stop!" he cried after her. "I brought the stuff you wanted."

"Just leave it. I'll get it later," she snapped without breaking stride.

"Wait, dammit! I ride all the way here from Markingham in the snow and muck, and all you can say is *leave it?*"

Maggie stopped and slowly turned. "I'm...sorry. Thank you for bringing me the things I asked for."

"Your wel—"

He froze, staring at her.

Maggie looked down and her heart sank. Her heavy coat had fallen open to reveal her swollen belly.

"You—you're pregnant!" he cried.

She nodded.

"No. You can't be!"

A harsh laugh escaped Maggie. "You mean you don't know how these things happen? Who would've thought your Marauder training would be so deficient?"

Sikes' face turned red. "I mean, I just can't believe it."

"I keep telling myself the same thing every day, but this damn bump keeps getting bigger."

Flustered, Sikes looked away. His eyes widened at the sight of a table laden with saddle tack and a mound of neatly organized supplies.

"You going on a trip?"

"That's none of your business."

Sikes looked at the canvas bag in his hand then back at the table. His shoulders slumped. "You're leaving, aren't you?" he asked in a small voice.

Maggie sighed. Bradley, although often a pain in the ass, had always been her most loyal follower. He deserved better than her barbed quips and sarcasm. She approached him and grasped his arm.

"Yes. I can't stay. I've done some evil things, Bradley, things I have to pay for."

"You mean the issue with the prince? Are you worried what people will think?" He dropped the supplies. "We can say I'm the father. No one will ever know otherwise."

Maggie snorted. "Do you really think I give a shit what anybody in that city thinks?" She shook her head. "No, I just can't face, Tal.

"But he doesn't need to know either."

"Don't you get it? *I'll know!* This baby is evidence of my deceit, my shame. Every time I see Tal, it will feel like the scab has been ripped off and force me to relive what I've done. I just can't do it. I'll fall to pieces." Her voice fell to a whisper. "It's the only way I can keep what little shred of self-respect I have left."

Sikes clenched his fists. "The bastard, that puffed up hypocrite! It's all his fault."

Maggie grabbed his coat a shook him. "How many times do I have to tell you it was me! I lied to Tal, I led him to this place, I tricked him into taking the witch's potion! He never knew, and still doesn't know what happened."

"Then I'll go with you. You'll need help—"

"No!"

Silence fell between them relieved only by Bradley's ragged breathing. Frustrated, he stalked to the supply-laden table and collapsed in a chair. "Where will you go? Don't you think I at least deserve to know that?"

Maggie threw up her arms, then reluctantly joined Sikes at the table. "Alright, if you must know, its Travers Crossing. There's a farmstead there that's still in pretty good condition."

Sikes cleared his throat. "Will—will you ever be coming back?"

Maggie shook her head. "I don't know. Maybe, maybe not."

"You have to let me come with you." Desperation dripped from his voice. "I love you, and I—I don't know if I can live without you."

Maggie moved to stand beside Bradley. Although awkward with her protruding belly, she hugged him. He clung to her like a drowning man.

"I'm sorry. I have to do this."

"Yes, but…" Sikes began, then fell forward, unconscious.

Maggie caught him and gently lowered him onto the tabletop.

She examined the back of his head where she struck him with the butt of her dagger. A raised lump had already formed, but other than a headache, he should be none the worse when he regained consciousness.

She kissed him on the cheek and smoothed his hair. "It's for the best, Bradley," she whispered. "For both of us."

An hour later, she had Hanley saddled and ready. It would take several days to reach Travers Crossing, and although Hanley was a strong flyer, she was taking only the most essential provisions. She couldn't take a chance of overloading the flying horse.

Maggie mounted Hanley and took one last look around. She stroked her belly. "It's just you and me now."

With a nudge of her heels, Hanley broke into a trot. He spread his wings, and they soared into the snow-spackled sky.

CHAPTER 53

MAGGIE WADDLED FROM THE BARN TO THE FARMHOUSE. She carried a brace of rabbits she snared, and a bag of mushrooms she had discovered in a dank corner of the barn. She planned on adding the hares' meat and mushrooms to the stew already simmering over the hearth. She had collected winter nettles and wild tubers, and once salt was added, should make for a hot, savory meal.

Hanley lifted his head from grazing and snorted at her. She smiled at the flying horse, her lone companion since arriving a few months earlier at the abandoned farmstead. The only problem he'd given her was his steadfast refusal to enter the barn, even during winter storms. The lingering scent of the night walkers' lair spooked him.

The house was remarkably preserved, and she needed to make only minor repairs to the doors and windows. The roof, miraculously, didn't leak. That left her with more free time to gather food. As a Marauder, she had learned early how to hunt and use the forest as her larder. The only necessities she brought with her from Markingham were those she knew would be hard to find in the wilds. This included seasonings like salt.

Maggie paused abruptly in mid-step at the sensation of warm liquid running down her leg and into her boot. She dropped the rabbits and mushrooms, then scrabbled at her skirt and ripped the hem up. She stared in shock. Her wet thighs glistened in the morning light.

My water has broken.

Maggie rushed for the farmhouse as fast as her ungainly condition would allow. She reached the porch when the first contraction occurred. Although brief in duration, the birth pangs still forced her to stop. They passed and she managed to continue. Throwing open the door, she hurried into the kitchen.

Another of her pleasant discoveries was the well pump in the kitchen. Once primed, it still functioned. She pumped the handle furiously, and water gushed out into a bucket. Before it could be filled, another contraction gripped her. She groaned and slid to the floor. It faded and she pushed herself back to her feet. Breathing hard, she took the water and stumbled to the hearth. She removed the bubbling stew and poured the water into another pot. Shoving it over the fire, she hurried back to the kitchen. Halfway there, she suffered another round of labor cramps.

Moaning in pain, Maggie forced herself to continue to the kitchen. A basket sat on the rough-hewn counter. It contained a spool of thread, a small knife, clean rags, a blanket, and lastly, a rare bottle of aged whiskey. She grabbed the basket.

Maggie hurried back to the fire and poured the now steaming water back into the bucket. She carried the bucket and basket to a narrow hallway separating the home's bedrooms. She took the blanket from the basket and spread it out beneath her. Then she retrieved a pillow from her bed and sitting, placed it behind her back.

The last thing she did was stretch out her long legs. Her feet fetched up against the opposite wall…the reason she had chosen the hallway to give birth. With her upper back against one wall and her feet against the other, she could brace herself to push with force.

Maggie took a deep breath and waited for the next contraction. She didn't have long to wait. It gripped her like an iron fist, the pain unlike anything she had ever experienced. It passed, and she wheezed with relief. Her head lolled against the plank wall, a chilling thought passing through her mind.

This is just the beginning.

Maggie's hair hung in damp locks about her face.

A steady drizzle of sweat dripped off her face. She had labored the entire day and was now, into the night. Her throat, parched from thirst and raw from screams of pain, issued a constant series of moans, the ceaseless contractions allowing no relief. Exhausted, she didn't know how much longer she could go on. The baby didn't seem any closer to delivery than when her labor started.

Cold fingers of fear gripped her. *Am I going to die in childbirth?*

Despair threatened to overwhelm her. Angrily, she rejected the defeatist impulse. She didn't become leader of the Marauders by letting fear rule her.

"No!" she shrieked. "I won't give up!"

Maggie placed her hands on her swollen belly, then squared her feet against the wall. When she felt the next contraction begin, she clenched her teeth and pushed.

Her shoulders grinding against the wall, she fought to push with every ounce of her flagging strength. One strangled breath followed another, her muscles straining. She felt a building pressure and unbearable pain. Screaming nonstop, she pushed one last time.

The pain and pressure disappeared.

Chest heaving, Maggie spied a tiny figure lying between her legs. One glance told her she had a son. A lusty wail left his lips, and he wriggled in her hands as she picked him up and used a damp cloth to clean him. She dug into her basket, poured whiskey on the knife and thread, then cut and tied off the umbilical cord.

Her son continued to squirm as she examined him. A full head of hair crowned him, the same golden brown as her own. There could be no doubt as to the father. His eyes were a brilliant green— just like Tal's.

More wails came from her baby, these tinged with hunger. She unbuttoned her sweat-soaked tunic and gave him her breast.

He suckled vigorously as if introduced to the world starved from the womb. Maggie kissed him and shifting position, lay down on the hard floor. Too exhausted to move, she cradled her son and closed her eyes.

She fell asleep.

❖

Drusulla soared, her sharp avian eyes searching.

Below, tree-canopied foothills stretched upward to rocky, granite crags. The witch alternated her attention from the ground below, to warily scan the sky above. She had barely survived several attacks by predators, the last being a young griffin. The beast launched itself at her from a bluff, then chased her until she lost it in the thick forest.

A growing sense of hopelessness filled Drusulla. She had searched for the dark lord's fortress for months without success. One peak looked much like the next, and she feared she was now traveling in circles. Worse, half her feathers had gone from black to white, a sign her aging had resumed. If she didn't find the dark lord soon, her death would be swift and certain.

A dark speck appeared in the distant sky. Cautiously, she flew toward it, ready to dive for the safety of the trees. As she drew nearer, she spied a large creature. It was covered in black, leathery skin, with huge, batlike wings carrying it through the air. She blinked in recognition.

A gargoyle!

She followed the gargoyle to a high cliff and watched the creature land in a cave-like opening. The rock facing was honeycombed with a countless number of these cavities. While she watched, another gargoyle emerged and launched into the air on the back of a giant, black bird. Her heart beat faster. *This must be the eyrie.*

She veered away toward the base of the steep ridge. An excited *caw* left her beak. A stronghold came into view at the foot of the crag. Carved from black granite, towers and crenellations circled a massive keep. Pinnacles rose from the battlements like spear-tips to point menacingly at the sky. A lake formed at the base of the citadel. Fed by a river that poured out of the escarpment high above, it created a waterfall that fell hundreds of feet. The thunder from the water's collision with the ground below could be heard even at the witch's great height.

Joyful squawks left her bill. *I did it!*

I found the dark lord's fortress.

CHAPTER 54

TAL SLID OUT OF BED.

"Where are you going?" a sleepy voice asked. "The sun's barely up."

Tal chuckled, then leaned down and kissed Alex. "Bozar has called a meeting this morning." He could hardly control his enthusiasm. "We're finally going to do something other than wait for our army to grow larger."

"But it's so early!" Alex complained. She sat up and yawned.

Tal couldn't tear his eyes away from her. The sheet fell from her bare flesh, and when she stretched, her breasts jutted toward him.

He swallowed. "I'll get back as soon as possible."

Alex rolled onto her stomach, chin cupped in her hands. "Maybe I'll still be here. Or," she sighed and turned over, the sheets now falling away completely, "maybe not."

"A challenge? I like this game." Tal pounced, Alex's happy shrieks echoing off the walls.

Giggling, Alex hugged Tal. "Go. I know you've been waiting for this. I wouldn't want you to miss a single moment. Besides, what would Bozar and Lord Gravelback do without you?"

"Your sage wisdom is equaled only by your beauty," Tal quipped. He tickled Alex to elicit one last squeal, then laughing, made his way to the door. He paused and turned. "But don't go anywhere.

"I *will* be back."

The spyhole was cleverly hidden within the bookcase.

The peephole, located next to a stack of books, lay in a shadow cast by the shelf above it, making the spyhole virtually invisible to the eye. Sikes stood on a platform and watched the prince dress and leave the room. Years earlier, Maggie had shown him the secret passageways of the keep, and as luck would have it, the prince and his new bride occupied one of the rooms connected to this hidden network.

Sikes snickered. Lucky for him, not so lucky for the prince. He took a drink from a jug of ale, then fingered a latch secured to a lever. When pulled, it released a section of the bookcase to allow entry into the room.

Motion drew his attention back to the spyhole.

The princess left the bed and rummaged through a trunk for clothing. Her nude figure caused a stir of lust which quickly subsided. His hatred for Prince Tal, combined with the staggering amount of ale he had imbibed, left little room for desire.

It's all the prince's fault! He drove away Maggie, the lone bright spot in Sikes' life, the only woman he ever loved. She tried to cover up what the despicable bastard did, but he knew better. Prince Tal used her then cast her aside like a soiled garment.

He checked the crossbow that lay at his feet. When the prince returned, he would get what he deserved. He cackled softly. Maybe he would even tell the princess what her precious husband had been up to.

Right before I kill him.

The earl's large conference room was already filled with imperial army officers and the earl's city officials when Tal arrived. A row of tables lined one side of the chamber, platters of ham, eggs, biscuits, milk and ale, laid out on them for breakfast. Chairs were arranged to face the front of the room where Bozar's table sat.

Tal helped himself to the breakfast bounty, then joined Bozar and Lord Gravelback. A sense of anticipation filled the air, and Tal felt his own excitement swell. *At last, we're going to take the fight to the foul Veil Queen.*

"Marital bliss seems to agree with you, lad."

Tal grinned at Artemis Thurgood. The garrulous grand master, his face a mask of good humor, sat a few chairs down from him. As usual, his robe of office was covered in food crumbs and wine stains.

"Yes, it does," Tal answered with a chuckle.

"It is good to see you so happy, Sire."

Pulpit sat next to Thurgood. Unlike the grand master, his white robe was spotless. When Tal had first met the monk, he found him to be a puzzling enigma. But since, he had developed a profound respect for Pulpit. Alex was especially close to the monk, something Tal counted of great value.

Bozar stood. "Let us begin." The room fell silent.

"We have completed repairs to Markingham's fortifications, particularly the wall. Crops have been planted and harvested, herds of sheep and cattle reestablished, and abandoned structures within the city either torn down or rebuilt. Our biggest problem is housing our invasion army which now numbers at fifty thousand."

Bozar paused to let his comments sink in. "Unfortunately, our pre-invasion plans call for a force of one hundred thousand legionnaires. The small size of the breach in the Veil continues to limit the movement of soldiers and supplies. It will take at least another year to meet this numerical goal."

A disappointed pall fell over the room.

"But," Bozar leaned forward, palms flat on the table, "we wait no longer. We start the search for the Veil Queen and King's lair today!"

A roar greeted the First Advisor's remark. Tal joined all the others in standing and cheering.

Bozar waited until the clamor died down. "Our next step is to approach the Duke of Wheel to join his forces with—"

The doors crashed open, and three cloaked figures rushed into the room. Tal and Gravelback shot to their feet, drawing swords. Close on the intruders' heels were the sentries on guard duty. A struggle ensued before a feminine voice cried out, "Please let us speak!"

Bozar held his fist aloft. "Hold!" he commanded.

The guards released the three trespassers. One-by-one they pushed their hoods back. The first revealed a young man about Tal's age with sandy blond hair and blue eyes. The second, another young man, had cinnamon-colored skin, dark eyes, and tightly curled black hair. But it was the last figure that elicited a gasp from Tal.

Half the size of her taller companions, a young woman stared at the assembly. Large, pointed ears swept up on either side of her jade-green face. Long, amber-colored hair fell about her face and shoulders. Lavender eyes were framed by thick lashes, below which was a petite, button nose. Full, red lips completed the picture.

A gnome!

"Who are you?" Bozar demanded.

The gnome stepped forward. "I am Lark, daughter of Latimer the High Gnome of my people," she replied. Lark motioned and the two men stepped forward. She pointed at the sandy-haired man and his dark-haired companion. "This is Morgan, son of Magnus, and Rafael, son of Henri."

Lark spread her arms. "We represent the Lost Remnant. And we want to join your cause against the Dark Queen."

CHAPTER 55

RACK.

The whip's lash left a bloody laceration on the woman's bare back. Stefan chuckled at her scream of pain. A sharp knock came from the door. Frowning at the interruption to his entertainment, he carefully coiled the whip and placed it on a table.

"Come!" he barked.

A large, wingless gargoyle led an old crone into the room. "She insists on seeing you, lord."

Stefan studied the ancient hag. Greasy white hair straggled down her back and thin shoulders. Her face was a map of creases and wrinkles, her eyes a rheumy blue. The frayed and torn gown she wore looked as timeworn as the woman. With each step she took, she left a trail of white and black feathers. He sniffed the air. A hint of wild magic followed her.

A witch.

"Why have you brought me this bag of bones?" he demanded.

"She—she claims to have valuable information you would want to hear, Lord Stefan," the gargoyle quavered.

"Get this hag out of my sight," Stefan snarled. He turned away and retrieved the whip.

The witch fell to her knees. "Please, lord, hear me. Travers Crossing!" she cried.

Stefan stiffened. He whirled around and reached the witch in one stride. He yanked her to her feet.

"A lucky guess! The name of a location you overheard someone say," he spat. "What proof do you offer? Be quick about it before I have you torn to pieces and fed to the squarks."

"A—a tall man possessed of powerful magic? His lover is a woman with hair of gold," she babbled.

Could she be describing Alexandria? And the man with her whose traps killed most of his band of raiders and gargoyles?

Stefan could hardly contain his excitement. "Leave us," he commanded the gargoyle. He pointed at a nearby table. "Sit." The witch scrambled for a chair.

Stefan gestured with his whip at a naked young woman tied to two wooden posts sunk into the floor. Her arms were secured to iron rings above her head, her legs to another pair of rings leaving her suspended and spread-eagled.

He chuckled at the witch's reaction. She wore her terror like a second layer of skin. "Let me introduce you to Cecily, my servant and concubine. Can you greet our guest, Cecily?"

A muffled sob was his reply.

"Please forgive my dear Cecily," Stefan smirked. "As you can see, she is...indisposed."

He uncoiled the whip. "The trick with the lash is to never strike the same place twice." With a quick snap of his wrist, the end of the whipcord struck the bound and helpless woman. She screamed as a red slash appeared on her left shoulder, a twin to one still oozing blood.

Stefan glanced at the witch. She looked like she might swoon. He coiled the whipcord and sat next to her. "You see," he continued, "if you strike an old wound, of course there's pain. But inflicting a fresh wound is so much better, the agony delicious and exquisite."

Stefan gave a brief wave of his hand. Cecily's bindings fell off, and she collapsed. "Come here, my dear," he commanded. She staggered to her feet and to Stefan. He motioned to his lap, and she sat.

Her back was crisscrossed with old scars. Stefan dipped his finger in the fresh blood streaming down her shoulder. He put it into his mouth. "Ah, you taste just as sweet as the first time you felt my lash. Now, tell our guest why you are being punished."

"I-I spilled wine on Lord Stefan," Cecily whispered.

"Tut, tut, there's a little more to it than that," Stefan admonished her. Cecily cringed. Her eyes filled with tears, and her breath came in quick gasps. He continued. "You see, I reached under my dear Cecily's gown, and she spilled a drop of wine on my sleeve."

"It won't happen again, lord," Cecily rushed to say.

Stefan pushed her off. "Clean yourself up, then go to my bed and wait for me." Cecily scurried away.

Stefan leaned closer to the witch. The smile left his face. "Now, if I'll whip a loyal servant for a dribble of spilled wine, imagine what's in store for you if you speak even the smallest of lies."

The witch's face went as white as one of the feathers which continued to drip from her. "I swear everything I've told you is true," she gibbered.

"Good. Now start at the beginning—and leave nothing out."

When she finished, Stefan sat back, amazed. *Markingham occupied by an invading army? The Baleful destroyed and Varg killed?* The witch could be lying, but the terror on her face was plain to see. She wouldn't dare lie.

"Tell me again about the woman and the potion you made."

"Her name is, Maggie, and she needed a love potion to enthrall the man she desired."

"This is the same man who was with Alexandria?"

"Who is Alexandria, lord?"

"The woman with golden hair, you fool!"

"Yes, yes, the same," the witch jabbered.

Stefan stood and paced, deep in thought. "One last question. Once enthralled, Maggie planned to take this man to Travers Crossing, then use the potion on him over and over again?"

"Yes, lord."

Stefan couldn't believe his good fortune. A cruel smile crept across his face. He now knew Alexandria's location, and that of the man who had helped her escape. With any luck, this Maggie might still have him under the potion's spell at Travers Crossing. Of course, his mother, Marlinda, would need to know about Markingham and the demise of the Baleful, but she would be especially keen to learn he had located Alexandria.

First, however, he needed to take a trip to Travers Crossing, the place he had suffered his greatest humiliation. He rubbed his hands in anticipation. When he dragged Alexandria back to Wheel, she would have company.

Her lover's severed head.

He helped the witch up out of the chair. "Your information has proven to be indeed valuable. You shall be richly rewarded."

"Thank you, Lord Stefan, thank you," the witch gushed. "I only need a few children to complete a potion."

"And you shall have them," Stefan said as he guided the witch to a large, open window. Far below, the battlements rose from the foot of the black granite mountain. "I just need you to do one more thing for me."

"Anything, lord Stefan," the witch exclaimed.

"Since you flew your way in here," he picked her up and threw her out the window, "then fly your way back out."

Screaming, she plummeted to the ground.

Nancy E. Durham

CHAPTER 56

B OZAR ORDERED THE ROOM CLEARED.
Tal watched the trio as everyone filed out. Only Gravelback, Thurgood, and Pulpit remained. Bozar motioned to Lark, and she and her companions joined them at the table.

The First Advisor got right to the point. "Who are the Lost Remnant?"

Lark shared a look with her companions. They nodded and she spoke. "We are all that remain of the free peoples not enslaved by the Dark Queen."

"Then why haven't you allied with the Duke of Wheel?" Bozar asked. "That would seem to be a logical next step."

Lark remained silent for a moment as if choosing her next words carefully. "We have contacts in Wheel, and prudence demanded we keep our existence secret."

"You mean spies," Gravelback growled.

Lark nodded.

"Why?" Tal asked. "What do you fear?"

"Wheel is infested with followers of the Veil Queen and has been for generations. It has progressed to the point that they now occupy important positions in the duke's court. We dare not approach the duke lest we reveal ourselves to the Dark Queen."

Tal's thoughts raced. Lark confirmed what Alex had been saying all along, specifically that her stepmother—the duchess—and Rodric, were Marlinda's puppets.

Pulpit spoke up. "Then why approach us if you fear treachery? Might the Dark Queen have spies among us as well?"

Lark shook her head. "We have watched you for months and have come to the conclusion that is unlikely."

"Why?" Bozar asked.

"Because you are not from here. In fact, although you have taken pains to conceal it, you are not from anyplace within Dalfur."

A long silence followed. Bozar steepled his hands together. "Interesting. You realize that we can't let you leave now. The Veil Queen cannot know of our presence until we are ready to strike."

Eagerly, Lark leaned forward. "Don't you understand? We want to help, to join you. We have been forced to live for generations in hiding, always in fear one day we would be discovered."

"You keep saying *we*, but I see only three before us, each young enough to be my own children," Gravelback retorted. "Do you speak for all or only yourselves?"

Lark hesitated, and the three companions glanced uneasily at each other.

Gravelback slapped the table. "*Bah!* I knew it. You have no authority. Likely you're here on some foolish notion you took upon yourselves to follow."

Lark spread her hands. "You're right, Lord Gravelback. We did take the initiative. At first, we didn't know what to make of the sudden appearance of a strange army, much less of Prince Tal, a powerful wielder of magic only the legends hint of. But we saw what you did for Markingham and its people, how you cared for them and rebuilt their city. Then, you defeated the Baleful, long a plague upon our land. Those with evil intentions would never have done this. So we waited and we watched. While we still don't know where you came from or how you traveled here, that is a secondary concern. There is a much higher priority."

"And what would that be?" Bozar asked.

Lark took a deep breath. "Persuade our leaders to join you against the Dark Queen."

"You spin a fanciful tale with absolutely no proof," Gravelback shot back. "You could be leading us into a trap. For all we know, *you* are agents of the bloody Veil Queen."

Artemis Thurgood cleared his throat. "*Ahem*. We have all remarked about the deserted nature of this entire region. The population has virtually disappeared. Maybe the lass speaks the truth. If so, her explanation makes sense." He turned to Lark. "How do you suggest we meet with your leaders?"

The gnome answered, "Come with us to Sanctuary."

A squeak of surprise escaped Alex as the door flew open and Tal dashed in.

He picked her up and laughing, swung her around. She recovered from her surprise and said, "It must have been a *very* good meeting."

"You wouldn't believe it," Tal gushed. He put her down. "Three strangers burst into the meeting, and one turned out to be a gnome. They want to join our—"

He whirled around, dagger drawn as a section of the bookcase swung open. Bradley Sikes emerged with a cocked and loaded crossbow.

He brandished the weapon at Tal. "Drop the dagger." Reluctantly Tal obeyed.

"Move away, Princess Alexandria," he ordered. "I have an issue to settle with your husband."

Shocked, Alex couldn't what was happening. "Bradley, what are you doing? Put that weapon away. You might hurt someone with it."

Sikes giggled. "Oh, I *do* plan to hurt someone. In fact, I plan to kill the Prince."

He lifted the crossbow, menace in his eyes. "Now move!"

Alex jumped in front of Tal. "No! I won't budge. Why are you doing this?"

Sikes, his face a florid red from rage and ale, spat, "Because the bastard drove away Maggie. She left because of him! He got her pregnant and she couldn't bear to face him."

The crossbow wavered, and Sikes' speech became slurred. "I love her! She should have loved *me*, not him. I would have been a good husband and father. Now, because of him, I'll never get the chance. I won't ever see her again, *and it's all his fault*," he shrieked.

"Step away from me, Alex," Tal said quietly.

She clung to Tal. "No! Can't you see he's drunk and hurt and doesn't know what he's saying?"

Alex spun to face Sikes. "You don't have to do this Bradley, we can talk—"

She screamed as Tal picked her up and flung her away. She sailed through the air, landing on the bed.

Grim-faced, Tal turned to Sikes. "I didn't even know Maggie was pregnant, but it doesn't matter because it wasn't me."

"Liar! I saw you with her. You were both bare-assed together in bed. *It was you!*" Sikes screeched, spittle flying from his mouth.

He pulled the trigger and a bolt shot toward Tal's chest.

Alex screamed…and time slowed to a crawl. Magic burst from her with a blinding incandescence. She lifted her hand and light shot from her palm to form a shield between Tal and Sikes. The bolt struck the shield and bounced off.

Alex jumped off the bed and ran at the Marauder. Using both hands now, ghostly cords burst from her to wrap around Sikes' arms and legs. He cried out in pain as they tightened, and he dropped the crossbow.

"Don't you dare threaten him," she howled. Sikes was jerked upward as if by invisible hands. He hung suspended in midair. "I'll kill you first!"

The cables of magic tightened, and Sikes began to wheeze, his lips turning blue.

"Alex, stop. He's suffocating!"

Vaguely aware of Tal's arms around her trying to pull her away, Alex dropped her hands. The spectral shackles evaporated. Released, Sikes fell to slam into the floor.

Alex felt dizzy and disoriented. She heard Tal calling for guards, but the sound traveled as if he were a great distance away. She shook her head, and the room slowly stopped spinning.

When her vision cleared, she found Bradley Sikes on the floor, a dozen guards restraining him. Bozar burst into the room just as they finished binding him.

"What's this? What's happened?" he demanded.

"Sikes tried to kill me," Tal answered, his voice shaking with anger. "And he would have succeeded if not for Alex."

Tal took a deep breath. "One moment Sikes shot at me with a crossbow, the next, everything froze, and I couldn't move. I could even see the bolt from the weapon, but it just hung in the air, suspended. Then, magic shot from Alex to form a protective shield around me, the arrow bounced off, and time started again. I could move."

Bozar looked at Alex for confirmation, and she burst into tears. "He was going to shoot Tal. I just reacted, and I don't know how I did it," she sobbed.

Tal reached for Alex, and she buried her face in his chest.

"Sikes claimed some nonsense that I got Maggie pregnant," Tal continued. "He also blames me for her leaving Markingham."

Bozar motioned to the guards. "Take him to the dungeon. Make sure no harm comes to him." They hauled him to his feet and carried him away.

Bozar shook his head. "He must be afflicted by some kind of madness."

He placed a hand on Alex's shoulder and gently squeezed. "You saved Tal's life. There's no need to worry about the how's or the why's. We can sort it all out later." Alex nodded, her face still pressed against Tal's chest. His heart pulsed a reassuring beat in her ear.

Her stunned mind tried to process the rapid sequence of events, and she barely heard the rest of the First Advisor's conversation with Tal. One moment Tal held her in a happy embrace, the next, Bradley Sikes tried to kill him. When she saw him fire the crossbow, her power responded instantly. But still, she couldn't have reacted fast enough to save him—except that time *did* actually slow. She could still see the bolt as it headed straight for Tal's heart, only to be stopped by her buffer of magic.

She hugged Tal tighter. *I almost lost him.*

A painful ache filled her. Despite the stunning chain of events, it was overshadowed by something far larger. Though Bradley Sikes might be afflicted with madness, the conviction in his voice was unmistakable.

And he claimed he *saw* Tal and Maggie together in bed.

CHAPTER 57

AL WAITED IN THE JAILER'S ROOM OF THE DUNGEON.

Bozar was interrogating Bradley Sikes in his cell. Because of the animosity the Marauder held against Tal, his *Eldred* insisted that he talk to him alone. Tal had grudgingly complied, but as the questioning dragged on, he now was having second thoughts.

Tal paced about, his mind churning. *Why did Sikes believe he was responsible for Maggie's pregnancy? It was a ridiculous accusation.* Before he could consider it further, the dungeon's door opened, and Bozar came out. He ordered the soldier behind him to secure the door and guard it. Then he signaled Tal to follow him, and they went outside.

It was late in the day, the winter sun low on the horizon. Bozar wore a troubled look, his breath white plumes in the cold air. "I want to make sure no one hears us."

Tal tried to swallow the hard knot that had risen in his throat. Rarely had he seen his *Eldred* in such a state. To be so fearful of eavesdropping that he led them outside was a bad sign.

A very bad sign.

His First Advisor started with a question. "Think back nine to ten months ago. Can you recall any endeavor, anything at all, you did with Maggie?"

Heat crawled up Tal's neck. "You mean did I bed her? You're as mad as Sikes," he snapped.

Bozar clutched Tal's shoulders. "Answer me. By the Creator's love, *think!* Stop reacting with anger."

With some effort, Tal managed to reign in his emotions. His mind worked furiously as he sifted through his memories. He finally shook his head. "I'm sorry. Maggie went off by herself not long after I gave her Hanley. I saw her only a few times after that, and then only from a distance. The one and only time I spoke to her was when she showed me her family's old country estate."

Bozar closed his eyes in dismay. "Maggie claimed the empire might be able to use the manor to house soldiers, didn't she?"

"Yes, but how did—" Tal stopped, "What aren't you telling me?" he demanded.

Bozar ignored the question. "Is there anything else you can recall?" he persisted.

Tal's face flushed. "I-I drank too much wine, and I might have passed out. Other than being sick to my stomach, that's all I remember. We went back to Markingham, and I never spoke to Maggie again."

A deep sigh left Bozar. "I'm sorry, Tal. It all fits."

"Stop talking in riddles!" Tal cried. "What fits?"

"Do you remember the witch escaping? And how we couldn't determine how she managed to bewitch her jailers?"

Irritated, Tal snapped, "Yes, but what's that have to do with Maggie?"

"Because she set the witch free."

Tal's mind spun. "No. You're wrong. She wanted to kill the witch. Why would she let her go?"

"Maggie did it in return for a potion, one she used on you. I'm sorry, Tal, but you *were* with Maggie. And you are the father of her child."

Alex's supper had gone cold. It lay untouched beside her on the table. The sight of it made her nauseous, and she pushed it away.

Lost in thought, she was startled when the door handle rattled, and Tal walked in. She bolted up and flew to him.

"Well? What did you find out?"

Tal hugged her but wouldn't meet her eyes. He gently pushed her away and went straight for the flagon of wine beside her uneaten meal. Pouring wine in a goblet, he gulped it down and refilled his cup. Seconds later, he drained it again. He retrieved his sword and shoulder sheath from beside their bed, then buckled the weapon across his back.

Alex grabbed his arm. "Tal, what is it? What are you doing?"

Tal braced his hands on the table, his head hung low. When he looked up, his eyes were haunted. "I'm going to be gone for a while. I don't know when I'll be back."

Stunned, Alex stared at her husband. "Gone where? Why?"

Tal did not immediately answer. At last, he straightened. "I'm sorry. I'm so sorry," he managed to say.

Alex studied Tal. The look on his face was one she had never seen. He appeared devastated, the sorrow so thick, it looked like it might crush him. "Tal, please tell me what happened."

His shoulders slumped. "I have to find Maggie. She's probably had the baby by now, and I need to bring them both back to Markingham."

Tal's words shocked Alex. Numb, she asked, "But why you? She's the earl's daughter. He can send an entire escort for her."

"You don't understand. It *has* to be me."

Tal sat heavily in one of the chairs beside the table. "About ten months ago, Maggie took me to the earl's old country estate. She claimed it could be used to house some of the imperial soldiers. She led me to a room, and over wine, I told her I didn't think we could use the old manor. That's the last thing I remember until I woke up stinking of wine and with a throbbing headache."

Tal pounded the table. "What I didn't know—until now—was that Maggie used the opportunity to slip a potion into my wine."

Alex couldn't breathe. With growing dread, she knew what came next. "Bradley was telling the truth."

Miserable, Tal nodded. "He followed us there. Later, he confronted Maggie, and she admitted to making an agreement with the witch we had captured. In return for her freedom, the witch made Maggie a potion to capture a man's ardor."

Tal looked up at Alex. "And she used it on me."

The numbness Alex felt was quickly replaced by another sensation.

Cold anger.

"You bedded Maggie? *Before you even bedded me?*"

"Yes, but—"

"I threw myself at you, practically begged you to make love to me, and each time you refused! Do you remember your words? That I might get pregnant and produce a bastard child? *Yet that's exactly what you did with Maggie!*"

"She tricked me! She slipped the witch's potion into my wine."

Alex laughed harshly. "Oh, poor, Tal. Here I've heard you referred to in grandiose terms such as the blood prince, the heir to the throne of Meredith, yet you're so powerless you can't even resist the potion of a backcountry witch? I *watched* you bring fiery hail down on the heads of the Baleful. I *saw* you produce a bramble thicket right from the bare soil. Don't tell me you couldn't defeat the magic of an old hag."

Tal shot to his feet, the chair falling to the floor with a crash. "Is that what you think? That I wanted Maggie?" he demanded, red-faced.

"She never bothered to conceal her desire for you, now did she? She shamelessly pursued you, sometimes with me right there beside you. Maybe you decided once, just once it wouldn't hurt to have a roll in bed with Maggie."

Crack. A plank on the table splintered as Tal's fist struck it. "I would never do that, never betray you." He started for the door, shaking with anger. "Maybe you'll have come to your senses by the time I get back."

"Wait!"

Tal stopped, and Alex marched right up to him. "If you go after that—that woman, then don't bother coming back to me. Just find yourself another room…and another whore."

Tal reached for the doorknob and paused. He took a deep breath, then turned back to Alex.

"Whatever happens, I want you to know that I love you. And despite what you may believe, I have never loved another. You took me at my worst, angry and full of rage when mercy wasn't part of me, kindness even less so. But you showed me another way, a reflection of your own life. I can't go back to being that man, and I won't leave a helpless babe and woman to fend for themselves."

"Maggie is the least helpless woman—or man—that I know," Alex retorted.

"Could you continue to love me knowing I turned my back on my own child? On Maggie?"

A vise gripped Alex's heart. The hot jealousy which filled her ebbed away. She clutched Tal's hand. "Please don't go," she whispered. "Stay with me."

Tal squeezed her hand. "I'm sorry. I have to find them."

He opened the door, turned the corner, and disappeared from her sight.

CHAPTER 58

BEDROSIAN RUBBED HIS TIRED EYES.

Stacked in front of him were teetering piles of books, manuscripts, and scrolls. He'd spent many months searching for any clue that might explain why Alexandria was so valuable to the Veil Queen. Both he and his fellow gnome, Pandathaway Pandergast, thought they had found the key in Alexandria's parentage. They discovered, Diana Dane, a powerful healer, had married Corbin Duvalier, the Twenty-Fifth Duke of Wheel. More importantly, she was the great grandmother of Sonja Salterhorn, the creator of the orb. Here was the possible reason the Dark Queen coveted Alexandria. Her lineage might tie her to the orb.

Unfortunately, despite his exhaustive search, nothing more had turned up. The problem was the genealogical trail ended with Sonja. When Marlinda, the Dark Queen, seized the orb from Sonja and perverted its magic to create the Veil, she had slaughtered Sonja and her entire household. Sonja had perished childless. With no direct pedigree to Sonja, their theory on the Veil Queen's interest in Alexandria was moot.

Or so history would lead them to believe.

Bedrosian had spent much of his life following his passion—the written record of Meredith and the myriad of tomes that chronicled the history of the empire from the founding kings and queens to the present. No detail, large or small, escaped his attention. What others considered dry, dusty work, he attacked with relish. The greater the mystery, the more dogged he became. His position as Chief Archivist of the Library of Wheel—second only to the Imperial Library at Meredith City in its collection of historical documents—gave Bedrosian the perfect platform to indulge his pursuit of knowledge.

Hard-earned experience taught him the problem with history were the hiccups, the blanks in the sequence of events where no written authentication existed. In Sonja's case, the gap in her life's story was almost twelve months. She had interrupted her studies and left the Academy of Magic at Locus, only to re-enroll a year later. While this was a well-known fact, Bedrosian's research had never uncovered the reason *why* Sonja abruptly left the academy.

The gnome hated to admit defeat, but it seemed futile to continue his fruitless search. He reached to deactivate the light crystal at his desk when his hand brushed against a thin book. Buried under layers of manuscripts, he pushed them off to view the title.

Goodwife Toomey was inked on the soft leather cover. Curious, Bedrosian picked it up and opened it. He leafed through the pages, absently scanning the names of mothers and their babes the goodwife had helped deliver. He noted goodwife Toomey was meticulous in her citations. Besides the names, she also listed whether the delivery was easy or difficult, complications, if any, weight, hair color, and gender of the baby. And one last notation.

Date of birth.

Bedrosian's breath left him in a rush as he stared at the date of one particular delivery. He scrambled to locate another book he had already viewed and cast aside. His hand closed on it, and he frantically opened the tome.

"It's here. I know I saw it," he chattered to himself. He stopped, his lips moving as he re-read a passage.

He leaped to his feet, almost upending the desk. Manuscripts, books, and scrolls went flying in a blizzard of paper.

Bedrosian grabbed the two books, then raced out of the library and into the night.

A persistent knocking awakened Pandathaway. It soon transitioned into pounding.

Irritated, he yawned and climbed out of bed.

"Who could be calling at this time of night?" his wife asked.

"Go back to sleep, Lillian," Pandathaway replied. "I'll see who it is and send them on their way."

The gnome snapped his fingers, and the candle next to their bedstead flickered to life. Grumbling, he carried it down the stairs. When he reached the first floor, he realized the beating didn't come from his store's front door.

But from the back.

The gnome hurried to the rear of his shop. Along the way, he armed himself with a stout walking cane he grabbed from a shelf. With the cane held above his head like a club, he unlocked the rear door and cautiously inched it open. His jaw dropped.

There stood Bedrosian.

His friend pushed the door wider and brushed by him. Pandathaway closed the door and locked it. Bedrosian frantically motioned for him to join him at a dusty table he swept clean of curiosities for sale.

"This had better be good. You woke me from a—"

"I found it! I found out why the Veil Queen wants Alexandria!"

Any residue of sleep instantly left Pandathaway. "What?"

He joined Bedrosian at the table, and his friend opened a book titled *Goodwife Toomey*, then pointed at a notation.

Infant girl, blue eyes and fair of hair, born to a maiden with blue eyes and hair of gold.

Pandathaway knew "maiden" meant unwed but still didn't see how that related to Alexandria and the Dark Queen.

As if reading his thoughts, Bedrosian said, "Note the date the infant girl was born, then look at this." He opened another book and pointed to a passage.

The foundling was left at the doorstep of Lord Westcamp's manor. The lord's wife, Lady Marcella, had recently given birth to a stillborn daughter. The foundling was received with much joy, and Marcella prevailed upon her husband to take the infant into the family as their own.

"This was chronicled by Lord Westcamp's seneschal who kept a record of all the lord's activities." Bedrosian quickly went back to the goodwife's book. "Goodwife Toomey delivered both the stillborn daughter and the foundling. The dates listed show both deliveries were only days apart."

Pandathaway squinted at the passage. "So? I don't see the correlation."

Bedrosian slapped the table. "The foundling was born to Sonja."

Stunned, Pandathaway tried to make sense of his friend's statement. "I don't understand. How can you make such a connection? They don't seem related at all."

Bedrosian stood up and paced. "Sonja must have learned from the goodwife about the stillborn delivered to Lady Marcella. She knew if she left her daughter on Lord Westcamp's doorstep, the Lady Marcella, devastated at the loss of her own baby, would take her in."

Pandathaway held up his hands. "Wait! This presumes Sonja was pregnant and gave birth. Even I know there's no historical evidence for this. She died childless at the hands of Marlinda."

"Let me correct you, my friend. The *existing* historical accounts verify what you've said. But what about the year of Sonja's life that history offers not a bare whisper? The year she left the academy? We have no account to explain why she left, where she went, or what happened to her."

Bedrosian picked up the thin volume. "I believe *Goodwife Toomey* answers this. Sonja left the academy because she was unwed and pregnant. Think about it. She was one of the most exceptional students ever to attend the academy. Beautiful and gifted, she was sought after by the sons of nobles from both the minor and major houses. Her pregnancy was a disaster that threatened her entire future."

"So she did the only thing open to her," Pandathaway mused. "Leave the academy and go somewhere far away, deliver her baby, then slip back, re-enroll, and resume her life with no one the wiser."

"Precisely." Bedrosian picked up the second book. "Lord Westcamp's seneschal kept an account of all the notable events of his lord's household. Twenty years later, their daughter Anna, married Bolden, the son of a minor lord. Later, their daughter Melissa wed Steven, the son and heir of the Duke of Wheel."

Pandathaway gasped. "That's it! That ties Alexandria as a direct descendent of Sonja!"

Bedrosian nodded. "But there's more. All the historical accounts agree that as new students, Sonja and Jack Morley were close—very close. Later, after Sonja left then returned to the academy, she had very little to do with him. We know Jack attacked her in a jealous rage after learning of her engagement to Lord Will, the Royal Governor's son. Imprisoned, he managed to escape and somehow found his way to Marlinda, only a wildling witch at the time. They killed Sonja, seized the orb, then created the accursed Veil. Jack became the Veil King, the Dark Queen's paramour."

Impatient, Pandathaway waved away the comments. "Yes, yes, this is all well known. Get to the point."

"The point, my friend, is that I believe Jack to be the father of Sonja's baby. It all fits. They were close, intimately so, then Sonja leaves and when she returns, rejects Jack. What transpired between them to cause such a rift, we may never know. What we *do* know is before their falling out, Jack helped her with the making of the orb. He knew its potential and had an idea about how the magic of the orb worked. Marlinda needed him in order to use the orb to form the Veil."

Pandathaway's mind worked furiously. "So Alexandria is descended from Diana, Sonja, *and* Jack? What a combination."

Bedrosian's countenance sobered. "Yes. And it's this combination that chills my blood. The Dark Queen has used the past thousand years to subjugate Dalfur, all the while shielded from the empire by the Veil. But the Veil hasn't moved an inch in all that time. Don't you think the Dark Queen would have expanded the Veil if she could? That means her control is limited. But what if she gained the means to fully control the orb, to employ its magic whenever and wherever she desired?"

The consequences of this possibility staggered Pandathaway. It would mean the end of Wheel, the end of the empire, the end of all of them.

"She wants Alexandria not just to control the orb but to expand its reach," he breathed in a voice suddenly gone hoarse.

He jumped up. "I have to warn her. She doesn't know what she's facing."

Bedrosian frowned. "How do you plan on doing that? You don't even know where Alexandria and the lieutenant fled to."

"But I do know. I just haven't told you or anyone else."

Pandathaway wagged a finger at his friend's questioning look. "Don't ask. The fewer who know, the better." His thoughts raced, already planning on what he would need.

He faced a long and perilous journey to Markingham.

ACKNOWLEDGEMENT

A big shout out to my critique group for reading every word and making me a better writer. Thank you, Lisa, Galand, Gary, Skip, and Vicki. You're the best!

ABOUT THE AUTHOR

 Multi Award-Winning Author Michael Scott Clifton, a longtime public educator as a teacher, coach, and administrator, currently lives in Mount Pleasant, Texas with his wife, Melanie. An avid gardener, reader, and movie junkie, he enjoys all kinds of book and movie genres. His books contain aspects of all the genres he enjoys...action, adventure, magic, fantasy, and romance. His fantasy novels, The Janus Witch and The Open Portal, received 5-Star reviews from the prestigious Readers Favorite Book Reviews. Edison Jones and The Anti-Grav Elevator won a 2021 Feathered Quill Book Award Bronze Medal in the Teen Readers category. He has been a finalist in a number of short story contests with Edges of Gray winning First Place in the Texas Authors Contest. Professional credits include articles published in the Texas Study of Secondary Education Magazine. The Open Portal, won The Feathered Quill Book Finalist Award, and launches the fantasy book series, Conquest of the Veil. Michael's latest release, Escape From Wheel—also a 5-Star Readers' Favorite Review—is Book Two in this fantasy series. Visit Michael's official website michaelscottclifton.com or google him @ authormsclifton.

Made in the USA
Columbia, SC
29 April 2021